THE TROPHY
WIFE EXCHANGE

D1601449

THE TROPHY WIFE EXCHANGE

CONNIE SHELTON

W🌐RLDWIDE

TORONTO • NEW YORK • LONDON
AMSTERDAM • PARIS • SYDNEY • HAMBURG
STOCKHOLM • ATHENS • TOKYO • MILAN
MADRID • WARSAW • BUDAPEST • AUCKLAND

W⊕RLDWIDE™

Recycling programs
for this product may
not exist in your area.

ISBN-13: 978-1-335-42520-1

The Trophy Wife Exchange

First published in 2018 by Secret Staircase Books,
an imprint of Columbine Publishing Group, LLC.
This edition published in 2024.

Harlequin Enterprises ULC
22 Adelaide St. West, 41st Floor
Toronto, Ontario M5H 4E3, Canada
www.ReaderService.com

Printed in U.S.A.

As always, I have a huge amount of gratitude for everyone who helped shape this book into its final version.

Dan Shelton, my husband and helpmate for nearly twenty-eight years, is always there for me. And thank you, Stephanie, my lovely daughter and business partner, for giving my business and writing career a burst of fresh new energy this year!

Editors Susan Slater and Shirley Shaw spot the plot and character flaws and help smooth the rough bits in the prose. And topping off the effort are my beta readers, who drop everything in their own lives to read and find the typos that inevitably sneak past me. Thank you for your help with this book: Christine Johnson, Debbie Wilson, Marcia Koopman, Judi Shaw and Sandra Anderson. You guys are the best!

ONE

THE BANK HAD been crowded all morning. By the time Sandy Warner glanced at her watch, it was eleven-thirty and she felt as if she were starving, although she'd had a decent breakfast and really should cover for the tellers as they began taking their lunch breaks. A glimpse of the lobby told her they had fewer customers than an hour ago. The tellers at windows one and four were standing around, while at window three a plump woman in a shabby T-shirt and noticeably worn denim capris stood facing the teller, her back to Sandy's office.

Sandy motioned the two idle employees to take lunch and caught the eye of Lisa, the slightly flustered teller at window three.

"This client wishes to close her account," Lisa said when Sandy approached. "I'm not sure…"

"I'd be happy to take care of it," Sandy told her, noting a couple more customers had walked in and waited in the velvet-roped lane a few feet away.

The woman turned, averting her eyes as she followed Sandy toward the manager's private office. Sandy pushed aside two folders on the desk—loan applications that needed her attention before close of business, settled into her chair, and indicated the one across the desk for her customer.

"Now, what's the name on the account?" she asked, tapping her computer mouse to awaken the screen she'd signed off from a few minutes earlier. "And I'll need to see your driver's license."

Without a word, the woman took a good quality wallet out of a cheap faux-leather purse, opened the clasp and fumbled for her identification. Sandy accepted it and looked at the name.

"Mary? I'm so sorry I didn't recognize you when you came in. You've, uh, done something different with your hair." And added twenty pounds. And taken a gigantic plunge off the social ladder. The regular clientele at the Scottsdale branch of Desert Trust Bank were never, ever seen in public looking less than perfect.

The address on the license was in nearby Mesa, but Sandy recalled they'd done their banking in Scottsdale because their kitchen and bath design business was here. She tried not to stare as she compared the woman before her—blonde hair with two inches of mousy roots showing, dull complexion, red-rimmed eyes—with the Mary Holbrook she remembered, the athletic one who ran a very successful business with her husband, dressed young for her age and probably would have never worked in the garden in the clothes she wore now, much less come into the bank dressed this way.

"Mary, is everything okay?"

Mary opened her mouth to speak but her eyes welled up and she merely shook her head.

Sandy stood and crossed the room, gently closing her office door and giving a small twist to the adjustment rod on the mini blinds, blocking the view from the lobby.

"I just need to close my account, Ms. Warner," Mary said, not making eye contact.

Such formality. They'd been on a first-name basis for

years, and Sandy tried to remember the last time she saw Mary, one of her favorite customers. More than two years, she guessed. Mary and Clint Holbrook had been among the guests at the bank's Christmas soiree—was it really almost three years ago now?

She pulled her keyboard closer and entered Mary's name. When the account information came up, she saw a savings account had been closed last January. It had been Desert Trust's Gold Star account, meaning the balance had normally been maintained in the six-figure range.

"So, the account you want to close is checking?" Sandy asked.

Mary nodded. Still minimal eye contact.

Sandy tapped a few more keys. The only checking account with Mary's name came up. It contained less than two hundred dollars.

"May I ask—are you switching banks?" Perhaps the Holbrooks had become unhappy with Desert Trust's service.

Mary shook her head and stared out the window facing the parking lot.

"All right. Just a few more steps," Sandy said, her thoughts torn between simply performing her job and asking after Mary's welfare. "Would you like your balance in cash or as a cashier's check?"

"Cash, please."

Sandy printed a form and pushed it across the desk for Mary to sign. When she returned from Lisa's window with $197.41 in notes and coins, Mary finally looked up at her. Tears brimmed in her eyes and the tip of her nose was bright pink.

Sandy closed her office door, laid the little bank envelope in front of Mary and sat on the edge of her desk. She reached out and took both of Mary's hands.

"Whatever's going on—I realize it's none of my business—but I want to help. Clearly, you're distraught and something's not right."

Mary snuffled loudly and pulled one hand away to rummage in her purse for a tissue.

"Mary, we used to have lunch now and then. You came to our social functions, invited me to your business's open house. Can I help in some way?"

"No one can," came the muffled reply. "Clint left me last year, took all our money and hooked up with someone new."

"But, he can't *do* that. The court would have awarded you half of everything, and you guys had a successful business."

"Well, he did it anyway. I got our house—mortgaged up the wazoo—and what was in our checking account. By the time the judge ever saw any paperwork at all, Clint had drawn all the accounts down to nearly nothing. The house was foreclosed eight months ago."

Sandy felt her own eyes dampen, her heart going out to her friend. She noticed more details—Mary's shirt and capris could have come from Goodwill, and although her wallet was of good quality, the purse was a cheap one.

"If you feel up to it, let me take you to lunch. Two of my tellers are back now and I was about to grab a bite anyway." She put on a perky smile. "My treat. Really. I insist."

The mention of food brought a flicker of longing to Mary's face. She nodded. They walked out into the searing midday heat—September seemed the longest month. While the rest of the nation enjoyed autumn weather, Phoenix area temperatures would hover in the high nineties for several more weeks.

Offhand, Sandy couldn't think of anyplace in Scottsdale that would make Mary feel comfortable enough to talk about her situation. She ended up steering her blue Mazda sedan onto the 101 Loop and parking at a Denny's a few exits away.

They took a corner booth and ordered sandwiches. As the story came out, Sandy found herself growing angrier by the minute. Clint's deception and betrayal struck close to home, vivid reminders of an early relationship. Sandy had supported her man through law school, only to have him turn the laws to his advantage when he left.

"I have an idea," she told Mary. "Let me speak with some friends of mine and get back to you. What's your number?"

TWO

"SHE SAID SHE would have to come back to the bank and find me. She doesn't have a phone or a car. She sold her vehicle four months ago and barely got enough for a few months' living expenses. I don't know how she's surviving."

"My god, the poor woman." Over the phone, it sounded as if Penelope Fitzpatrick had come to a dead stop. She'd told Sandy she was watering the potted plants on her deck, but Sandy could sense Pen's one-hundred-percent attention.

"I'd like to get the group together and tell everyone what I learned. Maybe there's a way we can help Mary."

"By all means," Pen agreed.

Within thirty minutes, Sandy had received text message replies from Gracie Nelson and Amber Zeckis; a meeting was set for seven o'clock at Sandy's home. The four women had followed the trail of a missing diamond necklace last April—maybe they could track the money Clint Holbrook had taken and find a measure of justice for his struggling ex-wife.

Sandy left the bank a few minutes early, picked up take-out Chinese for her dinner and went home to tidy up. Her two black cats, Heckle and Jeckle, greeted her at the door with plaintive meows to suggest they were starving. She knew better. She put food out for them, then dug into her carton of moo goo gai pan with her favorite pair of chopsticks, purchased on a banking trip to China a couple of years earlier. She walked through her living room, deciding once she'd picked up some stray magazines and taken her morning coffee cup to the kitchen it looked good enough for an impromptu meeting with friends. She changed from her business suit to cotton slacks and a loose top, wishing she could drop the spare twenty-five pounds that never seemed to leave her hips these days. The joy of menopause.

Pen Fitzpatrick was the first to arrive. Stately, in her seventies, with a Lauren Bacall aura that never seemed to wilt in the summer heat. It was Pen's stolen necklace the group of friends had searched out, dubbing themselves the Heist Ladies as they trailed a gang of jewel thieves last spring. Pen immediately asked about Mary, inquiring whether Sandy had come up with some ways in which the group could help.

"We had a long talk over lunch today," Sandy said. "Let me relay the information to everyone and we'll see what we come up with."

Pen nodded, dropped her small Versace bag onto a chair and knelt to scratch one of the cats behind the ears.

The doorbell rang a moment later. Gracie and Amber had arrived at the same time. Sandy admitted them, offered iced tea and everyone settled in, both cats immediately curling up on Amber's lap. She smiled and shifted her iPad to the small side table by her chair.

"A few months ago, we all jumped on board to help a friend, and I think we had some fun in the process."

Gracie groaned in a playful way, turning it into a smile.

"Well, aside from Gracie's one injury on the job." Sandy took a deep breath. "One of my customers, who's also a friend, is in a pinch. Ex-husband, younger woman... Mary and Clint had a fairly successful kitchen-and-bath business they both worked in, taking jobs with some of the major builders, and money wasn't a problem. Three years ago, Mary had to quit to take care of her ailing parents, and she trusted her husband to handle business as usual. With everything else on her plate, she admits she didn't know their true financial picture.

"By the time Clint left her for a younger woman, apparently he'd obtained second and third mortgages on their house and either spent or moved money from the bank accounts. Mary has no idea where it went. During the divorce proceedings, he didn't put up a fuss about giving her the house, even said he would continue to make the payments. Well, that promise was easily broken and she lost the house to foreclosure. It wasn't as if this couple lived beyond their means—it was a lovely home in a nice neighborhood."

Gracie spoke up: "So what's his explanation? He just quit making house payments and doesn't say why?"

"Apparently, that's pretty much the way it went. Mary had a few thousand in a savings account, but the bulk of their cash had disappeared. Her parents only passed away this summer and she hasn't had a chance to get work yet. She cleared the last two hundred dollars from her checking account today, and I really fear for how she'll manage to eat."

"Does she have any ideas about what she'll do next?" Penelope asked.

Sandy shook her head. "She's clearly not taking care of herself—she's put every scrap of her energy into her parents' care. I'll do some more checking but, seriously, she looks like a street person. Mary Holbrook was never that way. She used to be slim and athletic, well-groomed. Never flaunted money but never lacked it either. She didn't come right out and say so, but I have the impression she's living in a shelter. She's devastated."

Amber, Gracie and Penelope exchanged glances and each gave a small nod.

"Well, then," said Amber. "It looks like the Heist Ladies have another job. Last time it was diamonds, this time it's cash. And this time we know who the crook is."

Pen raised her iced tea glass. "All of you helped me when it meant recovering a family heirloom. Absolutely—we must help Mary take back her life and her dignity! Those are far more important."

The others raised glasses as well. "All right, then. To the Heist Ladies!"

THREE

SANDY SAW MARY tentatively hovering outside her office door the next day and motioned her to come inside. She noticed Mary was wearing the same clothes as yesterday, although her hair looked freshly washed.

"I was hoping you would come back soon," Sandy said. "I have good news—my friends are very much interested in helping. We want to get your money back for you."

Mary gave an inquisitive look.

"I think we can do it." How much to tell? Sandy wasn't sure giving details about the million-dollar necklace heist would be a good thing. "Let's just say a couple of our members have been pretty successful at tracking money and other missing items."

"I don't know…"

"Please. Let us at least try. Obviously, your ex isn't going to willingly give you anything. Otherwise, he wouldn't have hidden assets from the court and cheated you out of your share, right? We want to help you."

"I can't pay for an investigation."

"Right. I'm sure you would have already pursued it if you could. Mary, I assure you it isn't a problem for us. It's purely a matter of doing the right thing, of correcting the wrong that's been done to you."

"All right. But I'll do something in return. I'll pay you back somehow."

"We'll deal with that later. First, let's see if we can solve this thing."

Mary fidgeted with the clasp on her vinyl handbag, sending nervous glances around the office. "Where will you start? How will you know what to do?"

Good questions. "We'll think of something. First, I'd like you to meet the group and tell your story. Any little detail might be of help. Can you come to my house tonight?"

Mary's gaze drifted toward the door.

Of course. The woman didn't have a car. "How about this? Come back here to the bank around five o'clock. I'll take you home with me, we'll have a salad or something and I'll drive you home afterward."

A tilt of her head was all the acknowledgement Mary gave before she basically bolted out the door.

Oh my, Sandy thought. She's like a skittish fawn adrift in the city.

She picked up her phone and sent a text to Gracie, Amber and Penelope. My house, 6:30 tonight. Within a few minutes each had confirmed she would be there. Now, if Mary would actually come back.

Meetings consumed her afternoon and the tellers had balanced their cash and left by four-thirty. Sandy glanced at her watch. It was too late to call the home office. Although she had paperwork to review, her mind wasn't on the task and she found herself staring out the window. At 4:45 a bus pulled to a stop across the street, discharging one passenger. It was Mary.

At least this explains how she gets around town, Sandy thought. With her own car always at her disposal, she'd never realized the logistics needed to plan even a simple trip across the valley to another part of the huge city. It couldn't be easy to do everything you needed to without even the basic freedom a car provided. She gathered her purse, closed her blinds and met Mary at the front door.

"I'm so glad you came," she said as she locked up.

They walked together across the parking lot and Sandy unlocked her vehicle. Mary's eyes met hers across the top of the car.

"Thank you. Earlier, I didn't mean to sound like I didn't want your help. I guess I'm just not used to asking for it. I've always been so capable. Together, Clint and I were self-sufficient. Nothing has felt normal for the past year."

Sandy gave a sympathetic smile. "I know. This whole thing must have been so difficult for you."

For the first time, a hint of the old Mary came back when she pulled a wry grin. "You could say that. Ah well, I'll end up okay, no matter what happens."

Sandy wanted to ask a dozen questions but could see the shy little fawn still hovering below the surface. She drove quietly, letting Mary enjoy the car's air conditioning, pulling into her driveway twenty-five minutes later.

"Here we are. I hope you don't mind cats—I have two and they're always around."

She caught herself looking at her home afresh, through the eyes of someone who'd never been there before. The tan stucco, so similar to all the other houses on the block, the tile roofs, most landscapes done in rock, cactus and other native plants that could withstand the brutal summer heat. Walking inside was where differences became apparent. Without a male in her household, she'd opted for soft peach and pink colors, scented candles and pastel artwork. Her furniture tended toward the European—Queen Anne chairs and tables, cushioned sofa, television hidden inside an elaborate armoire. Her love of books was evidenced by the wall of shelves, and she treated herself weekly to fresh flowers both in the living room and at the kitchen break-fast bar, as well as in her bedroom.

"This is lovely," Mary said, gazing around the entry and living room. "It's been awhile since…"

Sandy filled the awkward pause by bustling toward the kitchen. "I have a lot of salad greens right now, so I thought that would make a nice dinner—if it sounds good to you?"

Mary nodded, standing beside the breakfast bar and run-ning her hands over the gleaming white granite top.

"Have a seat. How about a glass of wine? There's a nice pinot grigio chilling in the fridge or I have some reds…"

"Whatever you're having."

Mary accepted the cold glass of white wine, and Sandy sipped from her own as she pulled a variety of lettuces, celery, cucumber and sliced almonds from the fridge. A ginger-sesame dressing, a few mandarin oranges and crispy chow-mein noodles would complete the dish. She worked quickly, filling the silence with busyness rather than the dozen questions she really wanted to ask.

"We had no children, Clint and I," Mary said. "I sup-pose it was by choice. Our business kept us so occupied there wouldn't have been time to give kids the attention they need. What about you? Any kids?"

"No." Sandy had learned over the years it was the sim-plest answer.

"And now my parents are gone. I have a sister in Texas, but we have absolutely nothing in common, haven't spoken in years." Mary paused. "You're wondering if there isn't someone in the family I could have turned to. It's what most people assume—that you'll turn to your family when things get rough, right? So, no. There's no one."

"I'm sorry." Sandy slid a pile of cucumber slices on top of the lettuce she'd placed in the salad bowl.

"All our friends were really Clint's. Business acquaintances that he turned against me with lies. It's amazing how you find yourself not able to name a single person you know outside your husband's circle." She toyed with the stem of her wine glass. "Former neighbors... I never knew them well. Besides, I'm sure gossip is all over the neighborhood how the house at 2418 was foreclosed, and everyone has to be wondering what went wrong. That, or scared their own positions are every bit as shaky."

Sandy nodded. The huge rush of mortgage foreclosures had happened a few years ago in the Phoenix area, but she knew people were still feeling the effects. She added dressing and tossed the salad, then dished up two equal plates of it. Setting one in front of Mary, she circled the bar and took a seat beside her.

"It must have been hard, watching so many aspects of your life change so quickly."

Mary nodded. She forked up a large bite of her salad and chewed, her gaze focused somewhere in the middle of the kitchen. Sandy decided to let her guest set the conversational pace.

"I know you were shocked when you saw me yesterday," Mary finally said when she'd eaten more than half her salad. "I know how different I look. Cheap fast food isn't the way to stay in shape, and a gym membership is pretty much out of the question anymore. Geez, I haven't even had a few bucks to spend on a home hair color kit, much less a place to—"

"Mary, I don't want to get too personal but could you at least tell me where you're living? I'm worried about you."

Mary set her fork down. A long sigh escaped her. "Well, up to the beginning of summer I stayed in my car. Moved it around, kept out of sight. But when it got hot, the car had to go. It brought me enough cash to afford a motel I found with weekly rates. And a bus pass works okay."

"But now? Yesterday you said something about having no place to go."

The doorbell rang and Mary's frightened-deer eyes came back.

FOUR

SANDY HURRIED TOWARD the door, but not before she caught the word *shelter*.

"Sandy, sorry, I'm a touch early," Penelope said, breezing in. "So hard to judge the time it takes to drive anywhere in this city, especially during rush hour."

"You're fine," Sandy assured her. "Mary and I are just finishing our salads. Have you eaten?"

"I'm afraid I've become one of those septuagenarians who eats only once or twice a day, and only when I feel like it. Until this weather cools, I've hardly an appetite for anything."

"Come in then, and let me pour you a glass of wine. Or there's tea."

They walked into the kitchen and Sandy saw the way Mary practically shrank in stature when she saw the elegant, platinum-haired Penelope who retained her very proper British accent despite having lived in America her entire adult life. Luckily, Pen had a way of putting most any person at ease.

"Mary, I am so happy to meet you," she said, extending a hand. "Sandy has, of course, told us you've always been one of her favorite clients at the bank."

Mary actually blushed a little as she shook Pen's hand.

"I absolutely mean it, my dear. You won't find a better friend than Sandy Werner. Months ago, she stepped up to help me. I must say, she has a group of the most loyal and generous friends one would want to meet."

Pen accepted the wine glass Sandy held out. When the doorbell rang again, Pen offered to answer, giving Sandy and Mary a chance to finish their salads. Voices came from the front hall and by the time they drifted toward the kitchen Sandy had the plates cleared and an assortment of cookies set out.

Pen ushered in Amber Zeckis, the group's youngest member, the computer-whiz girl who'd dropped out of college because she was smarter than most of the professors. The caramel-skinned pixie whose corkscrew curls defied taming.

"Wine?" Sandy offered, holding up bottles of both red and white.

Amber pointed to the merlot and tucked her iPad under her arm, her dark eyes sparkling as she accepted a glass.

"I wonder if it's pleasant enough to sit outside," Sandy mused, glancing at her shady deck surrounded by wispy-branched acacia trees.

"It's nice out," Amber said. "Maybe eighty-five? And the sun will be down in a minute."

"Gracie should be along any time, so let's go ahead," Pen suggested.

They chose cushioned chairs around the glass-topped outdoor table. A small cactus garden grew in a talavera bowl in the center, one of Sandy's few concessions to the native Arizona flora. Elsewhere in her yard, she favored leafy trees, hibiscus and other flowering shrubs, and kept a small patch of lawn—Bermuda grass during the hot summers—which her landscape service man would seed with a less heat-tolerant winter grass in another month or so.

"Since we've agreed to assist Mary," Sandy said, "I want

her to tell the story, give as much information as she can so we'll have an idea what to do. But it's best if we wait for Gracie, I think. Meanwhile, maybe a quick introduction from each of us? Let Mary know what skills we each bring to the group."

A hesitant glance passed between Pen and Amber.

"Okay, then, I'll start," Sandy said. "You already know me from the bank, and basically the knowledge I contributed to our last little caper related to money. I can read financial reports, profit and loss statements, balance sheets and things like that. If we can get our hands on some of the data from your ex-husband's business, maybe I can figure out how much money is at stake and get some clues about where it went."

She turned to Amber, who picked up the narrative.

"Well, I love computers and digging around to find information," she said with a dimpled smile. "Basically, if someone is trying to keep a secret but they've posted any clues online, I'll find them."

"The girl scares me sometimes," Sandy said with a laugh. "She certainly has gotten into some banking information that I, as a banker, should be horrified about. As her cohort in solving crime...well, I'm happy to have her on our team."

They both looked toward Pen.

"Frankly, I don't know *what* I contribute. I went to Sandy when I needed her and she very generously stepped up. I booked some flights for travel, I suppose."

"And you know everyone who's anyone here in the valley. Most likely in the whole country," Sandy said. "She's a bestselling novelist, Mary, and seems to have entry to social events everywhere. I might remind—we found important information last time at one of those, plus, there are her contacts in other countries... And Pen's gentleman friend is retired prosecutor Benton Case, and I have to admit we've mined a bit of legal strategy from his trove of knowledge."

Pen tilted her head, small acknowledgement that Sandy's statements were true.

Mary smiled at Pen with more confidence now. "And this other lady, the one who's coming later?"

"Ah, that would be Grace Nelson. Gracie is a wife and mother—super organized. She keeps schedules and always knows who's doing what," Amber said.

"Except that it isn't at all like her to be late."

As if in answer to Sandy's concern, the front doorbell chimed.

"See?" Sandy said, jumping up. "Ask and you shall receive."

Gracie bustled through the house, like a perpetual motion device that ran until suddenly it couldn't sustain itself. She collapsed into the empty chair beside Amber. Strands of her long, dark hair strayed from the clip at the top of her head and a sweaty sheen glistened across her forehead. She accepted both a tall glass of water and one of the wine glasses from Sandy.

"So sorry, gang. It's always something with my family. This afternoon, it's an unannounced extra practice for next week's ballet recital. I had to drop my daughter off; Scott will pick her up and take the kids for pizza after. I swear, they only keep me around as their social secretary."

"And here I was, just now bragging about what a great organizer you are," Sandy said with a laugh.

Gracie rolled her eyes as she drank from her water glass.

Sandy straightened slightly in her chair. "Well. Enough about the rest of us. We've agreed to try to help Mary, so it's time we gather facts. Mary, I know this is weird for you, and maybe somewhat uncomfortable, telling a group of people what's happened. But you are among friends."

Amber reached over and gave Mary's shoulder a pat for emphasis.

"What can you tell us—about your ex, about his business, his actions, how he handled money—whatever we need to know to unravel this mystery?"

Mary downed the remains of her wine and took a deep breath. "Well. I pretty much told you yesterday, Sandy. He met a younger, prettier woman." Her voice became thick.

"Don't they all?" Pen popped up, already on her second glass of wine. "At some point, every man meets a younger, prettier woman. It doesn't give him the right to dump the woman who contributed to his success and leave her stranded while he trots off with the new trophy wife. It doesn't make him young and virile—it makes him a bastard."

There was a moment of silence. Pen had once been married, and now Sandy wondered… But the tension evaporated instantly when Mary broke out laughing.

"Yes! That's the thing I never could make myself say. I kept thinking I wanted him back, that I wanted our lives to go back to the way they were when we worked side by side. But you know what? I'm done with that. He had no right to leave me penniless—this is now about the money!"

"Hear, hear!" Pen called out.

Mary sent the older woman a look of such gratitude Sandy could tell a strong friendship had just formed.

Gracie had finished her water, switched to the wine, and now pulled an organizer notebook from her roomy handbag. "Okay, let's get started with details. Mary, we need names, addresses, contacts—everything you can remember."

FIVE

DETAILS EMERGED IN BURSTS, the first one in a rather startling manner.

"It's Kaycie Marlow," Mary announced.

"What! The blondie-chick weather babe from Channel 3? That's his trophy?" Amber's mouth actually hung open. "The girl can't even read the teleprompter without moving her eyes back and forth. Meteorologist? What a joke—she probably can't even spell the word."

Mary gave a gentle smile. "Surely she's not quite that dumb."

"Oh, I didn't mean to say your ex would—"

"No, no, it's fine. I'd like to think I have *some* qualities which surpass her perfect little face and cascades of golden hair." Mary picked at a cuticle. "But you can see why it's a little intimidating to compare myself to her."

Sandy put up one hand. "Mary, we're not even going there. No bit-by-bit comparisons. The truth is you supported your husband and helped build his business to a level of financial success. There is no justification for the way he and Kaycie Marlow treated you."

The others jumped in to agree.

"Okay, let's take down those names and addresses. Anything and anyone you can think of who might help us figure out where the money went." Gracie held her pen poised to make notes.

"Well, to start with, there's the bookkeeper who took over my position at the office when I had to leave," Mary began. "Two of the business accounts normally had better than six-figure balances, but I realize I can't get a judge to listen on my word alone. I need proof. I'd already thought of simply going to the office one night, letting myself in and finding the financial statements, but my key didn't work anymore. He'd actually changed the locks."

Gracie and Amber exchanged a secretive little smile. Sandy didn't want to ask what that was about.

"I guess finding the new locks was the point where I realized he wasn't welcoming me back into the business." Mary seemed wistful for a moment. She took a deep breath. "We could check out a couple of his buddies from Stardust Resort where he plays golf—he might have confided something to one of them."

Gracie wrote notes in her book; Amber was tapping away on her iPad.

"What about neighbors, social friends?" Pen asked.

"I don't know...he seems to have turned most of them against me with his story of how I abandoned him."

"Yes, but those are the ones he would have bragged to, giving his own justification for why he would move money out of your reach. Think about it."

"His home," Pen said. "Most men want their secrets nearby, so he'll have a safe or a desk or some place at home where he's locked away account numbers and such. Where is he living now?"

"I actually don't know. I assumed he'd moved in with her when they got married. I mean, if money was running low...and she makes a good salary..."

Amber stared at the screen on her tablet and said something, which Sandy had to ask her to repeat. "Vandergrift Towers. That's their address."

"Seriously?" Gracie peered toward the lighted screen. "Holy crap! It's one of the most expensive condo complexes in the state."

Pen gave Mary a firm stare. "Money was *not* running low—get that through your head right now. What he told you—it's all poppycock."

Mary looked as if she'd been punched in the stomach. She reached for the wine bottle and refilled her glass, downing half of it in one gulp. The others exchanged glances and Sandy quietly moved the bottle to the other end of the table. They needed their friend coherent tonight, although no one could argue with the emotions raging through her.

Amber made eye contact again. "Okay, there's a personal bank account at Scottsdale Bank, although the balance in it at the moment probably wouldn't cover two months' rent at the Vandergrift condo… Oh, but look—here's an account in Barbados with more than a hundred thousand dollars in it." She gave a devilish smile and turned the tablet toward Mary, whose face hardened when she saw the screen.

"All right, girls," she said. "This is war."

Sandy stood. "This is an area I'm very uncomfortable with. As an officer with a major bank I really cannot be privy to this sort of knowledge and *shouldn't* even be acquainted with anyone with the hacking skills to learn such things. So, let's just say that I went into the house to make us a snack. Say that was ten minutes ago and I never heard any of this last bit. And let's say that when I come back out with a tray of cheeses and crackers, the topic will have turned to things less specific about Mr. Holbrook." She picked up one empty wine bottle and gave a wink as she left the table.

"Are there more accounts?" Pen asked, once Sandy was out of earshot.

Amber nodded. "Several."

"I think it's best if we leave direct knowledge of them to a very small circle—let's say only Amber and Mary—while the rest of us concentrate on other things. I'll be happy to see what I might learn from the golfing friends. Benton is a member of the same club, among others, so I'll have a way to ask around and perhaps make acquaintance."

"How about if Amber and I check out the offices of Holbrook Plumbing, see if there's a way into the records," said Gracie. "I mean, you never know when someone may forget to lock a door or a secretary may leave some vital piece of paper out in plain sight…"

Mary spoke up: "I can surely walk into my old office during the day—say I just wanted to visit everyone."

Sandy came outside just then with a bowl of salsa and a bag of tortilla chips. "Sorry, I was out of cheese. And this was quicker." She set the items down. "Mary, I heard your idea about visiting the office and I'm going to suggest against doing it. We already know Clint is able to move money around and he's certainly not above doing it again to hurt you. A visit would come as a surprise to him right now, since you say you've had no contact in almost a year. I think you need to stay out of his sight completely, so as not to alert him that we're suspicious."

"I agree," said Pen. "Let him believe he's succeeded, that he's pulled off his shenanigans without being caught."

The others nodded.

"In fact, we all should be careful about meeting with Mary in public places for awhile. If Clint suspects anything at all—and it could come from a casual mention by an acquaintance such as 'oh, I saw your ex-wife having lunch with Penelope Fitzpatrick the other day.' The smallest thing could alert him. Let's gather facts, put together a case and then surprise him with it."

"Sandy is right. I'll consult Benton on this, but I'm fairly certain if you want a judge to reopen your divorce settlement case on the basis of fraud, you'll need plenty of evidence. It's too risky to let Clint know what we're up to."

"But, I feel like you girls are doing all the work and I won't be contributing anything," Mary protested.

Sandy set a hand on her friend's shoulder. "You will be doing plenty, especially behind the scenes. Plus, you've done quite a lot already by giving us the information you provided tonight. For the near future, we'll limit face-to-face visits to your stopping by the bank to see me. We'll get you a phone so staying in touch will be easy."

Gracie looked at her watch. "That's a beep from hubby, wondering if I'll be much longer, so I think if we're set for tonight I'll take that as my exit cue." She stood and tucked her notebook into her bag.

Amber, who had been frowning intently at her iPad for the past ten minutes, tapped a couple of times on it and closed the cover. "Me too. Looks like I'll have a busy day tomorrow."

Sandy and Mary gathered glasses and the remaining chips to carry indoors. Pen had gone to the powder room and Sandy turned to Mary.

"I have a spare room," she said, "and I'd really rather you stayed here than going to the—wherever you've been staying."

Mary's reluctant demeanor returned. "I can't ask that—"

"You didn't ask. I offered."

"I'll stay at the shelter at least one more night. I have to go back for my clothes and things anyway. And then I'll let you know tomorrow. I'm going to get a job. If nothing else, you and your friends have given me the hope and confidence to get out there and make something of myself. It's been two months since Mom died, and it's ridiculous that I haven't already taken action."

Pen emerged from the bathroom in time to hear Mary's words.

"May I offer an idea?" she said. "A small loan—"

Mary sputtered.

"Only a loan, dear. Only enough to get you into an apartment of your own and get set up with some basic things." She made a *stop* motion with one hand. "It's only practical. You cannot be conducting this sort of business, having these types of private calls from such a public place as a shelter. You need your own place. You'll get that job quickly, and the loan will be repaid in no time. Really. I'm only looking out for the interests of the entire group."

"In that case, thank you," Mary said with tears in her eyes. "Thank you so much. I'm going to contact the owner of a gym where I used to be a member. He was always so nice to me, even after the split with Clint. I'd love to teach self-defense or lead workout classes, but if all he offers is for me to mop the floors, I'll do it."

Pen took both of Mary's hands and squeezed gently. "I do believe there are great things ahead for you."

As Pen drove away, Sandy turned to her friend. "Are you sure you don't want a room here for the night?" Privately, she couldn't see how on earth Mary would be teacher material for a gym, but Pen's offer for the apartment was nice and eventually something would come along.

Mary shook her head. "I'd feel more comfortable going back, if you don't mind driving me? I'm pretty sure the buses have quit for the night."

"Okay. I am going to insist on a stop along the way though." Sandy picked up her keys and purse.

Mary gave the address of the women's shelter and Sandy planned the drive so they could stop at a 24-hour Walmart store along the way. A half-hour later, Mary was equipped with a new cell phone and enough prepaid minutes to keep her in contact with the rest of the team for a couple of weeks.

"Add this to my loans to repay," she said when they were back in the car, although she was beaming as she played with the buttons on the phone.

"It wasn't much. Consider it a gift."

SIX

CLINT HOLBROOK SUPPRESSED his elation as he scrawled his signature on the bottom line of the document in front of him. It was the single largest business deal of his life, the one that put his construction company truly on the global map. A five-hundred-million dollar deal—who'd have thought it? Little old Holbrook Plumbing had come a long way from its fledgling days in Apache Junction, Arizona. He reluctantly credited part of that rise in success to his ex-wife's suggestion that they move the business to Scottsdale. If you wanted to bring in wealthier clients you needed to be nearby. But Mary hadn't been involved for more than two years now; his own brilliance had led him to get his contractor's license and to cultivate the contacts needed to put this mega deal together.

His lawyer pushed another sheaf of papers toward him, indicating two more places to sign.

Clint rarely thought of Mary these days, other than to make unfavorable comparisons with his new love. Sad, really. Mary used to be a knockout—trim and fit, she played softball on a team when he met her. She played well on the golf course, and her suggestion that they join a club had paid off big when he got his first contracts with some of the more prestigious Scottsdale builders. Of course, that's when they handled only the plumbing aspects of jobs, installing bathrooms elegant enough to put Buckingham Palace to shame, and then with the trend toward all-out gourmet kitchens, well, his reputation only spread.

He penned his signature, his eyes focusing on the dollar figures on those pages, which made him think of the bunch of bills arriving soon and reminded him—the deposit money for today's deal had better reach his bank account soon.

Derek Woo gathered the signed pages, took one final look through the stack of documents and seemed satisfied. He nudged Clint; contractor and lawyer stood. Across the table, attorneys for Clint's customer chattered in their own language, so speedily Clint couldn't catch a word. Finally, the lead attorney gave a slight head-bow toward Clint.

"Gentlemen, thank you very much."

Clint returned the little motion.

"Your engineers will be at the job site first thing on Monday?"

"You bet," Clint said, realizing his speech pattern made him sound like a hick compared to the formality of those across the table. "I mean, yes. I am personally flying to Shanghai the day after tomorrow."

Handshakes, bows, a quiet exit as the foreign men left.

"Well," said Derek Woo. "That went smoothly."

"I didn't doubt it would," Clint said. "Hey, can I get you a drink? I think this calls for a celebration."

"Thank you, but no. I've another meeting across town. I'm certain your wife will be in the mood to celebrate with you." He gave a grin as he picked up a thick briefcase and walked out.

For a nano-second, a picture of himself and Mary clicking champagne glasses flashed through Clint's head. He shook it off. Mary had turned into a sour old frump, and once she'd left him and the business so she could stay with her ailing parents, everything between them went downhill. Dammit, when you were married almost twenty years, Alzheimer's was no excuse to duck out on all the important things in life.

Kaycie was his wife now and he liked it that way. Young, gorgeous, locally well-known as the main draw on the Channel 3 evening news. If contacts in business were important, Kaycie could certainly bring him a ton more of them than Mary ever did. And, she was the ultimate arm-candy. He was a lucky guy. He picked up his phone and instructed it to call her.

"Well, Babycakes, it's time to put on your best dress and those high heels that always get me fired up—we're celebrating tonight with dinner and dancing."

"You signed the deal!"

He pictured those sexy dimples framing her perfect, brilliant-white teeth.

"I did. And I've got a big surprise for you. Tell that boss of yours you need some time off."

Her perkiness went down about six notches. "Oh, Honey Bear, I gotta work tonight. I've got the six o'clock show and the ten, and Johnson wants a staff meeting in between. I think we're all supposed to grab some kind of quick dinner at our desks."

"Tell him something's come up. Tell him you got a headache or some female thing. I don't care—this is important to me."

"My career is important to me, honey. The staff meeting is about the new fall lineup and there could be network people here. My chance to hint around at a promotion—"

"Is some network promotion more valuable than the half-billion I'm making on this overseas project? More important than hobnobbing internationally?"

He could practically hear her wheels turning. Kaycie was a climber, for sure. "Do your first gig then figure a way to skip the rest. I'll pick you up outside the studio at seven o'clock."

"O-kayyy…" She sounded reluctant but he could hear the excitement in her voice. It was a good thing he'd not told her the surprise was a pair of first-class tickets. He couldn't wait to see the look on her face. Collecting his thank-you gift later in bed would just be the bonus for her gratitude.

SEVEN

SANDY WERNER DROVE her little Mazda past the address Amber had given, the upscale condo where Clint Holbrook and his new little sweetie were living. It was a gated complex, four buildings, each four stories tall, typical Arizona style—tan stucco exteriors with some rock accent trim, large windows to let in maximum view, tinted to minimize the glaring sun. Additional sun protection came from tall palm trees, and it appeared there were inner courtyards with acacia, Desert Museum trees, leafy hibiscus and purple sage. A stately row of royal palms led from the guardhouse at the gate, down a two-lane entry road with oleander bushes groomed within an inch of their lives, to a twenty-foot water feature where impossibly blue water crashed over a series of boulders to a mini-lake.

Just outside the high fence stood a carved sign with the name: Vandergrift Towers. And in much smaller print: Exclusive Adult Living. As if anyone would allow a child to leave so much as a footprint in the perfectly raked pea-gravel which covered rolling mounds of earth. Amber had told the Heist Ladies the average condo price here was in the neighborhood of 1.5 million dollars. Nice neighborhood.

So, how did a contractor manage a place like this? Sandy wondered. From what Mary had told them, the home she and Clint had lived in was an average three-bedroom and was what they could comfortably afford. Even so, he'd taken out extra mortgages on it. None of this made sense unless TV weather babes made a lot more money than Sandy would have guessed. She processed enough loan applications at the bank she highly doubted that was the case. Unless the minor celebrity's bonuses included a place like this, then either the kitchen and bath business had taken off like a rocket to Mars, or Clint was living way beyond his means.

Then again, Mary had told the group there had been money in the bank, way back when. Clint absconded with it, and this address might be exactly where it all ended up. Sandy turned left at the end of the block, hoping for a better view of the whole complex, but a high fence and tall oleander bushes squelched that idea.

Two blocks later, she made the turn onto the 101 Loop and headed toward the bank. Sooner or later, they would find out the rest of Clint's story, and if it meant he had to downgrade his fancy new lifestyle and live in a regular neighborhood again in order to do right by Mary, well that was just too bad for him. At the moment there were too many possibilities for Sandy to know how the story went—and it was exactly why she and her team were looking into it.

She had hardly set her purse on her desk when her phone pinged with an incoming text message. It was from Amber. Sandy automatically began to compose a reply when it occurred to her the questions would consume a dozen or more back-and-forth messages. She opted for a real call instead.

"Hey, Sandy. What's up?" Amber sounded as if she were multi-tasking at least four other things.

Sandy told her about the condos she'd checked out this morning. "I'm going to request a file and see if my bank handled the loan for Clint and Kaycie Holbrook, but I doubt that's the case. Once he drained his and Mary's assets, he seems to have moved on to other institutions."

"Yeah, probably. What I found last night was elsewhere. But it's worth a look."

"My main question is where they got the money for such a place. Unless Kaycie's a much bigger celebrity than she seems, most local television talent don't make enough to qualify for a million-dollar home. The few I've known personally live in average, middle-class neighborhoods."

"Yeah, hold on a second," Amber said.

Sandy could hear computer keys tapping in the background. Something crackled in her ear, like a sheet of paper being wadded.

"Let's see… Kaycie Marlow, meteorologist, Channel 3, Phoenix, Arizona. Her salary is listed in the directory of entertainment professionals as sixty-thou' a year. Certainly not the low end of the scale, but about average nationally."

Okay, thought Sandy. Sixty thousand would qualify you for a smallish house in one of the less-pricey valley cities, not much of anything in Scottsdale and certainly not Vandergrift Towers.

"So, Clint is taking home a half million a year as a plumber?" Her voice sounded incredulous—she meant for it to. Simple math told her it was close to the range he would need to qualify for that place.

"Well," said Amber, "that's the thing I was texting you about. I visited the state Construction Industries website and looked up mister Clint. Looks like he expanded and became a building contractor just about the time Mary was no longer at the office to keep an eye on the financials."

Sandy sensed more was coming.

"Holbrook Plumbing went under the umbrella of Holbrook Construction Inc. when he got his general contractor's license, although the plumbing branch of the company stayed at the old location. Apparently, there were still enough kitchen and bath remodels to keep his original, core business going. Holbrook Construction Inc. now operates from a high-rise in downtown Phoenix. He leases the top two floors, but I think he leaves clients with the impression he personally built and owns the whole building."

"Interesting."

"Yeah."

"And this happened during the time he's crying the blues to the court about not having money to split with Mary?"

"He's sneakier than that. He waited until the ink was dry—barely—on the divorce papers before he branched out. Doesn't look like he waited quite that long to hook up with Kaycie Marlow. They were photographed together at several social events while he and Mary were still a legal couple. The jerk didn't even have the decency to help out with her parents' situation or lend emotional support to his wife through all that. I tell you, I hate him already."

Sandy smiled at her young friend's dedication to their cause. Still, something nagged at her.

"Last night you found several bank accounts," she said. "I wonder how it's possible for a brand-new contractor with a brand-new business to get the large jobs and make the profits those balances would seem to indicate."

"Dunno," said Amber. "You want me to keep digging?"

"Unless he took government contracts, I doubt specifics on his bids and costs will be anywhere in a public record," Sandy said, "but it's worth a try. Mary's going to need hard figures and good data if she hopes to make a court case of this."

"Got it. I'll let you know what I find." Amber clicked off the call before Sandy thought to ask whether she'd printed copies of those questionable bank transactions she'd found the previous night.

A tap on her door, one of the tellers with a question, reminded Sandy she still had her day job. It felt as if she'd barely tackled the day's emails when her personal phone buzzed. A glance at the readout showed it was Penelope.

"Yes, Pen?"

"Oh. I meant to leave you a message rather than interrupt your workday."

"It's all right." *I need to get communications under better control if I hope to* have *a job by the time this is finished.* "What's happening?"

"Just a quick report. We've found Mary a furnished apartment. She chose it because it's on the bus line and near the place she hopes to be working soon. I've put down the required deposits and first month's rent, and I gave her a ride from the shelter with her belongings. She wouldn't accept cash but I left a little anyway, tucked beside a lamp on the nightstand. She'll need food, for heaven's sake."

"Thank you, Pen. You've been most efficient this morning, and it was sweet of you to consider the cash."

"Well, I'm off to lunch at the country club. Purely work, you know. I mean to seek out a couple of those golf chums Mary told us about last night."

"Thanks."

"And I thought I would suggest—perhaps we should each send you a little report at the end of day, then we either confer by phone or email once. It seems better than these little dribs and drabs of information you must be receiving from all of us."

"Agreed. And it's a better way to report to Mary without using up the limited minutes on her new phone."

Sandy put her phone away and looked at the dizzying

number of bank emails awaiting her attention. She couldn't think straight and decided it was because she'd skipped breakfast. She went to the break room where she brewed a cup of tea and found a picked-over box of donuts someone had brought. Hardly brain food.

The thought that continued to nag her was what she'd asked Amber earlier. How on earth had Clint Holbrook managed to take a small-time plumbing business to a multi-million dollar construction company in less than three years? Overnight successes happen, she told herself, but the timing of this one smelled very fishy.

EIGHT

GRACIE NELSON PULLED her gray minivan into the parking lot at Amber's building a few blocks from the Arizona State campus. She'd been here before—to the tiny efficiency apartment with the personality of a shoebox. The lack of ambiance didn't especially surprise her. Amber lived in a mental and virtual world where her enjoyment came from cyberspace. A dwelling with no views and few other amenities, and the constant traipsing of college students probably didn't bother her at all. For Gracie, college and that whole scene felt a lifetime away.

Her own home in Mesa was a decently sized split-level, nothing grand. At least they enjoyed a few niceties such as a spacious kitchen and a backyard swimming pool, which saved her sanity when the outside temperature was a million degrees and her two kids and all their friends began to make her crazy within the confines of the house. She leaned back in her seat, took a deep breath and composed a short text message on her phone.

Within a moment, the response: BTS

What? Oh—Be there soon.

Amber emerged from the walkway between two buildings, dressed in black leggings, black hoodie, a black backpack slung over her shoulder. Seriously? Although dark, it was more than eighty degrees outside. The outfit must be stifling.

"Hey," Amber said, plopping into the front passenger seat, tossing her backpack behind.

"Hey."

"So?"

"I'm still up for it. You?"

A row of shiny white teeth glimmered in the darkness. "Oh yeah. Let's do this thing."

Gracie put the van in gear and backed out of her parking spot.

"Oh, I printed out those bank statements I found last night," Amber said with a nod toward her pack.

"Sandy's gonna have a blast with that."

Gracie made the turn onto University Drive where the traffic was backed up. College towns. The same anywhere, she supposed. By the time they reached Price and the 101, the quieter roadway felt more like that in her own area. People here had eight-to-five jobs and many had to arise before dawn to do their hour-plus commutes. Bedtime came early, with dinner and homework occupying the early evening hours.

She exited at Thomas Road in Scottsdale and made her way to the address Amber read off for Holbrook Plumbing. She could have programmed her GPS to take her directly there, but all this cloak and dagger stuff had made her paranoid about some authority later being able to go back to her logs and find out where she'd been this date and time. Tonight's little foray needed to stay completely anonymous.

They drove past the Holbrook shop once at normal speed, Amber studying the building while Gracie concentrated on not being noticeable. Holbrook Plumbing had display windows showing sinks and bathtubs, softly lit with low indirect lights. A metal grate protected the large plate glass from bricks hurled by smash-and-grab robbers. As if someone would go to all that effort and then try to haul away a bathtub. The neighborhood was one of small businesses, all closed at this hour. There was a sandwich shop, a dry cleaner, a shoe repair (did anyone actually repair their shoes anymore?), and a pawnshop with metal shutters over the windows and door. Several other storefronts seemed geared toward the same clientele as Holbrook's— hardware, carpet and an electrician's place. It was a small neighborhood completely devoid of big-box stores, like a slice of 1970 somehow out of sync with the rest of the mega-metropolis Phoenix had become.

Amber pointed at the pawnshop. "What's that?"

Gracie wracked her memory to think whether she'd actually ever been in one. Nope. "I remember my dad talking about them. When he was in the Air Force, there were pawnshops near the base. Guys who couldn't quite squeak by until payday would take something of value—their guitar or the ring they'd planned to give their girl the next time on leave—hock it for some cash, bail it out when their pay came, provided they weren't in even more debt by then. I suppose it was the days before kids just ran up credit card debt to cover everything."

Amber nodded as if she still didn't really get it.

Gracie circled the block and parked down the street from Holbrook Plumbing. "Was there any sign of somebody around?"

"No one," Amber assured her. "But there was a security company sticker on the front door."

"You could see that from the car?"

"Yeah, well, I'm blessed with excellent vision." She sat facing the darkened building.

"And how are we getting past that?"

Amber turned to face Gracie, taking the tone of a kindergarten teacher explaining the colors of the rainbow. "The company was Franklin Security. They sell one of two very basic alarm systems. The Bell 47206 or the Bell 38921. Either one is pretty much a piece of cake if you know the codes."

"But we don't know the codes."

"*You* don't know the codes. Don't sweat this, Gracie."

I'm risking arrest for this, based on a twenty-one-year-old telling me not to sweat it? Gracie nearly reached for the ignition key again.

"Hey, I've never let you down yet, have I?" Amber said with an impish grin.

"I've never done anything like this with you," Gracie pointed out.

Amber tilted her head, acknowledging the truth of the statement. "Come on. I looked it up on Google Earth. There's a fence around the back of the property, which we'll reach from the alley. It looks like chain link, which is an easy climb. The back door has a keypad and I'll get the alarm for us. Bada-bing—we're in."

"Bada-bing? Where do you come up with this stuff?"

"Eh, me and my mom watched *The Sopranos* a lot."

Gracie reached for the ignition again.

"Pull around the corner and go in the alley," Amber said. "But we probably shouldn't park directly behind. In case there's cameras or something."

"You know how to use the keypad and bypass the alarm, but you don't know whether they have cameras or not?"

A shrug was the only answer she got. *I need to go home right this minute, do not pass Go, do not collect anything*, Gracie thought.

She drove into the alley and followed Amber's instructions as they got out of the car.

The chain link fence surrounded a small dirt yard, a place where the discarded toilets and tubs went when they got replaced by shiny new ones during a remodel job. Three company trucks were backed into spaces to their right, two big dumpsters sat on the left, one of them sprouting the shaggy ends of nasty old carpeting. Amber paused in the shadows, taking a full two minutes to scope out the place from outside the chain link. The whole area was dead quiet. She coughed loudly—no response. When she was satisfied no guard or watchdogs were about to pounce forth, she slung her backpack off her shoulder and unzipped the front compartment.

"Whaaat's thaaat?" Gracie asked, stretching out the words in the singsong way she used when she thought her kids were smuggling Oreos to bed.

"Lock picks. I think it'll be quicker to get the padlock off this gate than to scale the fence and deal with the razor wire at the top."

"You didn't mention razor wire when you were talking about Google Earth," Gracie reminded.

"It doesn't show up real well in those images." Amber opened her little kit and inserted a tiny metal stick into the hefty padlock.

Gracie nervously scanned from one end of the alley to the other. Movement behind the pawnshop caught her eye, but it turned out to be a plastic shopping bag flapping in the breeze.

"Okay, done," Amber said. She slid the rolling gate open a few inches and squeezed herself through.

"Look, I've had two kids. I need a couple more inches of space than you, Miss Skinny."

The gate rolled easily enough for Gracie and they pulled

it closed behind them. "In case someone comes along," Amber said.

They edged their way through the clutter using small penlights from Amber's pack rather than going down the driveway, which felt a little too exposed by the security lights at the corners of the property. Gracie noted that Amber also hadn't mentioned those when she cased the place on Google.

A small loading dock filled the left half of the back façade of the building, nothing sized large enough for semi-trucks, but adequate for mid-sized delivery trucks to bring new stock. Perfect for Holbrook's own small fleet to load up the tubs and sinks and granite slabs they would take out to their jobs. To the right of the concrete dock was a walk-through door, solid metal, and beside that was a numeric keypad. Amber headed directly for it.

"See? Told you it would be a Bell." She pulled out her phone and went to some internet site she'd already book-marked.

Gracie felt like an actor on a stage, the way the back porchlight shone directly down on her head. She shrank to the shadows, her heart going into overdrive at every tiny sound. Amber pecked away at the phone until she found what she wanted. She took a deep breath and began pressing digits on the keypad.

"If this doesn't work we'll just jimmy the door and then I can disconnect the alarm wires once we're inside," she said, without looking directly at Gracie. No big deal.

Oh, god, what am I doing here? Gracie sent a silent wish heavenward that she would very soon be safely home in her own bed next to her sweetheart of a husband, rather than calling him from jail begging him to come bail her out.

NINE

SEVEN P.M. AND Sylvia Marlow was seated on a barstool in Flannigan's when Kaycie walked in. She'd stopped at the ladies room on her way in, as always, making certain her hair and makeup were perfect before walking into a public place. The day had cooled somewhat, as her six o'clock forecast said it would, but when the temperatures hovered in the low nineties it was impossible to walk from a parking lot to a building without feeling wilted. With a fresh spritz of cologne and a close-up check of her eye liner, she'd flashed her brilliant smile in the mirror. She absolutely understood what Clint Holbrook saw in her.

She still wore the form-fitted red dress from tonight's early broadcast and a few heads turned as she passed tables on her way to the bar. It never got old, people recognizing her in public. Would she miss the adulation? Yes, but she could get used to living off Clint's money and traveling the world with him in place of standing in front of a blank screen and pretending to be ecstatic over the weather.

Sylvia waved from across the room, her smile tired and the bags under her eyes more pronounced than usual. With an unlimited budget, Kaycie decided she would take her mother shopping for a wardrobe that didn't look as if it came from a discount store. A makeover wouldn't hurt, either. She set her smile in place and closed the distance between them.

"Hey, Mom, thanks for meeting me." Kaycie air-kissed a space beside Sylvia's left ear.

"Well, you said you had some special news for me." Sylvia's glance dropped toward Kaycie's belly. "I know what I hope it will be."

"Um, let's get a table in the corner where we can talk quietly," Kaycie said, signaling the bartender for a glass of white wine as she took her mother's arm. "How about that one over there?"

She aimed Sylvia toward the most deserted part of the large room, well away from the business crowd at the bar. Maybe she should have held this news until she'd had time to drive out to her mother's house in Glendale and deliver it privately. Well, they were here now. Plus, it was noisy in the room and Kaycie couldn't hide her excitement any longer.

"I'm not pregnant, Mom," she said, the minute they were seated. "There's time for that later."

Although she really should take steps in that direction soon. The one thing that would bind Clint to her forever would be a child. Every younger woman who married a rich, older man figured that one out—have a baby with him right away and he was locked in to supporting you financially. It was like a perfect storm—Clint's billion-dollar business deal and a baby in the same year. She automatically picked up her phone to add the task to her calendar: get pregnant.

But no—this wasn't something she would forget to do. She needed to think it through so the timing would be just right.

"So, if it's not a grandchild for me, what's the big news?"

Sylvia had brought a fresh beer to the table and a fleck of the foam clung to her upper lip.

"Clint and I are taking a big trip. First class tickets and everything! It's going to be even more fabulous than our honeymoon trip to Barbados."

"Really. Where you goin'?"

"Well, that's the real surprise—he hasn't told me our destination yet. He just said I should take a couple months leave from my job and go out and buy some pretty clothes while we wait for our visas to come through."

"Visas?"

"Well, yeah, I guess a lot of countries don't require them but some places do and it can take awhile. I don't know—the destination has to do with this new contract he just signed, so it's a big construction project of some kind. He talks about that stuff sometimes but I didn't hear much after he said the part about shopping for new clothes."

"What about Channel 3 and your job?"

"Well, I could do as Clint suggested and just quit." The idea was tempting, living the life of a millionaire's wife. Plus, now there was the idea of a baby. "But my career is important to me too. You know how I've talked since I was a little girl about wanting to be a TV anchor at a big station somewhere like New York or L.A."

Sylvia nodded. It was true, ever since Kaycie learned how much the camera loved her adorable little face, her daughter had wanted to be a TV star.

"Anyway, I'm giving it some thought. So, I was thinking this weekend we could hit some of the nicer stores like Neiman-Marcus. Want to come along? You could use a nice outfit or two."

Sylvia cocked her head. "I don't know. My job isn't a fancy one like yours. I can be a file clerk wearing any old thing."

"Come on, Mom. It'll be fun. You and me, like the old days." *The old days when you dragged me to Walmart because that's where the bargains were?* "My treat."

She sipped her wine and tried to imagine the first-class cabin on an overseas flight.

TEN

"So, THE NEXT thing I knew we were inside," Gracie said, holding her hand over her heart. "There I was—a burglar. I kept picturing charges of breaking and entering."

"Geez, it's not as if you haven't done it before—you and Sandy." Amber delivered the comment with a grin.

"We didn't break—we only entered," Sandy reminded.

"What a weenie." Amber rolled her eyes as she gathered the pages coming out of her printer.

Gracie sent a pleading look toward Penelope. "I'm not a weenie. Tell them! Tell them about my on-the-job injury."

Pen looked around the tiny apartment, taking in the whole group. "I've been thinking about that, about the danger we're occasionally putting ourselves in. Maybe we should look into self-defense classes."

"Can we get guns and carry-permits?" Amber's eyes gleamed.

"No… I think that would be taking it a bit far," Pen said. "Still, it couldn't hurt to know some, shall we say, *moves*."

Sandy seemed thoughtful. "Let me check with Mary. I think she used to take classes at the gym, and she's working there now. Did I tell you?"

Startled expressions all around.

"I talked to her this morning. Her old instructor hired her right away. For now, she's just helping out, cleaning up and laundering the towels and such. But she really sounded happy. She's finally doing something she enjoys and not thinking about Clint all the time." Sandy was genuinely glad her friend had found a niche. "Okay, much as we'd love to hear about the scary parts of your visit to Holbrook Plumbing, what we really need to know is what you found there."

Amber spoke up once more. "First off, there was nothing in the files we found to verify the banking activity I'd located online."

"Not surprising," Sandy said. "I would imagine he's keeping all that secret cash hidden very well."

"Right. We found and photocopied financial statements. That's another thing—the location we, um, visited…it seems to be strictly limited to Holbrook Plumbing's business transactions. There was no obvious reference to his contracting jobs."

Gracie piped up: "He had a private office though. The layout of the place included a showroom at the front, a conference room with a drawing table for blueprints and such, then there were separate offices for a secretary or bookkeeper and one for himself. That one was locked." She chuckled. "But the lock didn't stop Amber."

Amber took a mock bow, obviously a little bit proud of her contribution.

"So, once we were inside Clint's private office, I used my handy-dandy thumb drive to copy a bunch of stuff off his computer. I haven't had time to go through all of it yet. There seem to be several corporations and I'm not sure how they're related. Sandy and Pen—you guys might be able to figure it out easier."

"I'd be happy to give it a look," Sandy said.

"Benton might lend a hand, too," Pen added, "although

I'm trying not to pull him too deeply into this. The more he knows, the more obligated he'll feel to report Clint's maneuvers to the authorities. For now, we definitely don't want the law peeking around. We need evidence, which will get Mary a new hearing, not something that will let the Feds come in and confiscate Clint's assets."

Heads nodded all around. The thumb drive was passed over to Sandy.

"Next item of business goes to you, Pen. Were you able to learn anything about Clint's dealings by chatting with the golfing buddies at the club?"

Pen sat a little straighter on Amber's futon. "I must say, I did have a lovely lunch at the club. Benton readily agreed to take me there and even provided introductions to Roy McDonald and Stanley Piccard. The other name Mary gave—Joseph Rose—he wasn't about."

"How did you approach the subject with them?"

"Oh, I made it sound as if I'd known Clint Holbrook many years ago from a kitchen remodeling job, and I'd heard he had divorced—sadly, because I'd enjoyed working with his wife on the planning and cost estimates for my job. When I mentioned his remarriage, you should have seen the eyebrow-wiggles from the two men. Apparently, Kaycie Marlow Holbrook is every bit as fetching in person as she is on television."

She shifted in her seat again—she would avoid the saggy futon on future visits. "I moved the subject to the rumor I'd heard that Clint had greatly expanded his business, dropping the hint that one of the charitable boards I sit on has raised a great deal of funds for a new concert hall and we've been wondering which contractors we might want to solicit bids from. Perhaps Mr. Holbrook's company would be interested, I suggested."

"Any nibbles?"

"Roy McDonald was clueless. He went off on a tangent about where the concert hall would be located. I had to steer him away from what would have become a full hour's discussion. Stanley Piccard picked up my hint and told me he felt certain Holbrook Construction would be interested in bidding, making it sound as if Clint was a great admirer and supporter of the arts." She made a little face. "He did give me Clint's personal cell phone number, which is something even Mary did not have."

"Good job," Gracie said.

"Mr. Piccard did say Clint apparently won a sizable bid recently, but he didn't know the details. Seems Clint is being rather mysterious about the whole thing."

"There have to be records. Huge construction projects don't happen without a lot of paperwork and communications going back and forth," Sandy said.

"The thumb drive," Amber suggested. "It's gotta have something of value. I mean, surely he's not keeping all of it at home."

Sandy hoped the thumb drive would provide the key. Breaking their way into the penthouse suite of offices downtown or the gated condominium at Vandergrift Towers would not be nearly as easy as their first foray into crime.

ELEVEN

SANDY LOOKED UP from the pages spread over her dining table. Her head pounded and she wondered—not for the first time—why she'd given up a beautiful Saturday to delve into Clint Holbrook's accounting shenanigans. Practically on schedule, the first day of October had brought milder temperatures and she itched to be in her garden, setting out some winter vegetables and simply enjoying the feel of earth between her fingers. But no—she'd assured Pen she would have something to report by this afternoon when they'd all agreed to meet at Brimmer's for tea.

She wanted to make time for a call to Mary, as well. None of them had seen her for a couple of weeks now, in keeping with their plan to avoid being publicly seen together, but Sandy had spoken with her friend almost every day and was pleased to hear a chipper note in Mary's voice, especially when she talked about her job.

She looked out the window, sighed and turned back to the paperwork. So far, the flash drive had yielded some letters between Clint and an attorney, Derek Woo, who'd corresponded about contracts. Everything between them was couched in language Sandy found obscure—references to other business entities in addition to Holbrook Construction Inc. So far, she had a hard time knowing if these others were owned by Clint Holbrook or were simply other clients with whom he dealt.

The men's references to building contracts were seldom backed by other documents. Either Clint didn't keep the contracts on his own computer or Amber had not copied them, understandable in their haste to get in and out of his plumbing company office quickly. Or, most likely, he kept separate files and records at the downtown high-rise. It would make sense that he compartmentalize his various business entities. If only the Ladies could find a way to get into those offices.

She glanced again out the dining room window to her garden. *Enough of this head-pounding over paperwork— I deal with paperwork all week.* She quickly stacked the profit and loss statements in chronological order with the most recent on top; the correspondence went in another pile and the remodel bids in another.

I'll spend one hour in the garden and still have time to shower and make the meeting at Brimmer's.

As it turned out, a quick recon of the garden told her she would need a lot more than an hour to put it in shape. The shrubs needed pruning, a spikey old agave had died and would have to be dug out, plus the raised beds where she planned to plant the winter vegetables needed some work on the soil first. She checked the heads on the drip watering system and made a list of things to purchase at the garden center before stowing her gloves and heading inside.

Her cell phone, sitting beside the stacks of pages on the dining table, reminded her of the call she'd intended to make before the afternoon meeting. She could run some of the information past Mary and see if any of Clint's recent dealings rang a bell with her.

"Hey, how's things?" Mary sounded breathless when

she answered. Music with a heavy beat played in the background.

"Moving along at a glacial pace, I'm afraid. I've started going through those reports we got but I'm not finding anything that jumps out at me. The earnings from the plumbing business seem in line with what you remembered from several years ago."

In the background she caught the lively voice of an exercise instructor.

"I'm sorry—did I catch you in the middle of a class or something?"

"No worries. There's always something going on here. Let me just step out—"

At once, the music and voices became muted.

"Better," Mary said. "Sorry. Go ahead with what you were saying."

"Well, I'm meeting with the rest of the group later and I don't have much to report. I wonder if you recognize any of these names? Do you have a minute?"

"Sure. I'm taking a short break anyway."

"There's a lawyer, Derek Woo, whose name comes up in some letters."

"Hmm… I don't know of him. We always used Arnie Monroe for pretty much everything to do with the business. Although I suppose he's getting up there in age now. Maybe he retired."

"What about these business names—MRH Enterprises Inc. or Redwing Holdings?"

There was a pause. "The letters MRH, that's Clint's initials—McClintock Ray Holbrook is his full name. His buddies from childhood called him Mack, but he always liked Clint better—thought it was more grown-up."

Sandy had guessed about the initials, since Amber had already ferreted out Clint's background.

"The other one—did you say Redwing?"

"Yes, Redwing Holdings."

"No clue about that. The only slight connection I can think of is his high school baseball team was the Redwings. And I only remember that because he kept a team photo on his desk for a long time. But, geez, it was more than twenty years ago and I can't imagine what it would have to do with his business today."

Sandy couldn't either except she knew when inventing names for things, people often reached for a name or symbol which meant something to them.

She caught sight of the clock on her oven. "Thanks, Mary. I'd better grab a shower before I leave for the meeting. I feel badly you aren't coming along. I'll run it past the rest of the group to get a feel for when it would be safe for you to be seen with us. I've missed seeing you around."

"No sweat. I'm doing great, and everyone's been really good about telling me what's going on with the investigation."

"So, life is moving in a better direction for you?"

"Way better. I'll show you some new things when I see you next time."

TWELVE

PEN BUSTLED INTO Brimmer's Tearoom with a book tucked under her arm. Sandy noticed it was Pen's latest title in hardcover and there were a number of scrap-paper bookmarks tucked between the pages. She wore a tailored dress in a shade of lavender that set off her violet eyes and, if possible, made her platinum hair look even more elegant. Adding to the look was a stunning silver brooch on her left lapel and a heavy bracelet of the same style.

"On my way to a signing," Pen said, breezing her way to the far end of the table. "A good, bracing cup of Darjeeling is just what I need."

Sandy, Amber and Gracie had decided to share a pot of something with passion flower, so Pen ordered hers separately. A plate of delicate cookies already sat on the lace tablecloth. Sandy mentioned the phone call with Mary and laid out the names of Clint's various business entities: MRH Enterprises Inc. and Redwing Holdings in addition to Holbrook Plumbing and Holbrook Construction Inc.

"The problem is, these other businesses are barely mentioned in the documents we have—only as side notes in a couple of letters. Without financial statements we have no way of knowing if they generate any income or are merely for show. We can't possibly know where to find the missing cash if we don't know the names under which he's likely to have hidden it."

"Mary didn't know anything about them?" Gracie asked.

"Not a thing, other than to verify the names are some Clint would be likely to have chosen." She picked up the fragile china cup of tea Gracie had poured for her. "I feel like I'm spinning my wheels, since there's nothing conclusive among the information we have. I guess the banker in me is used to having clients come in with all their financials in order, ready to present, and they are normally trying to show off their assets to the max. Clint, obviously, would be doing the opposite. He's hiding things."

"That, in itself, is information," Pen pointed out. "The fact his documents are so obscure—doesn't it prove he's hiding cash?"

"Good point. And if I were betting, I'd say any real documentation for these businesses and for his construction firm will be somewhere in that high-rise downtown."

Amber's eyes sparkled. "Maybe we need to get in there some night, too."

Gracie grinned at her. "What? With grappling hooks and bungie cords as we dangle off the roof?"

Sandy cleared her throat. "You both watch too many action-adventure shows. There will be no dangling off the roof."

She noticed their server standing off to the side, probably taking in each juicy detail. She sent a warning head-tilt toward the others. Gracie signaled the waitress over and asked for a plate of sandwiches for the group. When the girl was gone, they put their heads together.

"So, how *will* we get in there?" Gracie asked.

"Do we really need to get in? Can we find what we need online?" Sandy posed the question to Amber.

Their youngest member shrugged. "I gave you pretty much what I came up with already. The bank balances, the bank offshore. But it's nothing Mary can take to court."

"I'd be willing to steal the money back for her but robbing a bank *in another country* isn't exactly practical," Gracie whispered.

"Why don't we go with the direct approach?" Pen suggested, looking cool and unflappable. "I'm due downtown in an hour for my signing. When it's done I'll simply walk into Mr. Holbrook's high-rise office and ask for the information."

Gracie sputtered and Sandy felt her own eyebrows rise. "You actually think he'll give it to you?"

"If I'm on the board of a large charitable organization looking to obtain bids for a multi-million dollar project, of course he will. I'll simply explain that we're required to perform due diligence and a complete background check on any contractors we hire. If the job sounds tempting enough and he wants it badly enough, he'll come through. There's probably a secretary who can put his or her hands on the information without even batting an eye."

"But will the information they hand out be the truth, will it give us what we need?"

"Those are two separate questions," Pen told Gracie. "The first answer is most likely no, it will not be the truth. Will it give us what we need? Quite likely. The report will contain enough nuggets of truth to get him past my *organization's* background check, and we can mine the data between the lines for what's not been said."

"That's brilliant," Amber said in a rush. "Not as much fun as rappelling down the side of the building and using gadgetry to get inside and bypassing an alarm system…"

Their waitress came with the sandwiches and conversation went generic until she walked away.

Pen pulled out her cell phone. "Let's set this thing in motion," she said, tapping a number she'd already programmed.

"Mr. Holbrook?" Her British accent became even more pronounced as she introduced herself. "I was chatting with Stanley Piccard the other day at the club and he thought you might be of help to me. I'm on the board of the Opera Guild and perhaps you've heard…well, I'm sure you're so well connected that most certainly you've heard…about plans for the new concert hall. No? Well, it's all very early days yet and we're keeping the details under wraps so I'd appreciate your discretion. We'll soon begin soliciting bids and, you see, your name rose to the top of the list."

A pause while she listened.

"Naturally, we investigate every contractor, and I thought perhaps having your financial details and company background information ahead of time would assure we give you primary consideration."

She rolled her eyes as he talked for a full two minutes non-stop. Before he finished she was sitting up straight, giving him full attention.

"Of course, of course, and I wouldn't be asking on such short notice but the committee meets Monday. I'm stepping out on a limb a bit here, but I thought if I had your dossier in my hands for that meeting…well, it might speed things along, especially as reaching you will become a bit more difficult in the coming weeks."

She sent a slightly panicky look toward Sandy.

"Of course, if it's inconvenient… I'm sure we will be receiving other bids… Oh, then perhaps this afternoon?" Pen said to the phone. "I'm downtown and could stop by your offices, say, around five? Six is even better. Yes, I'll see you then."

Her violet eyes flashed as she ended the call. "He admitted he's leaving the country. There's apparently a big project beginning soon."

"Where?" Sandy felt alarm bells go off. What if he completely absconded?

"He didn't say. I shall try to discover during my visit. Maybe I can get him to brag about it."

THIRTEEN

CLINT HOLBROOK HOPPED out of his golf cart and teed up for the tenth hole. The phone call from that British lady had piqued his interest. He'd heard nothing about a new concert hall to be built but that didn't surprise him. He and Kaycie weren't exactly patrons of the opera. Still, she worked at a news station and he'd have thought some big fund-raising effort might have been noticed.

He hit the ball, chiding himself because he hooked it. Stan Piccard was up next and he let the man take his shot before bringing up the phone call.

"Yeah, I kind of remember her. Classy woman on the tall side, older than you'd be interested in since you like 'em young."

"Did she ask about me?"

Stan shoved his club into his golf bag and walked around the side of his own cart. "Let me think…she did bring up your name, said something about some charity project she's tied in with. I gave her a little spiel, told her you were a big patron of the arts." He hit the pedal and the cart took off toward his ball, which had gone perfectly down the middle of the fairway. Clint hustled to where he'd seen his own ball go into the rough.

Okay, so the woman's story sounded legit, and Clint supposed he could name a few art events he'd attended if the need arose to sound as if he cared. He found the ball, took his time and sent it back on track, although he'd probably end up two shots behind Stan on this hole alone. Ah well, if the guy's mentioning his name resulted in another big contract, Clint decided he could throw a golf game or two his way. He pulled out his phone again and instructed his secretary which documents to gather.

"Make 'em look good, all in a nice folder or something," he said. "And if I'm not back by six, entertain the lady until I get there. I want to meet her in person."

So I can give her the razzmatazz about what a great company we are. He'd love to have another contract in the bag by the time he finished the current job. His mouth literally began to water when he thought of all that lovely cash going into his private account.

"Hey, you're up," Stan called out. He'd knocked his ball neatly on the green about two feet from the cup.

Clint dragged his mind from visions of money piles back to the golf course. He topped the ball and gave up any hope of winning. The rest was a matter of concentrating well enough to finish short of total humiliation. Stan was the kind of buddy who wouldn't drop him after a bad round or two, but he also wouldn't hold back mocking him thoroughly over this lousy streak.

By the time he walked into his office at 5:49 he'd graciously bought a round of drinks at the Nineteenth Hole, showered in the club locker room and thought of nothing else but how on earth he would manage to handle a project as large as a concert hall. Special acoustics plus all the considerations for a performance venue were completely beyond his experience. But the money…he couldn't refuse the job until he knew more.

Promptly at six o'clock a statuesque woman in her

seventies walked through the door. She wore a lavender dress and jewelry that whispered of quiet, good taste. Penelope Fitzpatrick extended a hand and introduced herself.

"It was fortunate I already had an appointment downtown," she said. "The timing couldn't have been better for me to present your name at our Monday board meeting."

"I'm happy to be considered."

He was glad he'd asked his secretary to stay an extra hour. Normally, Tamara wouldn't have worked a Saturday at all, but he'd decided to pony up the overtime to be sure everything was in order, the details of his current strip-mall job done, before he left the country. Tamara offered beverages but Pen declined.

"For the moment," she said in that enchanting British accent, "I'm on a mission to collect the financial data to be used in narrowing our choices for bidders. You understand, I'm certain, that a project of this size must be handled only by a firm with the proper resources."

"Come on into the conference room," he said, ushering her past a series of closed doors which were intended to make it look as if Holbrook Construction Inc. had a battalion of employees working out of the huge suite of offices. "We've got the portfolio all ready for you."

Before he handed over anything in writing, however, Clint wanted at least a few minutes to make his case.

"Sure I can't get you something—water, tea, some wine?"

He pulled a chair away from the table for her, waited until she approached it and then took the seat at the head of the table for himself. A folder with the company logo in red and white sat on the table in front of his place.

"You said Stan Piccard was the one who told you about our company," he began. "I don't know if he mentioned some of the projects we've already contracted." He opened his arms wide to indicate the premises where they now sat.

The Fitzpatrick woman merely nodded.

"Yes, we've done a number of malls and quite a few office buildings." Okay, so they were little five-tenant strips and the offices, so far, consisted of the refurbishment of two floors here. But the new one…now *that* would be a real high-rise.

His phone chirped, the tone telling him it was Derek Woo. He'd been wanting to hear from Woo for two days now.

"Can you excuse me for a minute?" he said. "My attorney. I really need to take this but it shouldn't be long."

"Certainly," she said.

He pulled himself up out of his chair and went to the connecting door to his private office. Pulling it discreetly shut behind him, he tapped the button to answer the phone.

"Yes? Have you got answers for me yet?" he asked.

"Calm down, Clint." The lawyer's tone was his usual inscrutable one. "Here's what you need to do."

Clint paced between the window and his desk.

"It's time to move some cash to the suppliers over there. Earthmoving is to begin on Tuesday and those guys have payrolls to meet. Write down this wire-transfer information."

"Right. But what about the extra? Am I going to run into trouble setting up bank accounts and all? I mean, they aren't exactly known for being friendly toward American businesses."

"No problem," Derek said. "I'm flying over tomorrow, paving the way for you."

"And I'm coming along Friday, me and my wife."

"She really needs to be there with you?"

"Not technically, but I promised. She's so excited about this trip, there's no way I can back out on her now."

"Fine, but she does know you're working this whole time?"

Clint laughed. "Working—the way you said we would? Some visits to the ladies, a fishing trip or two?"

"When I say 'working' that's just what I mean." Derek rarely showed humor; the small chuckle Clint heard was the extent of it.

"And my paperwork is all in order, visas and everything?"

"It's in the works. Don't worry."

Exactly the kind of man Clint liked to work with, the kind who handled things so he didn't have to worry.

FOURTEEN

PEN LEAPED AWAY from the door to Holbrook's private office only moments before it opened and Clint walked back into the conference room. She'd caught a glimpse of the name, Derek Woo, on his phone's screen before he excused himself.

"I was just admiring this painting," she said, pointing to a large canvas on the wall. "Van Gogh?" Actually, a very cheap knockoff.

He nodded vaguely. "Yeah, I think so. My wife's the real decorator, actually."

Pen didn't think so but she kept her mouth shut. She hadn't liked the man from first sight—his oily smile, the overt salesman-like conversation. Twenty years ago he'd probably been a good-looking man but he'd let himself become jowly with a big paunch, and the way he combed his hair straight back from the forehead did nothing to lessen the disturbing way his eyes bulged and his meaty lips pursed. For someone as young as Kaycie Marlow, the attraction had to be all about the money.

"So, are there any questions I can answer for you about Holbrook Construction?" he asked, reaching for the red and white folder on the table and handing it to her.

Pen gave the most sincere smile she could work up. "As long as all the information is included here, I'm sure everything will be fine."

She stood aside while he opened the door to the corridor, noting when they passed Tamara's desk that the secretary had left. The overhead lights were off, leaving two small lamps burning in the reception area. Holbrook showed her to the door and she rode the elevator alone. Her heart didn't slow down until the elevator dinged at the ground floor.

Interesting bits of the puzzle, she thought. It reminded her of plotting one of her books—take a lot of little, separate pieces and put them together until the whole picture emerges. She smiled.

When she'd arrived in the lobby twenty minutes earlier, she'd been greeted at a large semi-circular desk by two uniformed guards who asked that she sign in and be issued a Visitor badge. She paused there now to return it.

"So, the entire building houses Holbrook Construction?" she asked casually, as she signed out.

"No, ma'am," said the guard with the name R. Sanchez on his shirt. "Most of it's a big stock brokerage company. Being the weekend, that's why no one's around."

"Holbrook?" the other guard said. "He only moved in here a year or so ago."

"But he built the building, didn't he?" She feigned a naïve expression.

Both men chuckled. "Don't know where you got that," Sanchez said. "This place was built at least ten years ago. The construction company you're talking about, I'm sure they had nothing to do with this place being built."

Pen shrugged. "Obviously, I got the wrong impression somewhere."

Another puzzle piece, not a surprising one.

She retrieved her Mercedes from the parking garage across the street and sat a moment, deciding what to do next. A quiet dinner at home had been her original plan, but she was eager to share the new information she'd gleaned with the Ladies. Would any of them be available?

She phoned Sandy first.

"It's too soon to call everyone together again," Pen said, "but I did gain a few interesting tidbits from my visit to Holbrook's office. Would you like to meet for dinner somewhere or perhaps come to my house?"

"If it's not too far out of your way," Sandy said, "come by my place instead. I just made a chicken dish with a tangy mustard and asiago sauce. There's plenty for two."

While Pen would have loved to settle into her own home, out of her linen dress and jewelry, a glass of wine in hand, the idea of a ready-made dinner with Sandy appealed as well.

"I'll be there in fifteen minutes."

"How did the book signing go?" Sandy asked when she opened the door.

"Quite well." Pen held up the bottle of wine given as a thank-you by the bookseller. "Thank goodness I've got past the days when two people showed up and I read chapters to a room devoid of interest."

"Now, you probably sign books until your hand has a cramp," Sandy said, leading the way to the kitchen where the scent of the mushroom-chicken dish was heavenly.

Pen laughed. "Sometimes. This new book seems to be well received. Good reviews in the press and nearly rapt attention as I read my sample chapters. Would it be all right if I stepped out of these shoes? I'm seldom in heels for more than a couple of hours nowadays."

"Be my guest. I'd be happy to provide a kimono if you want to *really* dress down."

"That's all right. Pour the wine and over dinner I'll fill you in on my visit to Clint Holbrook's offices." She pulled the proposal folder from her roomy bag and set it on Sandy's countertop. "This might make for interesting reading. A quick glance before I left his office didn't make sense to me, but you'll have Amber's findings for comparison."

"Should be fascinating." Sandy handed Pen a glass. "Cheers."

Pen carried hers to the place Sandy indicated at the kitchen table. The chicken dish, buttered noodles and fresh broccoli looked wonderful; she hadn't realized how hungry she'd become. They tucked into the meal without a word for several minutes.

"So?" Sandy asked when Pen paused for a moment.

"Well, the offices themselves are an interesting dichotomy. On the surface of it, the décor is tasteful enough, but something's off. It's as if he called Interiors R Us or something. I don't get the feeling he had a hand in choosing anything in the place. For instance, I commented on one painting and he told me his wife had chosen it. It was one of those starving-artist things of a flower arrangement, and he thought it was a real Van Gogh."

"Seriously?"

"The furniture, as well. It's real wood and real leather, but so generic. All of it could be…"

"Leased?"

Pen brightened. "Exactly. There is nothing personal in the place. Something else—we walked down a corridor toward his conference room, closed doors the whole way, which he chalked up to its being a weekend so no one was working. Perhaps. But the place had a hollow feel to it."

"And yet his company occupies two full floors of the building."

"Oh, that's another thing. I gossiped a little with building security at the front desk. They said there's no possibility Holbrook Construction built the high-rise. It's been there much longer than Clint lets on."

"Why would he do that?" Sandy pondered, offering seconds on the veggies.

"Why indeed?" Pen turned down the offer of more food, although everything was cooked perfectly and tasted delicious.

"There's more," she said. "While we were in the conference room, Clint received a phone call from his lawyer, Derek Woo. I saw the name on his phone. He went into his office to take it but the door is so cheaply made I could hear most of what was said." She blushed slightly. "Of course, I followed him and pressed my ear up to it."

Sandy laughed at the image.

"Mr. Woo apparently advised Clint to begin moving money somewhere. There were references to setting up bank accounts 'over there' and Clint wonders if that will be a problem."

"Over where, I wonder. We still don't know."

"Actually, as of now, we do. There were little signs of evidence around the place, some travel brochures, a phrase book, and two letters on the fax machine on his secretary's desk. They're going to China."

"China!" Sandy looked dumbfounded.

"I know. I'd assumed, if it wasn't somewhere in Canada or Mexico, it might be Europe. But this explains the need for visas, which wouldn't have made sense for most other places."

"The letter I saw most clearly was addressed to Shanghai." Pen watched Sandy's reaction.

"I'm stunned. Construction in China is notorious for always being done domestically. It's still a fairly closed society to outsiders. I can't imagine why they would want an American contractor."

"A fairly new, inexperienced American contractor…"

"Yes…" Sandy's attention seemed focused somewhere in the distance. "There has to be more to it."

"It could possibly be a personal trip disguised as business so Clint can write off the whole thing." Pen passed along the remarks, as nearly verbatim as she remembered, about fishing trips and the hint of seeing prostitutes. "Which is also strange. He's taking his wife along. I distinctly heard him tell Woo that he and Kaycie were joining him at the destination on Friday."

"This coming Friday?" Sandy's eyes widened. "That doesn't give us much time."

FIFTEEN

CLINT WAVED AT the security guard as the automatic gate at Vandergrift Towers opened and he drove through in his pearl-white Escalade. He whipped the large vehicle through a couple of turns to his covered parking slot. He'd received their passports with the visas for China affixed. That was the good news. He'd also gotten a call from the client, Tong Chen Enterprises, and the conversation left him grinding his teeth.

He picked up his briefcase and a rolled set of blueprints and tucked his phone into his shirt pocket as he got out of the car. His toe began tapping the moment the elevator doors closed, and by the time he reached the penthouse his body felt like a tautly pulled rope that could snap at any second. He took a deep breath before letting himself into the condo.

"Honey Bear! You're home!" Kaycie rushed him like some kindergarten kid. Couldn't she just back off and smile a little less sometimes?

"Our passports came through," he said, hoping to distract her so he could think what to do. "So now you know the surprise—we're going to China."

She squealed and it was all he could do not to grimace at the decibel level.

"Here's some brochures about Shanghai. Have fun packing—we're leaving Friday."

She'd found the visa sticker in her passport. "Ohmygod, look! There's my name in Chinese characters. Honey Bear, this is so cool." Her eyes sparkled and the dazzle of her smile could light the room. He didn't have the energy for this right now.

"Yeah. Cool." He dropped his briefcase on the coffee table. "Look, I got some calls to make. Can you—?"

"Ooh, I gotta tell Mom. She's been dying to know all about the trip. And you know what—I think I'll need some different clothes for China." She walked toward the bedroom, flipping through the brochures.

She picked up her phone from the king-sized bed and punched a number. When her voice went all excited, talking to her mother, he gently closed the door between them. He went to the bar at the end of the living room and poured himself a generous single-malt Scotch. Half of it went down at the first slug, burning his gullet all the way.

He sat at the kitchen counter and brought out his phone, going back through the texts he'd received this afternoon, first from Rudy Tong at Tong Chen Enterprises. He reread to be sure he understood what the battered English message meant. They wanted to draft several million dollars from his bank into the Chinese escrow account for construction materials, but their deposit to him wasn't yet showing in his own account. Complicating matters was the fact that most of Clint's money existed in small amounts in multiple banks.

He logged onto his largest business account, entered a number and waited while the little circle whirled to indicate it was processing the information. After a frustratingly long time, a message popped up: This transaction is not allowed at this time.

Clint growled at the stupid website and tried again. Even

with a smaller amount, the transaction wouldn't go through. *Dammit—what's with the rush from these guys? I like doing things the way I'm used to doing them.*

He took another gulp of the booze and called Derek Woo, wondering, not for the first time, whether it had been smart to get involved with the Chinese at his attorney's suggestion. Well, it was a little late for that now. Once the funds landed in his account he would neatly shuffle the money around and no one would be able to simply draft what they wanted. He sat up straighter. Clint Holbrook was no fool—he'd done plenty of business transactions and he knew his stuff.

Woo didn't pick up and the 'leave a message' voice came on.

"Yeah, Derek, we gotta talk," he said, leaving it at that. Let the other guy come to him.

He drained his glass, feeling the muscles in his neck relax, and left his phone on the kitchen counter.

In the bedroom, Kaycie was strutting around in a little one-piece thing that barely covered her, all pink lace and blond hair and shiny toenails. A suitcase lay open on the bed and she crossed the room, bringing a dozen garments from the closet.

"I can't decide what to pack."

"Let's think about it later," he said, scooping the clothes into the suitcase and setting the whole batch on the floor. He took her hand and spun her into his embrace. "I got other things on my mind right now, Babycakes."

She giggled. "I'm supposed to meet Mom at Fashion Square in an hour."

"Oh, baby, it's not going to take *that* long."

SIXTEEN

FINISHING HER CONVERSATION with a banking client, Sandy hung up the phone and turned in her chair at the sound of a light tap at the partially open door.

"Come in."

A woman stepped in, smiling and holding both hands out wide. She wore trim black capris, a slim-fitting bright pink T-shirt and pink and black bangle bracelets.

"May I—?" Sandy's jaw dropped. "Mary? Oh my gosh. Mary!"

"What do you think?" Mary said, unable to contain her smile. "The hair—is it too much?"

Mary's formerly lank, blonde hair was now cut short, with soft spikes at the top and wispy ends hugging her ears, not to mention a fresh strawberry-blonde color and high-lights. The adorable style suited her features and made her look twenty years younger.

"I love it!" Sandy rose from her chair and approached, turning Mary to see the new style from all sides. "It's just— I'm amazed at the difference."

"The women's center had a free makeover day with some visiting beauty consultants. They showed us how to do our makeup, and the haircut is courtesy of discount-senior day at the beauty school."

"I never knew you had those little freckles," Sandy said.

"I used to hide them with makeup until the lady suggested that less-is-better when it comes to being over forty. I kind of like the result myself."

"Definitely. Still—wow. You've done something more."

Mary laughed out loud. "Been getting in on every workout class I could manage at the gym. Billy doesn't mind. He's been so supportive since I started working there. Size sixteen, down to a twelve. I'm aiming for ten."

Sandy hugged her. "I'm so proud of you." They both came out of the embrace with tears in their eyes.

"Pen's making lunch for us at her house, where we'll go over the information we've gathered on your ex and decide what steps to take next. You have to come along. The group is going to be every bit as impressed as I am."

They took Sandy's car, driving up the winding drive on Camelback Mountain to Pen's home with its incomparable views of the city below. Mary grew quiet, no doubt thinking of the money Clint had cheated her out of, the fact that with a portion of it she might be living on a much better scale. Sandy pulled into the circular drive and saw Gracie's minivan and Amber's little Prius already parked there. They got out and walked up the travertine steps to the beveled-glass front door.

The reactions were exactly as Sandy had anticipated— puzzlement when the Ladies first spotted Mary, then incredulity followed by congratulations and joy. Amber, in particular, couldn't take her eyes off the transformation she'd witnessed. She was like the awestruck little sister as they took their places at Pen's dining table.

"Naomi made us this huge Mexican salad," Pen said, "and there's a spicy dressing here in the pitcher." She scooped portions onto plates and passed them around.

"So, fill me in," Mary said. "I know you've already told

me about some of your progress. Did Clint's golfing buddies give you any clues?"

Pen told how she'd used Stan Piccard's name to come up with the pretense of the charity sponsorship of a new concert hall, and how the information had gained her access to Clint's top-floor offices downtown. "He seemed genuinely interested in being considered for the job but somewhat distracted by his current project—too distracted to ask any serious questions about what ours would entail. Which is good, since I had no specifics and am not very adept at making up such fabrications at a moment's notice."

"Amber and I have been finding more background on your ex," Gracie said. "It seems he got his contractor's license within months after the divorce became final. He must have been studying for the test and making his applications even while you were with him, Mary."

"I was in such a daze then," Mary admitted. "Living much of the time with my parents, working beyond exhaustion. Barely seeing Clint, even when we were in the same room."

"So, then, with his fresh new license in hand," Amber said. "He leased the top two floors of that high-rise downtown. He did not build the whole place—Pen verified that during her visit. We think he took cash he'd hidden from the courts and furnished the offices to make an impression on new clients."

"I think it's leased furniture," Pen said with a sniff. "It simply is not quality stuff, and the art is only a step above dime-store."

"He would give clients some song-and-dance about his experience and convince them he was a bigtime contractor. It was a pretense—he's mostly done small jobs—a strip-mall shopping center here and a little office building there, mainly out in the suburbs."

"My guess," Sandy said, "after looking at his financial claims, is that he padded expenses on these little jobs and stashed cash in a variety of accounts. Amber ferreted out some of those during her initial search."

"He's been putting feelers out for bigger jobs for a year or more. Now it looks as if he's found one."

"Pen did manage to get the information that Clint's newest project is taking place in China," Sandy said. "He and little-blondie are going there at the end of the week."

"Clint's audacious, I'll agree," said Mary. "One of those guys who thinks he's a lot smarter than he really is. But even so, doesn't this seem quite a bit out of his league— taking a job in a foreign country, any country, much less China? I mean, there's tons of construction right here in the valley—all over the U.S. Why China?"

Shrugs all around. No one seemed to have an answer, although Pen pointed out that his lawyer had a Chinese name—Woo could merely be an Americanization of Wu. Perhaps that was the connection.

"So, what does that mean to us? Can we somehow gain access to the money?" Gracie asked.

"I'd hoped we could find enough information about his finances and accounts to handle this completely above-board," Sandy said. "I know. It's the banker in me coming out."

Pen spoke up again. "It's just that it's difficult to get a judge to review a divorce decree, much less make any changes to it. Once the papers are signed, it's usually a done deal. I once researched it for a book."

"Unless it's proven there was fraud by one of the parties," Gracie added.

"And that's exactly what happened," Mary insisted. "He hid assets, moved money out of the country…"

Amber set her fork down and picked up the tablet that was nearly always with her. "Let's check. I like Gracie's idea of our getting access to the money."

Nods all around.

Amber focused on the tablet, typing access information at sites she had visited before, while the others finished their salads. A scowl creased her forehead. She tapped a couple more links then held up the tablet. "Ohmygod—this one has been cleared out. There's less than a thousand dollars where there was previously more than a hundred thousand."

Mary practically wilted in her chair. Amber continued to slide her fingers across the surface of the screen.

"And this one…the account no longer exists."

"What!" Gracie was on her feet. "How can that be?"

Amber shrugged. "Lots of reasons, I suppose. He spent it, he moved it somewhere else…"

"Or he knew we were looking and he hid it again." Mary's small freckles stood out against her pallor.

"Look, we cannot assume anything at this point," Pen pointed out, her tone sensible. "We know he is working on a large business deal right now."

"Large deals require the movement of large amounts of money," Sandy said. "I agree. Let's do some further checking and see where it leads before we panic."

"Has he left for China yet?" Mary asked.

"I don't think so. The conversation I overheard indicated they would leave on Friday."

"Then I've got two days to track him down and confront him," Mary said, her brows pinched together in a frown.

Sandy and Pen exchanged a glance.

"That probably wouldn't be a good idea," Sandy said.

"Right now he's not thinking about you and isn't suspicious that we're looking into his finances."

"We *believe* he's not." Amber had gone back to her salad.

"Right. If he saw an inquiry on his credit record, he would assume it came as a result of the information I requested on behalf of my make-believe charitable project."

Mary sputtered a little. "But what if he gets away with all that money? Puts it somewhere untraceable and then gives the judge a shrug and makes him believe I'm crazy for even thinking I could get part of it."

Sandy reached out and patted Mary's hand. "That's not how it's going to work. We'll track the money first, then we'll print statements and documents to prove it exists. *Then* we'll get a lawyer to look at everything and try to get it before a judge. There's no way we're going to jump the gun here and make things worse."

Mary sighed. "Well, it can't get any *worse* than before. At least now I'm not homeless and penniless, even though my first few paychecks are going to repay Penelope for her help with my apartment."

Pen smiled at her. "Let's just take each thing as it comes. There is absolutely no rush on the loan."

"So what *is* our next step?" Gracie asked. She made the first move to help clear the empty plates. "I mean, if it turns out he's moved his money to China, is there any real possibility we can get at it?"

No one had an answer for that question. When Pen served flan for dessert, conversation came to a halt.

"I hate to eat and run," Sandy said, "but my assistant manager can only cover for me so long."

She glanced toward Mary, who took the hint and said she would love a ride back where she could catch her bus. Amber busied herself at her touchpad for a few more minutes. Gracie looked at her watch and announced she'd better be home when her kids got there.

Amber hung back after the others left.

"What do you think about the possibility Mr. Holbrook moved his money to China?" Pen asked as she cleared dishes and tidied the kitchen.

"It's doable," Amber said. She fiddled a little more with something on her screen. "If he has the recipient's IBAN number and SWIFT or BIC code of their bank, he can transfer money there every bit as easily as he could send it from Phoenix to Los Angeles."

Pen pondered the information. This was all becoming so complicated.

SEVENTEEN

KAYCIE FLIPPED THROUGH a rack of sequined dresses, looking for the purple one in a size four.

"You know, the Far East is the place to go for cosmetic surgery," her mother said under her breath, her attention divided between the clothes racks and her daughter.

Unconsciously, Kaycie glanced down at her chest. There was nothing wrong with being petite. But Mom had planted that seed of uncertainty. Clint definitely liked women with curves.

"I'm just saying… Your trip would be the perfect opportunity and no one back home would be the wiser…" Sylvia looked at the dress Kaycie had pulled from the rack. "Oh, no, sweetie. That one's cut too straight. I mean, that is…"

It was the third remark Mom had made about an item Kaycie chose. She jammed the hanger back on its hook. This shopping trip was quickly losing its allure.

She thought back to what she'd read in the brochures and guidebooks. Shanghai was the business hub of China, so there might be lunches and dinners with Clint and his clients. Theater and shows.

Her on-air clothing was certainly presentable for business meals. She would toss in a gown and a cocktail dress in case there were more formal occasions, and she could certainly shop for something new if her existing wardrobe lacked anything.

"Let's go," she said, turning away from Sylvia.

"Are you hungry, sweetie? I'd planned on treating you to lunch out, although it's a bit early."

She was tired of her mother's company, but by the time she drove Sylvia all the way out to her home in Glendale and then came back to browse the shops again, half the day would be wasted. Kaycie had to admit she was getting a little hungry. The small carton of light yogurt at breakfast hadn't quite held her appetite at bay. She put on a quick smile and asked where they would eat. When Sylvia went into her advice-giving mode it was best to let her take free rein with all the decisions.

"The other thing that would fill out your figure a bit," said Sylvia once they had settled into a booth at Ramon's, "would be having a baby."

Yeah, right. Having a baby would fill out the parts she absolutely did not want filled out. She shook her head. "We're not having this discussion, Mom."

She stared at the salad section of the menu but her mind went elsewhere. A baby definitely should be in the plan, for all the reasons she'd previously convinced herself. If Clint was not just blowing smoke about the size of this new job, his profit on it would provide several million reasons. She decided to add some enticing new lingerie to this afternoon's shopping list.

She had budgeted most of the day for shopping; she didn't need to be at the station until five. This was the day she was handing in her notice.

Or, maybe instead of quitting her job outright, she should request a year's leave of absence. No one she knew at the station had ever actually done that, but it was worth asking. She and Clint would be gone a few months and she would manage to get pregnant during that time. Then come home, have the baby, extend her time off with maternity leave, then spend a few more months getting back in shape before going back to the cameras.

"—sounds good, don't you think?" Sylvia was staring at the menu and had apparently been talking during Kaycie's little brainstorming session.

There was no way she would ask her mother to repeat. The server was heading their way. "Sure, whatever. I'm going with the grilled shrimp salad."

Predictably, Sylvia changed her order to match Kaycie's. The two finished their lunch before the restaurant became crowded; they headed toward a mid-priced store Kaycie knew of, where she hoped to focus the attention on upgrading Mom's wardrobe rather than hearing more about her own flaws.

She settled her mother into the changing room with a dozen outfits and told her she needed to put more money in the parking meter down the street. Instead, she ducked into Victoria's Secret and plucked the first two skimpy things she spotted off the racks. This ought to get Clint on the same wavelength with her about their late-night activity for the evening.

EIGHTEEN

PENELOPE CHECKED HER image in the hall mirror as she clipped a diamond to her left ear. Light flickered across the wall, and Benton Case's car pulled through her circular drive and stopped at the front door. She adjusted a strand of hair that was out of place and picked up her evening bag. She didn't need another night out this week—her work with the Heist Ladies had eaten a goodly share of her writing time already—but she'd committed to be Benton's date for the bar association fete where he was to be honored for his years of service in the district attorney's office.

He hadn't noticed her through the beveled glass yet, and she watched as he got out of his Lexus SUV and walked up the steps. With his silver hair and tuxedo he was a very handsome man and Pen had to admit it was a pleasure to be seen with him in public. More important, though, was the bond they'd formed over the years. They'd been lovers for a few years after she, as a young widow, had moved to Phoenix but then the relationship settled into one of shared confidences and solid friendship.

He reached for the doorbell and she opened the door at the same moment. They both laughed.

"Ready for a thrilling evening of rubber chicken and windy speeches?" he asked, giving her a light kiss on the cheek.

She took his arm and looked up at him. "You're the honoree, darling. Anything they have to say about you will be brilliant."

He made a little yeah-yeah-sure noise and opened the passenger door for her.

"At least it should be over fairly early, and afterward we'll go have a drink."

The event venue was the Arizona Biltmore, where the bar was known for the who's-who of celebrity faces one might see there. Benton drove up the stately driveway, past the sweeping lawns and banks of flowering shrubs. At the front entrance he stopped before the clipped boxwood that spelled out the words Arizona Biltmore. A valet held the door for Pen and took the car after Benton handed over the keys.

Contrary to his dire prediction, the meal was excellent prime rib with an especially nice merlot. The accolades came after, a fitting tribute to a man who had served the city well, and Pen felt proud when Benton walked to the podium to receive his engraved plaque and say a few words. By the time they retired to the bar, with its deeply burnished woodwork and windows facing the pool and palm grove, he was noticeably more relaxed.

"It's not comfortable for you, is it? Hearing praise and receiving awards," she said after they'd placed orders for Italian Amaro.

Some of the bar's other patrons had eyed the classy couple, wondering where they'd seen these faces before. It was the type of place Pen dreaded someone pulling one of her books from a bag and making a fuss. Luckily, no one did.

"I wanted to talk to you about this newest venture the ladies and I've got ourselves working on," she said when their drinks arrived. "We're in hopes that our efforts will help a woman whose husband was so unfair in their divorce settlement that she's found herself homeless. We're trusting that new evidence might gain her a new hearing with a judge."

"Fill me in. What new evidence do you have?"

She went over the first meeting with Mary, how Clint Holbrook had defaulted on the payments on the home and how the paltry amount of cash she'd received was quickly gone.

"He's living at Vandergrift Towers in Scottsdale and showing off his business from a spacious suite of offices in a downtown high-rise. There are huge amounts of money in his bank accounts." Well, there recently had been.

She quickly skimmed back to the subject of Mary's new job and apartment, not wanting Benton to ask detailed questions about how she should happen to know how much money was in Clint's accounts. Amber's hacking into the bank records to learn that information would not be viewed kindly by the law. They tended to favor search warrants and gaining information through channels. Such a bother.

"If there was fraudulent reporting of assets during the divorce proceedings, wouldn't there be a possibility of having the settlement reviewed?" she asked. "I think we can definitely get the information to prove it."

Benton picked up his glass. "How does Mary know he didn't earn all this money after the divorce was already final? You said she wasn't active in his plumbing business for a few years before they split up."

It was a concern, Pen knew. Clint would simply claim his newfound success happened after Mary was out of the picture.

"Pen, when people have hidden, offshore bank accounts, it's often because the source of the funds was illegal or undeclared." He scoffed. "*Often*—I should say *nearly always*."

"What are you saying? He's been running drugs or something?"

He shrugged. "Could be that. Could be nothing so direct. Maybe he's taken construction jobs for mobsters, someone who's paying with illicit money, laundering it, and has told him it was an under-the-table deal. Advised him not to declare the money either. You know, a little nudge-nudge, wink-wink thing."

Mobsters? It was something the Ladies had not even considered. Pen watched the rich drink swirl in her glass.

"If he's been doing that—laundering money—how will we find it?"

"It would help to find records dating back to their time together," Benton said. "Mary should have copies of their joint tax returns, banking documents. If you can put your hands on older financial statements for the business, dated bank statements, that sort of thing, they can be compared to the more recent activity."

He swigged the last of his drink. "Of course, if you come up with enough information to show cause, this is exactly the kind of thing the Attorney General's office would take on. Racketeering and hidden money—the government loves to ferret out these guys."

Except once the government got hold of the money, it would take a miracle for Mary to ever see a penny. Pen became quiet. Sandy had gone through the financial data they had, but now it appeared they would need more. And from what Amber had told everyone at their last gathering—the fact that money had disappeared from some of the accounts she originally located—meeting the criteria for a new hearing could prove impossible.

He stared at her face. "Don't give up quite yet. If you ladies can gather enough information to make a decent case, and if there's no mob connection, there are a couple of at-torneys… I'll get some names for you. And there's at least one judge, Marta Eggers, who's shown a lot of sympathy toward women who've gotten raw deals in divorce."

Pen perked up at the news.

He noticed her expression. "You can't request a particu-lar judge, you know. Random selection is what keeps our judicial system impartial."

She chafed a little at the knowledge. It felt as though they had a long way to go to solve Mary's problem. What had started as a straightforward matter—they knew who took the money, they simply had to get it back—was now taking all sorts of convoluted twists.

NINETEEN

"I SAY WE get the money back for Mary *first*," Amber said, jutting her chin fiercely upward. "We can figure out how to take down Clint and Kaycie once we have her share of the cash."

The five women were at Gracie's house the morning after Pen's evening out with Benton. She'd reported his advice and caution about Clint's possible involvement with organized crime.

"I agree," Gracie said as she stooped to take a tray of hot cookies from the oven. "Let me know what you want me to do. If I can help with computer research, or running errands…well, once I've delivered these snacks for my daughter's class. Leave it to kids to remember stuff like this the morning it's due."

"Hey, I'm just thankful I had a meeting on this side of town," Sandy said. "Those kids are in for a treat. When I walked in here, the smell just about made my knees weak."

The house still held the aroma of vanilla and cinnamon.

"The first batch goes to us," Gracie said, removing the warm cookies to a cooling rack.

Amber couldn't wait. She reached for one, even though it wilted in her grasp. When she took the first bite her eyes rolled upward. "Ohmygod. Good."

"How do you propose we get the money, Amber?" Pen asked. She noticed Mary seemed withdrawn this morning.

Their youngest member paced through Gracie's family room and back. "I'll keep monitoring his movements online?"

Pen sat a little straighter on the stool she occupied at the kitchen counter. "I have a better idea."

All eyes shifted toward her.

"We need to get closer, to go inside his operation."

"And how…?" Sandy looked skeptical.

Gracie scooped cookie dough into mounds on another sheet. Her mouth curved in an impish smile. "We go there."

Puzzled glances. Pen nodded.

"We go to China," Gracie continued as she set the sheet into the oven. "Clint and Kaycie will get there and not know a soul. We can figure out ways to work our way inside."

"He might remember me," Sandy said, "from the bank. And, despite the fantastic transformation, I don't think we dare risk Mary being seen by him."

"Okay," Amber said, "but that still leaves three of us he doesn't know."

"And we'll need team members to stay here. There's going to be a formidable language barrier in China," Pen said. "I've only been there twice and managed to learn no more than a handful of words."

"I'm good with languages," Amber said. "I'll study hard."

"China requires travel visas," Pen said, biting her lower lip. "They normally take a couple of weeks to obtain."

"Clint and Kaycie are leaving tomorrow." It was the first thing Mary had said.

"More time for me to learn the language." Amber helped herself to a second cookie. "Plus, I've got a great translation app."

Pen tapped her toe on the rung of her stool. "There might be a way to expedite things. Let me make a call or two."

She hopped off the stool and retrieved her phone from her purse on the family room sofa. Seeking a quiet spot, she walked toward the living room.

"Another thing about traveling in China," Sandy said, "is limited internet access. The government blocks certain sites, and I'm guessing international banking might be one area with limits. I really don't know…just saying we need to be prepared. Amber might not be able to work her little magical hacks over there."

"So, it's better if I stay here?" Disappointment showed on Amber's face.

"Not necessarily." Sandy took a deep breath. "I *know* I shouldn't be saying this. I *really* shouldn't, considering my job. But if you mark the sites for me, I can get into them. Tell me what to move and when—I'll do it."

"You're willing to take that chance? For me?" Mary's voice caught.

"Trust me, it's *only* for you."

"I'll set you up with a fake—" Amber's eyes gleamed.

"Don't say it."

"Then I can give you a computer that's registered in my name and put it on a VPN," Amber said. "Any website you visit will, at worst, only have my fingerprints on it."

"I feel like I should be sitting here plugging my ears and saying la-la-la," Sandy said. "The less detail I know, the better."

Gracie set her oven timer and leaned against the counter. "Sandy, none of us want you to risk your job over this. You've worked your way up through the bank by being a hundred-percent ethical."

Sandy nodded, her expression sober. "True. But, you know, I feel like this *is* an ethical thing we're doing. Slightly different ethics than my superiors would acknowledge, yes.

But we're taking down a cheater and liar. It's the right thing to do."

Pen bustled back into the room. "Good news. I believe I can work it so we have our visas within a few days."

The mood brightened.

"A friend travels from here to Los Angeles several times a week. I've just been on the phone with her. If we complete the applications and get them to her by tonight she'll carry them along and walk them through the embassy herself."

"They'll allow that?"

"She's done it before. That's what made me think of asking her." Pen set her phone on the counter. "Sandy and Mary will stay in Phoenix to handle things here, so it's Amber, Gracie and myself who will go. We need the visa applications— I assume you can find those somewhere online, Amber?"

"I'm sure I can. Gracie, you have a printer?"

A nod.

"Show me to it."

Each of the three travelers took a turn, filling out the information on the online form and printing her application.

"This has to accompany our passports and there's a fee," Amber told them when they were finished.

Mary fidgeted.

"I'll take care of the expenses," Pen assured her. "For now. Once we retrieve that money, I can be reimbursed, if you insist."

Mary didn't look comfortable with the idea. "All of you are being so kind. I have no way to pay you back for all this."

Gracie spoke up. "For the cash outlay, Pen said she's happy to wait, so don't worry about that. As far as contributing something important to the mission, I can think of something."

All eyes turned toward her.

"Our last little adventure got a bit physical at one point when a bad guy turned on me. We talked about it at the time—our getting some self-defense training. Mary, you told us you used to teach classes? While we're waiting for the visas to come through, could you teach us?" She halted. "Well, I'm speaking for myself really. But it would be a good idea for all of us. If you don't mind?"

Mary beamed. "I'd love to. We could start today."

All at once, they became quiet as the enormity of the task hit them.

"Okay, ladies, we have a heist to pull," Gracie said. "Let's get organized. Mary, can you get us time at the gym for our classes? Try to line up something for this evening. Amber, find the quickest language course you can and get cracking. Pen, you know a bit about Shanghai. Can you give us an information sheet or something—let us know what to pack, what the city is like, the weather. Tell us how to fit in—obviously, none of us can pass as Chinese, but what will make us appear less touristy, more like Americans who are working there?"

"Bring your passports to class tonight," Pen reminded. "I'll arrange for my friend to meet me somewhere and hand over our papers to her capable hands."

Gracie whipped the cookie sheet out of the oven and put two more in. "I'll deliver these goodies to my daughter's school, find my passport and coordinate what it takes to let my husband know I'm going away and he's running the show at home for awhile."

TWENTY

KAYCIE SAT IN the Admiral's Club international departures lounge at Sky Harbor, casual as could be, reading a fashion magazine, her foot bobbing in time to some unheard song in her head. Clint had already visited the breakfast buffet and downed two loaded plates. Now he was standing near the windows with his cell phone to his ear. Business, it seemed, occupied all his thoughts.

Not Wednesday night, she thought with a little smile. That night she'd arrived home from work around eleven p.m. and put her pregnancy plan into action. And good old Clint—he'd fallen for her new teddy—hook, line and sinker. She ran a hand over her belly. She hoped she'd calculated her cycle correctly but with the excitement of the trip and this week being her last at work until her leave of absence was over, well, she couldn't be sure about the best dates for conception. Still, they would be living in a fancy hotel in a foreign country for several months. Hotels always put men in the mood, she'd found. And—oops—she'd *forgotten* to pack her pills.

Clint headed her way, staring at something on his phone screen and muttering under his breath.

"Hey, Honey Bear, everything all set?" She put on her most winning smile.

He sat on the sofa beside her. "Yeah, I guess. Derek's

already in Shanghai and says we'll love our hotel. He's got a driver and an interpreter all lined up."

Kaycie stroked the back of his neck. "Good. Nothing to worry about then."

His head waggled back and forth a couple times. "I just hope the meeting on Monday goes good. You know, since I haven't ever met these guys from Tong Chen. Hard to believe we transacted this whole thing by phone and email, sending documents clear across the world."

"That's what you have a Chinese lawyer for, right? Derek can handle everything you don't understand."

"Hey. I understand my business just fine."

"Honey Bear, I meant the language. He'll translate for you. He's on your team."

He reached over and squeezed her knee. "Sorry to snap, Babycakes. It's just been a lot of pressure. More to come when I have to hire and direct workers in another country."

She nodded sympathetically, pressing her leg against his hand. "Hey, there's nothing Clint Holbrook can't handle."

He began scooting his hand a little farther up her leg.

She glanced around the lounge, which wasn't terribly crowded although there were people near. She cleared her throat. "Um, we'll have more privacy once we're on the plane."

His face softened. "Did I hear some gossip between you and your mother, some mention of enhancing a certain anatomical area…?"

"Maybe."

He was openly staring at the edge of her scoop-necked top now. "Might be a lot of fun."

Fun? She forced herself to override thoughts of incisions and pain with a vision of the finished result. "I don't know. I haven't decided if I want to go through it—surgery is pretty drastic."

He didn't say anything.

"Clint, take your eyes off my blouse. People will notice." She swatted his hand with her magazine. "You know, there's another way. If I were to have a baby, the little girls would grow into bigger girls."

"Yeah, for a few months. Then they'll sag. You know I don't want the responsibility of kids, anyway. Never did."

"But you never had a vasectomy, did you? I mean, if we were to decide…"

"No doctor's ever gonna cut on me *there*," he said with a laugh. "No way."

You're happy enough to let a doctor cut on me. She pushed the thought aside. For all she knew, she might be pregnant already and that would settle the question. Once he really was going to become a father, Clint would come around. She would simply wait until it was too late to back out before she informed him.

"You want a muffin or something?" he asked. "I saw the lady putting some new stuff out on the buffet."

She shook her head and he walked away.

She'd always been able to get Clint to come around to her way of thinking in the past. She could do it again. She rummaged in her oversized purse for a breath mint. Her hand came across the brochure from the cosmetic surgery clinic. For a moment she felt overwhelmed—was she going to please her husband or listen to her mother? Shouldn't she really be deciding what *she* wanted for herself? She jammed the brochure back into the bag and peeked at her watch.

The plane would begin boarding in another ten minutes.

TWENTY-ONE

No matter what they did to it, Pen thought, by the end of the day a gym still smells like a gym. She walked in feeling somewhat uncertain. Were sweats the right thing to wear? Should she have pulled her hair away from her face? Had she remembered to refresh her deodorant? A young woman at the reception desk directed her down a corridor to a side room where she said Mary Holbrook asked her group to meet.

Amber, Gracie and Sandy were already there. Mary wore sweats and a T-shirt, too, which came as a relief to Pen.

"Okay, ladies, let's get started." She waved them toward the middle of the room, which looked as if it probably served several purposes—yoga studio, exercise classes, whatever. It had hardwood floors, a mirrored wall, and little cubbies in one corner where members could stash their things.

"All right," Mary said. "I'll start with some simple, basic things you can do to defend yourselves at close range—let's say a guy grabs you in a parking lot."

Sandy tensed a little.

"Simplest thing you can do is just punch him. If he's touching you or within arm's reach, just whack him. Drive from the ground and push with your hip and fist at the same time. Aim for a vulnerable place on him—eyes, nose, throat—and try to make contact with the knuckles of your index and middle fingers. Pinkies are kind of delicate for this." Mary picked up a protective pad and held it in front of her chest. "Amber, want to go first? Let me have it."

Each of the women took turns until they felt more confident.

"Whew, that was fun," Amber said, slightly out of breath.

"If you need more force than the punch, another good move is the old standard kick to the groin. Yeah, we've all envisioned taking a guy off his feet that way. To make it count, just picture your foot making contact between the legs and going right on up through the top of his head—pretend you're gonna split him in two. Then get your balance back right away. And remember, once he's down, you don't stand around staring at him or wondering if he's okay. You get the hell out of there—run."

Gracie laughed. "Definitely—I can swear to that."

"Here's a quick way to squiggle out of a bear-hug attack, say, someone grabs you from behind and pins your arms to your side." Mary asked Pen to simulate the attack, then simply bent her knees and wiggled out below the gripping hands. "Lowering your center of gravity makes it harder for him to get a grip on you, plus you're now in position to kick or punch him while you have the element of surprise on your side."

The ladies practiced everything Mary showed them until everyone was breathing hard.

"Thank you, Mary. I think we all feel a bit more confident now," Pen said, patting her face with the towel she'd brought. "Now Amber, Gracie, did you bring your passports?"

They scrambled to their purses and brought out the little blue booklets.

"I shall run these over to my friend's house tonight. She

leaves in the morning for L.A. and we cross our fingers that the approval process goes quickly."

For the next three days Pen chafed at the inactivity. Until those passports were safely back in her hands, she couldn't proceed with travel plans. Gracie phoned to say she and Amber had got together a couple of times to practice their punches and kicks. Once, the phone rang and a rapid phrase in Mandarin came at her.

"What do you think?" Amber said with a laugh. "I can greet waiters, hail a taxi, and ask where the nearest bathroom is."

"All very handy phrases, I'm sure. The big question is, do you understand enough to comprehend the replies to your questions?"

"Mei Ling, my friend who owns the Peking Palace, the lady I've been practicing with, says I'm getting pretty good."

"Excellent—I'm suitably impressed."

"Oh, I also discovered which hotel Clint and Kaycie are staying at—the Grand Plaza Peace Hotel. It's in the business district, so I assume his job or his client's offices must be nearby. We called—Mei Ling handled the query—and it looks like Clint and Kaycie checked in two days ago, right on schedule."

"What other hotels are nearby?" Pen asked. "We want to be close but we should avoid being in the same place. A chance encounter in a corridor or restaurant would, as they say in the spy business, blow our cover."

She could hear Amber typing on computer keys.

"There's one called Lotus Blossom. It looks like a small, boutique type of place. For big and anonymous, I'd probably go with the Hyatt Imperial. It's next to theirs but both hotels are such large places we could surely avoid contact."

"I'll book three adjoining rooms," Pen said.

Once they ended the call, she stared at the manuscript she was supposed to be editing and drummed her fingers on the desk. As if in answer to her impatience, the phone rang again.

"Good news—I have all three of your completed passports in my hands," came the greeting.

"Marty, you are a godsend."

"You owe me a fantastic lunch. I spent three hours at the embassy the first day, then had to go back this morning to pick them up. There was a little hang-up with your stating on your application that you are a writer. They don't seem very open to writers visiting and taking notes."

"How did you handle it?"

"I assured them your position was more of a secretarial one, that you make notes on manuscripts and such. I suppose if they really wanted to know what you write, a quick Google search would tell them everything."

"That I write novels involving heiresses with a penchant for getting involved with the wrong sorts of men? None of which could possibly be a threat to a foreign government."

"At least you now have your travel authorization."

"And you have a special lunch coming to you. Are you back in Phoenix now?" Pen made herself a note to order a gift basket and full spa-day pass at the Phoenician for her friend.

"Arriving tonight."

They made plans to meet and Pen immediately got online to book reservations. Within the hour she had three business class tickets (because they might as well arrive rested and ready to work) and three rooms reserved at the Hyatt. At last—the operation could move forward.

TWENTY-TWO

"WELCOME TO SHANGHAI, where the local time is seven p.m.," came the voice over the plane's intercom.

Pen looked out her window and saw it was dark already. Lights reflected off wet pavement on the tarmac. From her seat across the aisle, Amber practically sparkled. Her first overseas trip and she was wound up. Pen doubted her young companion had slept a moment of the flight, she'd been so busy fiddling with the gadgets around her seat, watching movies and playing games on the screen.

Gracie, on the other hand, must have been exhausted from the last-minute preparations, arranging for her family's needs while she would be gone, turning the reins over to her mother to run the household. She'd eaten the dinner served early in the flight then slept nearly the entire way.

Pen feared both her companions were in for a time-zone crash. Gracie would be awake and wired, all the way into the early hours of the local morning, while Amber...well, who knew what Amber would do. Youth was on her side. For herself, she'd remembered the practical advice which had served her well through much of her international travel—set your watch for the destination time and start thinking and acting as if you are in that zone. She'd eaten two meals and slept well during the fifteen-hour flight.

She gathered her belongings and herded her companions off the airplane and through the immigration lanes at Pudong International, a huge glass-and-steel modern structure with sweeping curves and acres of roof. She was thankful she'd arranged a limousine with English-speaking driver for their arrival. No matter how well Amber had learned Mandarin ahead of time, nothing could prepare them to negotiate the tangle of roads and newly created flyovers that comprised the current city. Not at night. Not in their jet-lagged state.

The car zigged and zagged through traffic on the ring expressway, where it felt as if they were flying when they passed upper-story windows in tall, high-rise buildings. The driver pulled off the freeway, made a few turns and slowed to a stop.

"Your hotel," he announced. "Hyatt Imperial."

He offloaded their bags at the curb and drove away. Apparently door-to-door service meant exactly that.

"From this point on, we aren't all seen together on the street," Pen said in a low voice as a bellman stepped out to take the luggage. "I'll handle the check-in and you girls find spots to wait in different sections of the lobby."

She tucked all three passports into her coat pocket and approached the reception desk. A bright-faced young woman greeted her with a practiced smile, and in only a few minutes she had a receipt and keys for three rooms on the tenth floor. When Pen headed toward the elevators, Gracie sauntered over from the gift shop and Amber tucked her paperback book into her purse and caught up just in time to step into the same car.

"That went well," Pen said, once the three were alone after stopping for an elderly couple to get out at the third floor. "Now, I recommend we all get some sleep, keeping in mind it's already nine o'clock here. In the morning, we can discuss our next moves over a good meal and with clear heads. Set your alarms for seven, come to my room at seven-thirty."

Clearly, Amber was coming down from her earlier restive state. She accepted her room key with glazed eyes, and Pen took her by the shoulders and pointed her toward the door. Gracie met the bellman with their baggage and showed him which pieces went to each room before the ladies bade each other goodnight.

China. Pen stared out her window at the endless lighted windows across the city. More than a billion people lived in this country. Would she and her friends be able to unravel the web one American man had woven here, to right the wrongs that man had created? She went to bed with the question weighing on her mind.

In the morning, she phoned room service and ordered a substantial quantity of eggs, bacon, sausages, toast, pancakes and an assortment of fruit and pastries. This should satisfy all tastes, she thought, when the cart was wheeled into her room.

Amber arrived first, fuzzy-headed and shuffling her feet, obviously not adjusted to the time difference yet.

"Good thing you told us to set alarms last night," she mumbled, holding her hand out toward the coffee cup Pen extended. "I could've slept another whole day."

"Some breakfast and getting into a routine will help."

A tap sounded at the door and Pen admitted Gracie, who looked freshly showered and dressed in lightweight slacks and a T-shirt.

"Oh good—food," she said. "I've been awake since four o'clock and the restaurant downstairs was cold and dark when I went to check. And the desk clerk—he popped up so quickly from behind the desk, I think he was actually asleep on the floor back there."

Amber laughed. "Seriously?"

"Yeah. Anyway, I've spent the time productively. I logged onto the hotel wi-fi and checked emails, sent a note to Scott that we've arrived and all is well."

Amber's expression went solemn. "Be careful on the internet here," she said. "I meant to warn everyone ahead of time. The Chinese have been known to get past visitors' passwords and spy on their communications. Just be careful what you say. Don't mention our mission here or anything about banking or business."

"Geez. Okay." Gracie exchanged a look with Pen. "So, how are we going to get information back and forth from Sandy?"

Amber held up her iPad. "For whatever reason, these are more secure. I'll send important messages through this. Sandy and I worked out a few code words ahead of time, too. Things we can say innocuously. For instance, in all messages, Clint is going to be 'Dad' and Kaycie is 'Sis.' We've also worked out ways to send account numbers and such by breaking the data into smaller pieces and coding it. When we need to talk about places, we'll do it through chatty emails making it sound like we went there on a tour."

Pen could see a hundred ways this could go badly, but she kept quiet.

Gracie eyed the table laden with food. "Is that for us?"

Pen gave a relaxed smile. "Absolutely. Help yourselves. I didn't know what you like so I basically ordered everything. Myself, I'm starving."

Amber took fruit, two muffins and a cereal bar that appeared to consist of a sticky substance coated with a million various seeds. Gracie went the all-American route with bacon, scrambled eggs, and two pancakes. They took seats in the small sitting area while Pen filled her own plate.

Conversation lagged for a few minutes until finally Gracie moaned and swore she'd better slow down or risk exploding.

"Now that we're here, I must admit I'm feeling a bit overwhelmed as to how we're going to locate our subjects and get the information we need," Pen said, after wiping her mouth with a napkin.

Amber brushed muffin crumbs off her hands. "I've got some basic info as a starter. For one, the address of Tong Chen Enterprises, Clint's client. Their offices are located on Tsing Bao Road. Apparently, this is a manufacturer of electronics—they're cropping up all over China as competitors to the big Japanese players such as Sony and Mitsubishi. A news release three months ago said they are expanding their manufacturing, breaking ground on a new factory in the Laogangzhen district. The contractor is Redwing Holdings."

"That's one of Clint's companies, isn't it?" Gracie asked.

"Yes. I'm not sure why they're going through that one—I had the impression it was simply an investment vehicle or holding company of some sort."

"Perhaps the Chinese were attracted by the name redwing—it has the sound of nature." Pen put forth the suggestion with no idea whether it had merit.

Gracie and Amber both nodded. "Anyway," said Gracie, "it's Redwing Holdings but what can we do with that information?"

"Reading between the lines of the press release, it looks like Tong Chen has given Redwing some space within their building. I think it said something like 'working under the auspices of'..."

"And?" Gracie wasn't understanding where this was leading.

"Well, girls, I'm going to work in their offices." Amber sent them one of her perky smiles.

TWENTY-THREE

SANDY WERNER SAT at her desk trying to make it appear as if she was doing her job on any ordinary day. This morning she'd received a cryptic email from Amber: Arrived. Dad and Sis at hotel. Will get together tomorrow.

Sandy pondered the words. Surely Amber didn't mean they actually planned to meet with Clint and Kaycie? It must mean the ladies had a plan for tracking the two.

Movement outside her door caught her attention. She closed the page with her personal emails, blanking her screen from view.

Tap, tap. Mary's face appeared at the edge of the door. "Are you busy?"

Sandy waved her in. "Close the door." She repeated Amber's message.

"So, they are in China," Mary said. "Amazing. And it sounds like they know for sure Clint has arrived, which is perfect for my plan."

"Plan?"

"I'm paying a little visit to my former business."

"Mary...are you sure that's wise?" Sandy had to admit, it must be tempting to go back and see old acquaintances after a life-changing makeover such as Mary's.

"The bookkeeper and I were pretty good friends. Even after I left her in charge while I cared for my parents, she and I would touch base, have lunch once in awhile. Debbie was the one who let me know he was sneaking around with Kaycie Marlow while we were still married."

"So, is this visit purely social or are you on a mission?"

"How about we say it's a little of each." Mary's eyes gleamed.

THE SIGN ABOVE the building had been repainted, Mary noticed. Holbrook Plumbing. Seeing it here in writing brought back too many memories—she and Clint working side-by-side to start the business, the day they'd installed that sign with their names on it. What was she doing, keeping Clint's name after all he'd done?

She looked away. Depending on how the next few weeks went, maybe she would change hers, go back to her maiden name or pick something she liked better.

The displays in the front windows were less inspiring than before, a collection of miscellaneous bathroom fixtures. In past times, she'd organized things herself, insisted each window depict a finished room—kitchen or bath—with the newest fixtures to showcase the company's capabilities. Now, it looked like a row of toilets in some public restroom. Clint had probably become so busy with his big projects he'd left something as mundane as window displays to one of the staff.

She pushed open the glass entry door, noticing that the bell she'd had installed to announce customers was no longer operational. It was the little things that told how successful a business was, not the money hoarded away in a bank somewhere. She walked up to the sales counter where no one was visible or acknowledged they knew she was here.

Formalities be damned. She swung open the moveable section of counter and walked through to the employee area.

The wall behind the desk held the same tile samples, rather outdated now, that she'd put up three years ago. She let the gate swing shut with a clatter. No response, so she headed down the narrow corridor that led to the offices. Clint's office door was closed and a quick twist of the handle told her it was locked. The one across the hall had once been hers. She started farther down, toward Debbie's small office.

"Ma'am?" came a familiar voice as she passed her old office. "Can I help you, ma'am?"

Mary turned and peered around the doorjamb. "Hey, Debbie. It's me. I was heading for your office."

"Mary? Oh. My. God. You look amazing." Debbie, at ten years older and thirty pounds heavier than Mary, stood up and emerged from behind her old desk. "Look at you, girl. You're doing something right—you look so much younger!"

Mary did a little turn. "Thanks. New exercise program."

Debbie folded her into a hug. "I hadn't heard from you in so long, I wondered if you'd moved away."

Another thing living in your car or a homeless shelter takes away from you, the dignity to stay in contact with old friends. She gave a weak smile. "Yeah, well. No, I've just been busy."

"Come on in, sit down." Debbie waved toward the guest chair, which felt a little awkward to both of them.

"It's a quick visit," Mary said. "Just wanted to say hi. Look, I noticed there's no one up front. We always had a strict policy about that."

"Yeah, I know…it's just…" She picked up her phone and hit the intercom line. Her voice echoed in the distant warehouse in the back. "Joey, Rob, we need a counter person up front."

She sighed and sat down behind the desk. "Hopefully, that'll bring one of 'em."

"Things feel different," Mary said, taking the guest chair. "I suppose because I've been away."

"Nah, it's not only that. It really is different since…"

"You can say it. Since Clint remarried. Since Clint expanded the business beyond this little shop?"

A nod and a shrug.

"I can say his name, Debbie. I can say Kaycie's name. I'm over it." Mary leaned forward and winked. "Unless you've got some juicy gossip."

Gossip had always been Debbie's weakness.

"Well…"

"Yeah? Something good?"

"He's out of the country now, so I guess there's no way he'll hear me from over there." Debbie tilted her chin toward the closed office across the hall. "He's been getting calls from women who aren't the current Mrs. H."

"What kind of calls?"

"The kind he goes into the office to take. Where he closes the door and speaks real quiet." She fiddled with a pen, moving it from one spot to another on the desk.

"The kind he used to get from Kaycie when I wasn't here?"

Debbie blushed. "I didn't want to say it that way."

"I know. It's okay. So, you think the gleam is off the romance between them?"

Debbie looked as if she didn't want to voice the opinion, but she gave a little nod.

"What else reminds you of that time before? Is he moving money around, getting it out of sight?"

"Oh, I wouldn't know about that, Mary. Really. He handles a lot of things he doesn't let me see."

Mary eyed a small stack of mail in a tray labeled Filing. The envelopes that were visible seemed to be from an investment firm and a bank she'd never known Clint to do business with. It appeared to be correspondence, not junk mail.

Debbie reached for them at the same moment Mary did.

"Uh-uh," she said. "He'd kill me if he knew I let you see stuff of his."

"Sorry. I won't jeopardize you, Debbie. You know that." Mary left her hand at the edge of the desk. "I'll never admit I was inside this office today."

Debbie met her gaze with surprising candor. "I'd better go see if one of those guys ever showed up to work the counter. Since you're *not here* today, you'll want to be sure I've sent him to the back room before you walk out that front door."

Mary nodded. Was it really going to be this easy?

Debbie stood up and walked out the door, heading toward the showroom. The letters still sat in the tray. Without a second thought, Mary pulled her phone from her pocket and put it in camera mode. She quickly removed the contents of the top envelope, a letter of credit from a bank. Zooming in with the lens, a snap. The page went back into the envelope. Same with the statement from the brokerage firm, where it appeared Clint had liquidated most of the investments. For good measure, she photographed two more documents, although she wasn't sure of their significance.

She replaced the envelopes exactly as she'd found them and tiptoed to the door. No voices in the hall. None from the showroom. She scurried across the room and out the door, feeling like a character in a spy novel—or like a sneaky ex-wife who'd just betrayed someone she'd once loved.

TWENTY-FOUR

CLINT HOLBROOK STOOD at the window of the small office Tong Chen Enterprises owner, Rudy Tong, had allotted him for the duration of the job. He'd visited the work site within hours after arriving in Shanghai, felt the excavation work was moving along slowly and had a come-to-Jesus meeting—or come-to-Confucius or whoever it was they talked to over here—with the phase-one foreman.

The office here in the Laogangzhen high-rise was a nice perk—a couple of furnished rooms including a locking door to separate his own space from that of a secretary. He'd envisioned being stationed in a trailer or mobile building on the jobsite and, as wet as the damn weather was proving to be around here, a leaky metal building was no treat. If the rainy season didn't end soon, he could see the construction stretching out far longer than anticipated.

So far, Tong had provided secretaries, a different one each day, Chinese women who were fairly adept at English. When he could make himself understood, the women had proved helpful in showing him the ropes—how to work the ultra-modern coffee maker, for instance. He'd not asked them to type correspondence, and he had no intention of letting them touch his computer where it would be too easy for someone who was being paid to spy to get hold of his financial data.

He turned away from the view—miles of nearly identical high-rises—and glanced at his laptop on the desk. He'd started it up when he arrived, but it was taking forever this morning to get an internet connection. He needed to verify that a payment from Tong Chen had reached his construction bank account, then he wanted to move it quickly—to a new account he'd set up days before leaving the U.S. He clicked his browser button and was pleased to see a connection. Rudy Tong had assured him all online equipment in the entire building was completely secure, so he logged onto his accounts.

With the funds transfer complete, next he visited his insurance company to take care of a few details, then on to place an order for lumber to build the foundation forms. A ping sounded and he clicked over to his email. The new message came from Kaycie.

Will you be free for lunch, HB? Heard of a great restaurant we should try. xoxo

She'd added some dippy little smiley faces, the kind that made him cringe.

Lunch with the wife. He couldn't seem to get her to understand he was here to work. What had he been thinking when he suggested she come to China with him? Hot sex— that's what he'd been thinking. Kaycie and her lingerie collection in a hotel in a foreign country. They'd gone at it like rabbits the first two days, until he'd absolutely had to spend time at the office. The client wouldn't keep paying him unless they saw him actually working.

He typed a quick reply: Sorry, baby. Swamped here at the office.

He hit Send before he realized maybe he shouldn't have

admitted where he was. She might pick up some box of exotic who-knows-what and show up, determined to feed him. That was another thing—finding a great steak had so far been impossible in this city. What was it with all the food being freaking Chinese? The place was supposed to be a mecca of international business. Did everybody eat this vegetable stuff *all* the time?

He grumbled a little and closed the lid on the laptop. If he beat it out of here quickly, he could legitimately be at the job site when and if Kaycie showed up at the office. As he jammed the computer into its leather case he looked out the window again. Across the way he saw the shimmer of wet leaves on the trees in the median and realized there were raindrops on his window, as well. Shit. More rain.

He grabbed a slicker, a crappy lightweight, baby-blue thing the job foreman had given him the first day. The man had seemed amused Clint would arrive in China without rain gear. Didn't the guy have a clue that people who live in desert climates don't even own such things? Clint slung the flimsy plastic jacket over his arm and picked up his computer bag. He should get the secretary *du jour* to order him a car. Waiting on the curb for a taxi, he discovered, was usually frustrating.

Another new girl sat at the desk, her back partially toward him. She was a tiny thing just like most all these girls here. The striking difference was her hair, which she wore pulled away from her face and tied with a cloth band at the crown of her head. He'd not seen any of the Asian girls with such curls. These looked like the natural, springy curls of someone with black or Mediterranean heritage.

"Hello..." he said tentatively, with no clue how much English she spoke.

"Hi," she said in a perky voice. She turned and looked up at him. "You must be Mr. Holbrook?"

"You're American. Well, you sound American."

"I am. San Francisco, born and raised." She gave a dazzling smile full of lovely, even teeth.

Too bad about the heavy-rimmed glasses. He would have loved to see those dark eyes more clearly.

"I… I'm heading out to the job site and need a car. Do you know how to order me one?"

"Certainly, Mr. Holbrook."

"Clint. You might as well call me Clint, since we're the only two Americans in the place."

The smile again. No comment.

She picked up the desk phone and punched a series of numbers. *"Qǐng sòng chē qù Zhōngguó wáng yīsìwǔ."*

The only word he recognized in the exchange was *Zhōngguó*, the name of the street.

"The car will be here in ten minutes," she told him.

He couldn't think of a witty response that wouldn't come out in a schoolboy stammer. "Thanks. You're very good at that. I'll just wait downstairs. Um, will you be here later?"

She gave him a coolish look.

"I just meant they've given me a different secretary each day, and so far you're the only one I could actually understand."

She graced him with another dazzling smile and one petite shoulder raised slightly. "I don't know. The agency just gives me an assignment each day. I can ask, though."

He felt the goofy grin on his own face. "Yeah, if you could, that would be great."

He stood straighter and sucked in his stomach while he told her he would be at the job site if anyone needed him.

He provided his cell number, which she dutifully wrote on a small scratchpad.

She pretended not to notice when he bumped into the doorframe on his way out. He caught himself whistling that old Tony Bennett tune as he rode the elevator to the ground floor.

TWENTY-FIVE

"IT WAS *SO* GROSS," Amber told Pen and Gracie that evening. "I mean, seriously, the guy could be my father and I swear he's looking straight down the front of my shirt. And that smile of his is so…so…smarmy. Ick."

Pen felt a wave of horror, even though Sandy's nightly message had included startling double news. One—Mary had brazenly walked right into Holbrook Plumbing the previous day, and two—according to her pal the bookkeeper, the shine was coming off the boss's new marriage. She supposed she shouldn't be shocked at his attitude toward Amber, but she felt a grandmotherly, protective wave of affection for the girl.

"The good news is I learned Clint gets assigned a secretary from among Tong Chen's employees and I gather it's been a different woman each day. I figured out enough Mandarin to tell today's lady she wasn't needed, so if I need back in there I think I could easily come and go."

Pen filled them in on Sandy's news from Arizona.

"Should she have done that?" Gracie asked, open-mouthed at Mary's boldness.

"I don't know about *should*," Pen said. "The bottom line is she did come up with some new information." She handed her tablet over to Amber, who looked at the pictures Mary had snapped.

"Hm, this is a new bank," Amber said, "not one of the ones I found before. Having the account number and balance will help me get into it. I mean, when the time is right."

"What's this letter from an insurance company?" Gracie asked. "They're talking about assets and such."

"He's probably being required to carry some kind of a construction guarantee policy. If something happened so that he didn't complete the project, the policy would pay the cost of having another contractor finish," Pen said as she stared at the photo, although it would have been a very unusual way of doing it. Normally, bonding companies handled that sort of thing.

Amber had plopped onto the sofa in Pen's sitting area and was tapping away at her iPad.

Gracie started to say something, but Amber held up her tablet with the screen facing her friend. On a plain notepad screen she had typed: We need to talk outside the room.

"Let's go for a walk," she suggested. She closed the cover on the device and stood up.

With umbrellas in hand, they rode the elevator in silence.

"I don't want to say too much in the rooms," Amber said, once they were on the street. "The government could be listening. I found a bug in the office the Chinese gave Clint," Amber said.

"What?"

Amber gave Gracie an indulgent smile. "Why do you think his client offered him a free office? Had to be so they could keep an eye on him."

"I've been wanting to get out and walk anyway," Pen said. "So, where *can* we talk?"

"Realistically, probably anywhere. We're of no interest to the government. We just need to keep in mind that we don't have an expectation of privacy over here, not like we think we have at home. And since we're actually spying…"

"On Clint? Do you think *he* matters to the Chinese government?" Gracie asked.

"You never know. I think they definitely take an interest in Americans doing business over here."

They followed the tree-lined boulevard, watching at intersections for the scooters that dashed everywhere with their silent electric motors. It would be easy to be bowled over.

"What are they monitoring?"

"Everything. Well, that's my guess. Somewhere in that building somebody knows about every phone call he made and every time he went online."

Amber pointed to a small park where they could pause, away from the throngs of people on the sidewalk. "While I was observing Clint's computer in his office, I spotted the digital fingerprints of some other entity who was also watching."

"Wait a second. You could actually see what Clint was doing on his computer?" Gracie seemed fascinated. Pen looked concerned as they walked a pathway that led past a modern-art sculpture.

"He got an email invitation to lunch with his wife, which he turned down, and he received a four-million-dollar payment from Tong Chen. The money went into the account we discovered—Redwing Holdings. Redwing didn't hold it very long, though. Clint transferred the money to an account in the Cayman Islands right away."

Gracie stepped gingerly around a pile of dog droppings. "I wonder…at this stage of the construction project that's most likely money Tong Chen has paid as a deposit to cover materials. The contractor usually gets payments in increments, with the bulk of his profit coming upon completion.

It seems like an unusual move to take it out of his operating account."

Amber sent a sideways glance toward her.

"My dad was a builder," said Gracie with a shrug. "I guess I absorbed some of this stuff through family osmosis."

"So, why *did* he move the money?" Pen murmured the question.

"Maybe to get it out of reach of the Chinese?"

Amber shrugged. "We might figure it out if we had a way to watch what's going on outside the office."

"He and Kaycie are staying at the Grand Plaza Peace Hotel, correct?" Pen asked. "I think I may have another avenue to reach him."

TWENTY-SIX

PEN STROLLED INTO the lobby of the Grand Plaza, dressed as befitted a well-off American tourist in a foreign country. She'd waited across the street in a curio shop until she saw Kaycie Marlow Holbrook approach the entrance. Her target was alone. Pen dropped the silk cosmetic bag she'd been pretending to admire and stepped outside, dodging a phalanx of motor scooters and crossing the busy street. By the time she stepped inside the lobby, Kaycie was entering the hotel bar, a faux-English pub called The Brown Duck.

Pen crossed the white marble floor, with its rococo gold light fixtures and intimate furniture groupings, at a leisurely pace. She couldn't let Kaycie realize she was being followed. Sure enough, by the time Pen entered the shadowy room the blonde had taken a seat at the long bar and the bartender was placing a heavy glass with about an inch of amber liquid in front of her. He turned to Pen.

She ordered a glass of Chablis, pretending to be busy with her wallet when she glanced toward Kaycie.

"Oh—hello," she said, putting just the right amount of puzzlement into her voice. "We've met somewhere, haven't we?"

She held up a hand. "Don't tell me. It had to either be the Phoenix Little Theatre gala or the Arizona Broadcast Awards."

Kaycie extended her hand and smiled her classic television smile as they shook. "It had to have been the Broad-cast Awards. I'm sorry I don't remember..."

"Penelope Fitzpatrick." Her name was familiar enough in Arizona social circles it was entirely possible for their paths to have crossed. She only hoped Kaycie wouldn't pin her for details of the event.

A nano-second's uncertainty crossed Kaycie's face, but she was social animal enough not to admit she didn't rec-ognize a member of the hometown glitterati. "Of course, Ms. Fitzpatrick. So good to see you again. What on earth are you doing in Shanghai?"

"Purely vacation for me," Pen said. "Of course, I might ask the same. It's unusual to meet another Arizonan this far from home. And how is Channel Three getting along without you?"

The bartender set her wine on the bar but Pen didn't sit.

"My husband's a contractor with a big job here. I thought it would be great to see the city and do some shopping. Thought we would get out more and enjoy the nightlife, but Clint's work keeps him pretty busy." She downed half her drink in a long gulp.

"I'm rather on my own today, as well. My friends had plans. Look, if you aren't meeting anyone right away, would you like to get a table and just chat?"

The rest of Kaycie's drink disappeared and she ordered another.

"Yes. I'd like that." She picked up a tiny pink purse from the bar and slid off her stool to follow Pen.

The hour was early enough the pub's tables were nearly empty. They chose a small one in a dim corner.

"It's just kind of lonely here," Kaycie said. "I pictured doing everything with Clint all day. Not that I'm not a per-fectly independent woman, you know. Well, back home I am. I've got a career and friends and all. I just thought I'd meet more women here who speak English. A little hard, you know, conversing with the hotel maids."

Pen nodded, sipping her wine while Kaycie continued to talk.

"We've been married almost two years, and it's been great. We had a smallish wedding—like, a hundred people or so, and they were mostly from the station and my friends. But then we had a fabulous honeymoon on Barbados. Oh my god, Clint knows how to treat a girl to the fine life."

Pen thought of Mary. A homeless shelter. A tiny, by-the-week apartment.

"I suppose you get to travel a great deal then?" Pen asked.

"Well, yes and no. My schedule restricts me a bit, so we usually only get away for long weekends and that kind of thing. I took a leave of absence to do this trip." She took another hefty slug. "Do you think my boobs are too small?"

Pen sat back slightly. "What?"

Kaycie giggled. "Sorry. Silly question to ask a woman. I just… I'd look better on camera with a little…" She jutted her chest outward. "Not to mention, Clint would love the result."

Pen sipped her wine to avoid having to comment.

"So, there's this really well-known clinic here in Shanghai. I've got their brochure here." Kaycie slipped a tri-fold color sheet from the small purse. "Seems really reasonably priced for what you get. There are recovery suites where you can hide away until your bruises are gone. That's appealing—not having Clint see me all…you know." She wrinkled her nose. "Plus, you get pampered a lot in the process."

"Is surgery what you really want to do?" Pen asked.

Kaycie tossed the brochure aside and sighed. "What I *really* want is for me and Clint to have a baby. I mean, can

you see a little boy, a tiny version of Clint? Or a little girl—
she'd have to be completely adorable."

Pen didn't have children and part of the reason was because she was well aware that in addition to being adorable
they were noisy, messy, smelly and basically took over a
person's life for a minimum twenty years. But she was here
to pick up clues from Kaycie, not to talk life-choices to her.

"Anyway, so far no luck getting pregnant and Clint's
sure not pushing for it. Says he could get along just fine
without kids."

"It's a big commitment. Good idea to have both partners
in agreement, I should think."

Some emotion flashed across Kaycie's face, a flash so
brief Pen wouldn't have caught it if she'd blinked.

"Anyway." Kaycie sat up straighter and her eyes were
suddenly clear. She picked up the brochure again. "I'm doing
what I need to, to keep my husband's interest. My appointment is set for the fifteenth."

"Next week. Isn't this a bit sudden?"

"It's not like I haven't thought about it for a long time."
Her manner stiffened, taking on a you're-not-my-mother
tone.

"Well, of course. I'm sure you'll be very happy with the result." Pen raised her glass and Kaycie smiled as they clinked.

Pen thought about what she'd heard through Mary's visit
with Clint's bookkeeper back in Phoenix, that the man was
already eyeing younger women again. She wanted to feel
sorry for Kaycie, sitting here in a foreign bar drinking too
much and contemplating changing her body to please a
man who, from Pen's observations, wasn't the type who
would ever be content.

When Kaycie excused herself to visit the ladies room,
Pen slipped the brochure from the table and hid it in her own
purse. A plan began to form.

TWENTY-SEVEN

SANDY STARED INTO her own blue eyes in the mirror, contemplating the latest round of messages from China. She'd stopped at home after work, just long enough to change out of her business suit and tidy up before going back out to meet Mary for pizza. It was Mary's second payday and she'd insisted on treating Sandy to dinner.

At her ankle, a black cat rubbed and said *mrroww*. She knew it was Heckle only because his brother had four tiny white hairs on his chin. Pets—they never failed to remind when dinner was due. She dropped her hairbrush back into the drawer and followed the cat out of the bathroom. By the time they reached the kitchen, Jeckle had joined the chorus of complaints. She opened a can of their favorite, tuna surprise, and scooped portions into two bowls.

"You guys watch the house for me," she said, a routine pep talk that never elicited responses from either cat.

So Clint had met Amber and immediately hit on her, Sandy thought as she started her Mazda and backed out of her driveway. Although it most likely wouldn't surprise Mary, she didn't think she would mention it. The bigger revelations came from Kaycie's candid conversation with Pen. She debated whether to pass the information along to Mary. It really was nothing more than salacious gossip but, then again, Kaycie's movements might dictate Clint's actions as well, and all the ladies in the group should be kept up to date.

She arrived at the Pizza Hut on East McDowell and parked three slots away from the door. Inside, she caught sight of Mary's red-blonde spiky hair at a table near the windows. Mary waved and smiled hugely when she spotted Sandy.

"Hey. I can't tell you how much I've been thinking about pizza all day," Mary said when Sandy dropped her purse on the opposite booth seat and slid in across from her. "I mean, I'm loving the results of my diet but, geez, I've missed some of my favorite foods."

"I know. It seems I've dieted my whole life, not that it does much good."

They studied the menu in silence for a few minutes before the waitress appeared beside them. With their order on its way to the kitchen, Sandy brought up the subject that was really on their minds, and ended up mentioning Pen's news about the boob job.

"I never thought I'd say this, but I'm kinda feeling sorry for Kaycie," Mary said, eyeing the plate of Italian breadsticks the server had brought.

Sandy gave her a surprised look. "Seriously?"

"Well, look at her situation. She's willing to have surgery to please Clint and he's already nosing around other women like some kind of old dog. It's just sad."

Sandy looked at her friend for some sign of sarcasm or disdain, but she didn't see it. "That's a generous attitude, Mary, considering what they did to you."

Mary succumbed and picked up one of the breadsticks. "Oh, I don't really blame her. Not her fault she was born cute and blonde and perky. Clint's the rat in this whole scenario."

Sandy couldn't disagree.

"What I don't understand is the part you said about him moving money around. Is this history repeating itself? I mean, if he's already looking for an exit to get away from Kaycie, maybe he's doing the same thing to her that he did to me, financially. I thought I knew our business and finances pretty well, but he managed to cheat me. I have to wonder how much Kaycie knows—if she's completely in the dark about what he does with money, or if she's in on it too. She could know exactly what he's doing."

"It's possible. But something else is going on and I think it's got to do with the Chinese and the job he's doing over there." Sandy reached for one of the breadsticks too. "I just wish I knew what."

Their pizza arrived just then, smelling of pepperoni and sauce, and neither of the women said another thing about Clint Holbrook for awhile.

"If we knew what he was declaring on his tax returns, that might help," Sandy said after she'd wolfed down her first slice. "Do you have copies of joint returns the two of you filed together? If I had his social security number and some past information I could see if there's a way to request more current data."

"I can give you the numbers," Mary said, "but isn't there all kinds of protection for personal information the government has on us?"

Less than you would think. Sandy didn't voice that concern. She pulled a scrap of paper and a pen from her purse, and Mary wrote down Clint's information.

Mary passed the slip back to her and glanced at her watch. "I guess I'd better wrap this up. I told Billy I'd lead his seven o'clock Zumba class."

"I can—" Sandy started to offer a ride but Mary had already grabbed the check and was pushing her way out of the booth. "At least take the rest of the pizza for another meal at home."

"You keep it. I've worked too hard on my new shape to get into a nightly pizza habit. But it sure tasted good, just this once." Mary gave a grin and headed toward the register.

Sandy debated the pizza for herself and decided Mary's argument against it should be hers, as well. She certainly wouldn't ever lose these extra pounds if she didn't say no to some favorite foods. She took the last swig of her wine and followed Mary to the door.

"I'll get the process started to request those tax forms," she said when they reached the parking lot. "Let's touch base again in a few days."

She watched Mary sprint for the bus stop as the big vehicle rolled to a stop.

TWENTY-EIGHT

"HEY, BABY," Clint said when he walked into their room. "Look what I brought you."

He flashed a huge bouquet of red roses from behind his back. Kaycie looked at them and turned away. After the third time this week, turning down her lunch invitation, yeah, he'd better be bringing roses.

"I got us theater tickets for tonight, too," he wheedled, snaking his arm around her waist with the tickets in hand. "We'll have the whole evening, just the two of us…"

She turned toward him when she saw the tickets. "Really?"

"I know you've been on your own a lot since we got here." He seemed genuinely contrite. "Work has been consuming me. I'm sorry, Babycakes."

And here she'd been, feeling sorry for herself and getting all weepy over the fact she hadn't gotten pregnant yet. She hugged him close before taking the roses and setting them on the coffee table in their small suite.

"So, is there time for me to show you the new black lace teddy I bought today?" she teased. "Or do you want to save it for later?"

"I'm kind of sweaty, and we'll need to leave in forty-five minutes to make our dinner reservation. I'd better shower now. We'll save the good stuff for later." He patted her on the butt and began tugging his tie loose as he walked toward the bedroom.

The good *stuff*? She tossed one of the sofa pillows at him, but it fell short and he didn't notice. All right, honey, you'll soon see the good stuff—the *really* good stuff—she thought. I'm gonna take your breath away with my new curves. She still hadn't told him about the appointment at the clinic, and it was coming up in only three days. Tonight would be a good time to spring the surprise. A nice dinner...an evening together...plenty of champagne. And afterward, when she got him back to the room she would introduce the subject playfully, tease him into admitting he would be thrilled with the changes. Then she could drop the bombshell that it was happening right away.

She heard the shower running so she rummaged in the closet until she came across the right dress for the theater tonight—a brilliant blue sheath that accentuated her eyes perfectly. She slipped off her robe and stepped into the dress, located the matching shoes and laid Clint's tuxedo on the bed. At the small bar in the corner of the living room, she checked the mini-fridge to be sure there was champagne already chilled. Perfect.

Muttered words came from the bedroom—Clint's reaction to seeing his tux ready to put on, no doubt. Wisely, he didn't make an issue of it. He was either still in make-up mode for the earlier neglect, or he knew better than to start something before a night of promised sex. Kaycie strolled into the bedroom, putting a little sway into her high-heeled steps, and crossed to the dresser where she'd left her diamond necklace.

"Could you fasten the clasp on this for me, Honey Bear?"

He paused, trouser-less, with his white shirt hanging open, to work the necklace hook.

"Thank you, darling," she said, stroking his cheek and blowing an air kiss his direction. His gruff expression melted into a goofy grin.

They arrived at the restaurant, and Kaycie noticed it had a Western menu. Clint had grumbled about the steady diet of Chinese food for two weeks now. It came as no surprise he would find somewhere he could get steak or chops. She settled in to the pleasant surroundings and ordered a glass of the best Petite Sirah on the menu.

By the time they arrived at the theater they were laughing together the way they used to, which was a good thing. The tickets turned out to be for a Chinese circus, an amazing display of acrobatics and hold-your-breath balancing acts—but hardly a black-tie affair. Most people wore casual attire. Clint and Kaycie laughed over their social blunder and carried the light-hearted attitude back to the hotel.

Clint poured the chilled champagne and they carried glasses to the bedroom. Kaycie dangled the black teddy in front of Clint's face before ducking into the bathroom to put it on. When she emerged he was already in bed.

She climbed across his lap and pressed her bosom to his face.

"Say goodbye to the old ones," she said with a playful grin, "because they're going in for an upgrade to the bigger version."

He practically drooled.

"You don't mind if I disappear for a week or so, do you?" She'd intended to show him the brochure from the clinic—the day spa facilities, the gardens and luxury recovery suites—but she'd misplaced it somewhere. "I signed up for the full package. You don't have to see me until I'm all healed up and gorgeous for you."

He ran his hands over her body. "You're always gorgeous, Babycakes."

She sent him a seductive smile and moved against him.

"Fine with me if you check yourself in and have a blast. Besides, Rudy Tong invited me to go along on a fishing trip to the Philippines. He's got a buddy with a boat somewhere near Manila."

She felt her smile droop. Geez, everything was always about him, wasn't it?

TWENTY-NINE

"GRACIE, YOU TOOK drama classes in school. You can do this." Amber's eyes sparkled with fun as she spoke.

"I did, yeah. But I always got the secondary roles and, trust me, nothing I ever did was Tony Award material."

Pen spoke up. The group had met in her room at the Hyatt. "What we're talking about doesn't involve anything nearly that difficult. It definitely falls into the supporting-actor category."

"Yes, but this is real life. What if I get caught?"

The room went silent.

"Um, you run like hell?" Amber looked so cute in her pixie-like innocence, they all laughed.

"See? That puts it in perspective."

"Okay, let's role-play this," Pen suggested. "Starting with what we're doing later this morning. You'll go to this clinic as a prospective client. Amber is your personal assistant. Do something different with your hair and makeup because by the day after tomorrow you're going to be an employee at the place."

Gracie flopped back on the sofa and rolled her eyes.

"Just…just wait. We have a plan." Amber spread the brochure on the coffee table, the one Pen had taken from Kaycie. It showed an employee in a pale sage green uniform handing a female patient a cup of tea. "We know what the uniforms look like and we're going to try to steal one—that's plan A. Plan B is we find you a dress or suit in the same color, so no one will question whether you belong."

Pen spoke up. "While you're touring the clinic this morning, getting the lay of the land, I'll call Kaycie and say I've arranged a personal escort for the day of her surgery."

"She'll be thrilled to have an American," Amber said. "Trust me. You should have seen the look of relief on Clint's face the day I acted as his secretary. Kaycie's going to feel the same way."

"She will," Pen said. "She confided to me that she's felt very much out of her depth in this country, few women to talk to and she can't seem to comprehend the accents of the Chinese who speak English to her."

"So, while she's dopey from the anesthetic I'm to question her about Clint's finances and find out where he's stashed all that money." Gracie's expression was skeptical. "Why would she confide that to a stranger?"

"Remember, dear, you are not a stranger. You've come on my personal recommendation and you are her American liaison with the Chinese medical facility. Of anyone in the place, she's going to trust you most."

"Scary," muttered Gracie.

"I shall tell her you will meet her at the lobby of her hotel and walk her through the check-in process at the clinic."

"How on earth am I supposed to do that?" Gracie looked frantic.

"That's what our recon trip today is all about," Amber said. "I'll sketch the layout, and we'll make notes about the procedures, the whole protocol."

"This afternoon, we'll role-play it until you're comfortable. Everything will be fine." Pen placed a gentle hand on Gracie's arm. "Don't forget, I'll be right there with you.

Kaycie thinks I'm her new friend here. She is under the impression we know each other through common social contacts back in Phoenix. When she learned her husband would be away on a fishing trip, she practically begged me to accompany her. A second American, unrelated to me as far as she knows, will help solidify her confidence in us."

Gracie looked only marginally assured.

"All right," said Pen. "You two should get going."

Gracie went into the bathroom and emerged a few minutes later sans makeup, her hair hanging straight at the sides of her face. She had adopted the look of a woman embarrassed by her features.

"Hey, I'm impressed with your character," Amber said with a smile. "You'll nail this thing."

THIRTY

MARY HOLBROOK LANDED a series of blows on a punching bag at the gym. Dammit, this whole thing with Clint was taking way too long. The bag swung toward her and she met it forcefully with a hard right.

She thought of Sandy's plan to request IRS copies of old tax returns. At the pace the government worked, it could be another six months before the Ladies even obtained one scrap of information.

She danced away from the bag, circled it and punched again.

Mary appreciated everything Sandy and her friends were doing, truly she did. But now that she felt stronger, as if she was gaining back some measure of control in her life, she hated the feeling of uselessness. The rest of them were out there doing things, coming face to face with Clint and taking action, while they expected her to sit back and wait for results.

Left—pow. Right—pow.

That's what was making her crazy—the waiting. She didn't want to wait another day, much less weeks or months.

"Whoa, Mary. You gonna kill that thing?" Billy stood in the doorway of the otherwise empty gym, grinning at her.

"Yup." She panted as she danced around to face him. "Picturing my ex. His face is on this thing and I'm having fun with it."

She gave the bag two more slugs before reaching out to stop it from swinging.

"You must have been here at the crack of dawn," he said. He came into the room and turned on three more banks of lights. "Jana's seven o'clock weight lifters will be arriving any minute."

"I'm done anyway," Mary said. She held out a glove so he could unlace it for her. "I'll shower and get out of the way, but I'll be back in time to take the afternoon aerobics classes."

He handed her the gloves and gave a pat on the shoulder. Last week he'd hinted that maybe one day they ought to be partners running the gym. Said he liked Mary's work ethic and the way she took charge of her classes and made helpful suggestions to the other trainers. She'd been so surprised by the idea she couldn't come up with a response. But she'd given it some thought. It might not be such a bad idea—she loved the work, now that she was fit enough to handle it. Only problem was, a partner was expected to invest something. She still had nothing but her weekly paycheck and, although Billy didn't know it, making the rent and buying groceries was all she could manage right now.

She dumped the gloves on the shelf with the other rentals and headed for the showers. A couple of the women from Jana's class were stowing their purses in lockers and they said hello. Mary grabbed a towel. In the shower she thought again about Sandy and the tax returns. A plan came to mind. She let the stinging spray pound all the shampoo from her hair. A smile formed on her lips. Yeah. Why not?

With Clint out of the country, none of his employees would arrive at the plumbing shop early. As she recalled, Debbie was the only one who'd ever shown initiative to put in even a few extra minutes, and that only when it was time for month-end closing of the books. Mary hastily dried herself and dressed, dropping her towel in the hamper on her way out.

She ruffled her hair and slung her pack over one shoulder. Her short style dried quickly as she dashed for the bus stop. One of these days she really needed to find a car. Out of the question on the money she made now but, hey, one step at a time. She caught the Valley Metro northbound line, made the connection heading west, and got off at the corner two blocks from Holbrook Plumbing.

The convenience store three doors down made a great lookout spot. She could see the front entrance to the plumbing shop from its wide windows. She went in and browsed the cinnamon rolls and fruit turnovers in their cellophane packaging, cringing at the amount of fat and calories in them. Once, not so long ago, she would have bought a couple and wolfed them down, simply because they were a cheap breakfast. Although not the healthiest alternative, she did find a packaged whole-grain bar and a bottle of fruit juice and carried them to the counter. The clock above the clerk's head said it was ten minutes to eight.

The store had a couple of tiny tables with attached chairs at the front. A man sat with a steaming coffee cup at one, busily scratching the silvery stuff off a lottery ticket. The other table was empty and Mary took it. She positioned herself to face Clint's shop. She figured Debbie would arrive in five minutes or so, take a minute to switch on lights and turn on her computer. Another five to load and start the coffee machine in the break room.

The guys would amble in over a fifteen-minute period, always a few of them running late. Their work orders would be all lined up and by eight-fifteen most of the trucks would be rolling, on their way to various customer jobs. Debbie and the two counter guys would hang around the coffee machine, finding out how each other's weekend went.

All Mary had to do was pick a time when no one was up front and pray like hell no one had taken the initiative to fix the inoperable doorbell. If she could make it past the counter and into the records storage room, she'd be nearly home free. No one ever went in there, other than Debbie stashing away computer printouts of the profit and loss statements at the end of each month, which was still more than a week away. Mary could quietly search boxes to her heart's content, as nobody would question the door being locked.

The clock over the convenience clerk's head said seven-fifty-eight when Debbie arrived at Holbrook Plumbing and unlocked the front door. Mary smiled and drank more of her juice. A couple of cars pulled through the gate to the back lot. Fifteen minutes later, she'd seen three service trucks drive away. Clint would be pleased to know the business ticked along just fine in his absence. She forced herself not to grit her teeth.

The man with the scratcher ticket had left and a young mother with two wriggling kids took his table. The kids wouldn't sit. They kept zooming around the store and coming back for swigs from the milk cartons their mom had opened for them. Mary became impatient with the distraction. She took the final two bites of her cereal bar, crumpled the wrapper and capped her juice bottle.

Outside, the sun was bright already, the day warming rapidly. She pulled her pink ball cap low on her forehead and crossed the street, walking a leisurely pace toward Holbrook. At the front windows, she paused as if she were interested in the display of toilets. She didn't see anyone in the showroom or at the sales counter. Lingering over coffee in the back—she knew they would be.

She pushed the glass door, listening carefully. No little ding-dong sounded. She edged in quickly and dashed for the counter. In under a minute she'd ducked through the opening and speed-walked past the tile display and into the storeroom on the east side of the building. She hadn't considered what she would do if it was locked.

She'd once had keys to everything here but no longer carried them with her. She should have thought of this ahead of time, dug around in her drawers back at the apartment. Oh well, it was too late for that now. She twisted the knob, breathing a sigh when it opened. Stepping quickly inside, her hand automatically went to the light switch. She flipped it on and locked the door behind her.

Jail cells probably existed which were larger than this skinny rectangular room. Shelves rose to the ceiling along both side walls, flanking a narrow center aisle. A quick scan told Mary things were pretty much in the same places she'd left them. Thank goodness Debbie wasn't a big innovator for change in the workplace. And she doubted Clint had looked in here more than twice in his life. He left mundane tasks such as filing to the women.

Outside, she heard voices. Her breathing stopped. Two men. One walked past the storeroom, most likely on his way to the parts room farther back in the building. The other must have picked up the phone because a one-way conversation ensued. Mary gingerly set her pack on the floor and began scanning the shelves. A flood of memories as she studied her own labels, handwritten in black marker.

She ran her fingers along the rows of boxes, searching for those containing profit and loss statements and tax returns. The markings changed, Debbie's slanted cursive on boxes representing the past two years. Mary targeted four boxes—the last two years she'd prepared the documents herself and the two ensuing years since she'd been away.

Reaching for the first one, she cringed when the cardboard squealed against the metal shelf. Held her breath.

The phone conversation beyond the door continued without a pause.

She lifted the box from the high shelf and set it on the floor, thankful for her recent fitness classes. The thing must weigh twenty pounds. Her fingers skipped along the tabs of the hanging folders that filled the box. Sales receipts, rubber-banded by month, filled half the space. Why hadn't they gone to digital record storage years ago?

The voice outside the door rose slightly as the man thanked whoever he'd been speaking to and hung up the phone. The ensuing quiet was worse, Mary decided. She couldn't tell where he was or gauge whether he'd heard her. She moved quietly in the small space as she pulled another box down.

Debbie's voice caught her attention. She asked the counter clerk a question about a customer's order and they discussed it for a couple of minutes. Mary held still. If Debbie heard any sound at all from the storeroom she would know something was up.

Eventually, the bookkeeper went away and the clerk greeted a customer who'd come in the front door. Mary resumed her search, more eager than ever to find what she needed and get out. It took another ten minutes of prowling through the folders but she located four years' worth of detailed profit and loss statements, balance sheets and company tax returns. There was no time to study them here. She stuffed the papers into her pack.

If there was ever an audit of the business, this would play havoc with Clint's ability to answer questions and provide evidence. She zipped the pack closed. Heh-heh. Too damn bad.

THIRTY-ONE

SANDY REACHED INTO her freezer, spatula in hand as she tried to scrape a stubborn hunk of ice off the uppermost wire shelf.

"Sorry about this," she said to Mary. "Everyone in the nation has frost-free freezers now, but I inherited this one from my grandmother…and it really does keep food better than the other kind."

She wore stretch capris and an old T-shirt with the logo of a charity Fun Run she'd done a dozen years ago, and a headband held her hair away from her face.

"It's just a pain in the neck those couple times a year when I have to defrost the thing." The ice fell off in a chunk. She picked it up and plopped it into a plastic mixing bowl. "Almost done. Anyway, you were able to get into Holbrook Plumbing's records?"

Mary perched on a stool at the kitchen counter and watched her friend through the open door to Sandy's small utility room. "Getting in was the easy part. I thought I was home free—the place was quiet when I got ready to leave—until I opened the door. Debbie was standing right there, right by the sales counter."

Sandy's eyes went wide.

"I just kind of melted back into the storeroom and hoped neither she nor the guy she was talking to had seen the movement. I guess they didn't because they kept on talking. I thought that conversation would go on forever but, finally, they walked to the back. I guess they went into Debbie's office. I tell you, my heart was pounding so hard I'm surprised they didn't hear it."

"Mary, it sounds pretty chancy." Sandy dumped the bowl of ice clumps into the sink. She noticed the folders Mary was pulling from her backpack. "But it looks like you got some reports?"

"Yeah, the financial records from the past four years. Judging from the two years when I was there with an eye on the business, I don't think things look quite right. I'd love for you to take a look, especially in the banking sections."

"Sure." Sandy carried an old towel, saturated with water, to the kitchen sink where she wrung it out. "I shouldn't be much longer at this job."

"No rush. Since I couldn't make copies of the documents with no one the wiser, I darn sure don't intend to break back in and put them away. Keep them as long as you want."

"You sure? Will it look bad to the court that you got these papers without permission?"

"Does it look worse to the court that Clint basically embezzled from *our* company and that he lied to the attorneys about it at the time of the divorce?"

Sandy had to admit Clint's crimes were the greater of the two evils. She stepped to Mary's side and looked at the folder on the countertop.

"For instance, right here where it shows the gross sales for year before last." Mary pointed at the line item on the profit sheet. "I *know*, I mean I'm virtually certain we had about double that amount of sales."

She flipped to the balance sheet. "And this—the cash in the bank at year end. It's way off. I remember being shocked when Clint's attorney presented these figures, but I guess I was too stunned to argue. I can't believe I just sat there in that meeting and let him get away with it."

"Do you have any proof to the contrary?"

Mary's expression looked bleak. "I don't think so. I don't know. There was some paperwork that I stashed away when I moved out of the house. I left a few boxes with a friend. I'll see when I can go by there and get them. We might find something."

"Well, from what I remember of the tidbits Amber has come up with, I'd say this is suspicious. Clint moved a lot more money than this between his banks, and if he didn't earn it here, where did all that cash come from?"

"Exactly." Mary seemed mollified. "Thank you for believing me."

Sandy put an arm around her shoulders. "Why wouldn't I believe you? Clint's the guy I don't trust one bit."

"Sad to say, but I've lost all faith in that man. Let's just hope the judge is willing to take a serious look at all of it."

The phone rang as Sandy went back to her dripping freezer. "Can you get that?"

Mary picked it up and looked at the caller ID. "Hey, Gracie. How are things on the other side of the world?"

"Mary! You're at Sandy's house?" Gracie took a deep breath. "Well, I've been in acting classes for two days."

"Seriously?"

Sandy came in, drying her hands on a towel.

"I'm putting you on speaker so we can all talk," Mary said. She handed the phone over to Sandy, looking a little out of her depth with the buttons on the unfamiliar phone. In a moment Gracie's voice came into the room.

"So—acting?" Mary asked.

Gracie laughed. "Not actual classes—just whatever Pen

and Amber decided to throw at me." She went on to explain that the next day she would be tailing Kaycie Marlow, in the guise of being her escort, as she went in for surgery. "You should see my disguise. Well, actually, you can't because it's a surprise for the others tomorrow morning."

"Sounds exciting compared to what we're doing," Mary said. "Going through paperwork to figure out how my slimy ex managed to keep two sets of books without my ever figuring it out. I tell you, water torture is too kind a treatment for that man." She cleared her throat. "Never mind. Tell me what kind of place Kaycie Marlow is trusting her life to. Sorry, but having elective surgery in Shanghai sounds pretty iffy to me."

"Oh, you should see this place, Beautiful Life Haven it's called. The facility is huge. You walk into a reception area where you see nothing but gorgeous women—and some men—sitting around a large room on very modern couches. It's all done in soft colors, gray and pink with touches of sage. Once you pass through these double doors there's a whole warren of offices and rooms, doctors' offices and meeting rooms. Mirrors, nice furniture, plants."

"Is this doctor super wealthy or what?"

"It's way more than one doctor. I counted at least five, all milling around, each with a half-dozen assistants. I was worried about walking in there pretending to be an employee, but I don't think anyone will know. A bunch of the assistants are foreigners—Americans and Europeans—since that's where a lot of the clients come from. I was posing as a potential client and met with a 'beauty expert' who sat me in front of a mirror in a room with this ultra-clear lighting. When I said I was thinking of having my nose done, she tried to upsell me on eyelids, cheekbones and jawline."

"Ugh, that sounds creepy."

"I suppose. But the lady herself was so beautiful and she had such a friendly manner. You come away feeling that you want to be exactly like her."

"Gracie…"

"Me? No way would I sign up for that stuff. All I have to do is get Kaycie in there tomorrow."

"Isn't she worried about being recognized—being sort of a celebrity?"

"Well, for one thing, no one over here knows who she is. But they've thought of that. There are private entries and exits for the day patients on the opposite side of the building. A lot of them opt to stay in the adjoining spa facility where they have private rooms and nursing care in addition to pampering beyond belief. They assure the clients no one will see them until every bandage and bruise is gone."

Mary and Sandy exchanged a long look.

THIRTY-TWO

PEN AND KAYCIE stood in the lobby of the Grand Plaza Peace Hotel. Dawn hadn't yet penetrated to street level in this part of the city where skyscrapers rose in solid ranks. The early hour must be part of the reason for Kaycie's jitters, Pen thought. The younger woman wouldn't let go of Pen's arm.

"Are you certain you want to go through with this?" Pen asked, not for the first time.

"Oh, yeah, I *do*. It's just kind of… Well, it's also that I didn't sleep much. With Clint gone, it's amazing all the noises I heard in the night." Kaycie's gaze kept flitting toward the windows at the hotel entrance, her fingers fiddling with the handle of the small suitcase by her side. "I mean, it's weird being in a foreign country by yourself."

Pen knew she'd better steer Kaycie's thoughts in another direction. "So, your husband got away on his fishing trip all right?"

"Yeah, he was so excited. Deep sea fishing is something you don't get much of where we live." She laughed nervously. "And he needed a break from work. I think dealing with the language barrier and such different customs and food is starting to wear on him too. It was such a nice thing for Mr. Tong to introduce him to his friend from the Philippines, the man with the fishing charter business. Supposedly, the fishing spots are great there, although I personally didn't see why he had to go all that way. There's ocean all around the coast of China too."

Pen nodded absently, only half listening to Kaycie's babble. "Oh, here is your car, dear."

She pointed toward a long gray car that had pulled under the hotel's portico. Gracie stepped out of the limo, and Pen almost didn't recognize her. With her long dark hair pulled sleekly back into a bun, Gracie's high forehead and elegant cheekbones were accentuated. She wore more makeup than usual and had added designer eyeglasses with frames that accentuated her deep brown eyes. She wore the sage-green suit they'd found in a department store yesterday, and she carried a fabric-covered portfolio under one arm.

She walked up the two steps to the hotel's grand entry doors and allowed the doorman to hold one open for her. When they stepped toward her, Gracie greeted Pen like an acquaintance she hadn't seen in a long time—cordial but not chummy.

"And you must be Mrs. Holbrook?" She held out a hand toward Kaycie. "Or do you prefer Ms. Marlow?"

"Holbrook," Kaycie said. "Marlow is just a professional name now."

"I looked over your registration records on the way here, so I think we're all set." Pen had to admit, Gracie had the role down pat. She could earn a place in the hospitality industry quite easily.

Pen turned to Kaycie. "Well, my dear, you don't need me anymore—you're in good hands now. You have my number… We'll speak in a few days, once you're feeling up to it."

Kaycie hugged Pen as if she'd known the older woman all her life.

Gracie touched Kaycie's shoulder, gently guiding her

toward the door and Pen watched as they got into the limo and it drove away. Ignoring the curious glances of the bellmen, she hitched her purse strap up to her shoulder and walked out, heading toward the Hyatt where Amber would be waking and ready to have breakfast together.

GRACIE DIRECTED THE driver to the back of the Beautiful Life Haven building, watching for door number three, the one Kaycie had been assigned. From the outside, she realized how much like a warehouse the back appeared—a place to receive and ship, only this time people were the commodity and vanity was the business's mission. She shook off the feeling and made sure her smile was in place when the driver pulled up at the assigned door.

She ushered Kaycie out of the car, tucked her portfolio under her arm and rang the bell beside the green door. Within seconds, a female Chinese orderly opened it and greeted them in flawless English, which Gracie had noticed yesterday seemed to follow a set script. The woman probably didn't know more than a dozen phrases.

"Good morning. Please enter. Your doctor will be with you directly." She showed them to a plush sofa grouping where American and British magazines were fanned out neatly on a side table.

"I'll accompany you to the changing room but once you enter the surgical section of the facility," Gracie told Kaycie, "I'll have to stay behind. While you're in surgery I will handle the process of checking you into your private room. Your suitcase and belongings will be waiting for you at that end of the building."

Kaycie smiled. So trusting. So clueless that Gracie's real mission was to go through all her possessions to find usable information about her husband. Amber had showed her how to transmit the information on Kaycie's smart phone. Very soon they would know all her contacts and which, if any, of Clint's banks and brokerage firms his wife had access to. It might not exactly be playing fair to use her this way, but the Ladies had no doubt Clint wasn't hesitating to use his own wife. He certainly hadn't felt a qualm about dumping on his previous one.

A man in green scrubs and a white lab coat came into the small vestibule where they sat. Gracie didn't recall meeting this doctor yesterday but she avoided studying him. He would certainly be acutely aware of faces and might recognize her.

"Mrs. Holbrook," he said, "it is good to see you again."

Obviously, Kaycie had met this one. She stood and smiled. "Doctor Zhuge."

"Are we ready for your procedure?"

He went through a couple of standard medical questions, verifying she'd had nothing to eat or drink this morning and that she'd taken the pre-op advice on the paper she'd been given last week. She answered appropriately and he led the way down a corridor. Gracie followed, pulling Kaycie's travel bag, working to memorize the series of turns and the rooms they passed. To pull off the deception she would need to navigate her way back and find the room they'd assigned Kaycie to occupy for the next week.

A nurse greeted them in a room painted nearly the same shade of pale green as Gracie's suit. Neither she nor the doctor questioned Gracie's presence. The room contained a row of lockers, about half of which had keys on springy wrist bands inserted in the locks. A cotton gown and cloth slippers waited on the room's one chair.

"Place your things in a locker if you wish. I will meet you at the door," the nurse said. Again, Gracie had the feeling the woman spoke little English other than what she needed for her duties here.

"I can take your stuff to your room, if you'd rather not leave it here," Gracie said once they were alone again.

Kaycie stepped out of her shoes and had begun to peel off her lightweight sundress. Gracie turned her back until she felt a tap on her shoulder.

"I'm done. The gown isn't exactly fashion, but it's quick to put on."

Gracie unzipped the lid of Kaycie's wheeled bag and she dropped her clothing inside. She hoped she had memorized the corridors well enough, but supposed it wouldn't be unusual for an escort to need directions from one of the long-term employees. She could bluff her way through. Kaycie pulled open the dressing room door and Gracie spotted the nurse outside, her hands clasped primly at her waist. The smell of antiseptic cleaning products came strongly from the open door of a room across the hall, the room where Kaycie would be prepped for her procedure.

"Don't forget," Gracie told Kaycie, "I will be at the exit when you come out and I'll see you safely to your room. Meanwhile, I'll put your things there for you."

As the nurse reached toward Kaycie, suddenly a buzzer sounded from a small box on the wall. A voice came through, female, spouting a string of rapid Mandarin. She sounded agitated but everything in this language seemed that way to Gracie. The nurse replied and a short exchange took place. Kaycie stepped a little closer to Gracie.

"Is something wrong?" Gracie asked the nurse, who didn't seem to comprehend.

More quick conversation through the box.

Doctor Zhuge emerged from another room, his lab coat missing now, his hands in gloves. The flustered nurse said something to him. A flicker of impatience crossed his face but quickly turned bland as he faced the Americans.

"It seems there is an unusual circumstance. Mrs. Holbrook has a visitor who insists on being allowed to speak with her before her surgery."

Kaycie's brows pulled together. "I don't know anyone—"

"His name is Derek Woo. He says it's extremely urgent."

"Clint's attorney. I can't—" Kaycie indicated her flimsy gown.

"Is there a robe she can put on?" Gracie asked. "And a place she can speak with this Mr. Woo?"

Gracie tried frantically to remember if she'd ever met the lawyer. Would he recognize her? She decided her disguise would have to be good enough to fool him. She wasn't letting Kaycie out of her sight until she knew what was happening.

The doctor spoke quickly to his nurse and a robe appeared for Kaycie. Gracie kept a hand on the suitcase which now contained all Kaycie's clothes, her purse and phone—other things that weren't leaving her side right now. When an orderly appeared, the two women followed him through the labyrinth of corridors until they came to a small reception room. Gracie's sense told her it was somewhere near the front of the building but, truthfully, she was beginning to feel very disoriented in the vast space.

An Asian man in a dark suit greeted them with a solemn expression. Gracie knew Woo was an American but he could certainly blend seamlessly into the culture here, she thought, watching him interact briefly and send the intern away.

"Who's this?" he asked Kaycie, nodding toward Gracie.

"My friend from the hotel arranged for her to accompany me today, to help with my accommodations and everything.

What's going on, Derek? What's so urgent? Didn't Clint tell you I had…um…a private matter to deal with this week?"

Woo bowed slightly at the waist, again giving Gracie the impression he fit right into Chinese society.

"I'm afraid it's not good news," he said, reaching to take Kaycie's hand. "There's been an accident. A storm came up at sea and Clint was tossed overboard off the fishing vessel. I'm afraid he's dead."

THIRTY-THREE

"KAYCIE'S FACE WENT white as a sheet. I thought she was going to faint. I mean, she hadn't eaten anything and, well, we were both stunned," Gracie told Pen and Amber when she arrived at the Hyatt. "She just kept saying 'how could this have happened?' while I got her dressed and out of the clinic. The lawyer took over and all I could think to do was grab a taxi and come back here."

"You did the right thing," Pen said, "although I wish we knew what she's doing right now."

"I'm surprised she hasn't called you," Amber piped up, looking at Pen. "I mean, she thinks you're her best friend here in China."

"I'll call her, tell her I heard the news. I shall simply dodge the question of exactly how I learned it."

Pen picked up her phone and scrolled through the list to find Kaycie's number. The others sat perfectly quiet while she listened to it ring. As she became certain it would go to voice mail, a tentative voice answered.

"Kaycie, dear, I heard about your husband. How are you?"

"Pen. I'm so glad it's you." Her voice was subdued, shaky. "I don't know… I'm just in shock. I can't believe it."

"What are they telling you?"

"Derek is here. He got word from Rudy Tong, who heard it from his friend with the boat. They said a terrible storm blew up very quickly and they were caught in very rough seas. Clint was knocked overboard and they searched all night…" She dissolved into tears, apologized.

Pen heard scuffing sounds, a tissue rubbing against the phone, perhaps.

"He says I should go back to Arizona and start making arrangements. But my Honey Bear… I can't even think what to do about a funeral."

"It must be so very hard for you," Pen said, as gently as she could. No matter what a rat Clint Holbrook had been, Kaycie was in dire pain right now.

"Derek is going to Manila this morning to see what he can find out, and I suppose there's nothing I can do here in China." Her voice trailed away in distraction.

Pen could hear a male voice nearby.

"Yes, Derek says he'll tend to the legalities for me over there. He's promised me he'll bring Clint home. I'll have to deal with a funeral and insurance and all that. I just don't know how I…"

Pen thought rapidly. It wouldn't seem logical for her to offer to fly home with Kaycie. They weren't that close, and she'd already told her new friend she was here for another two weeks. Although she supposed…

"Well, Derek's ready to take me to the airport," Kaycie said. "Bless him, he made emergency travel arrangements for me and he's helped pack all our bags. I couldn't even think what to wear, but he chose something and set it out. I guess I'm ready to walk out the door. I just don't know if I can—"

She broke down completely and a man's voice came on the phone.

"Thank you for calling. Mrs. Holbrook very much appreciates your concern. Perhaps she can call you back later—when she's arrived at home in the States."

Pen felt her throat tightening as she choked out a good-bye. Poor Kaycie. It wasn't supposed to go this way. She plopped onto the small sofa in her suite and turned to Amber and Gracie who both wore solemn expressions.

"Well, I never in a million years would have thought our trip would end like this," Gracie said. She paced from one end of the room to the other. "We were supposed to catch Clint with a fistful of cash and guilt him into making Mary's financial situation right."

Mary. None of them had thought about breaking the news to her.

"Should we wait until we get back to Phoenix?" Gracie asked. "I mean, it would be better if she has someone with her."

"True, but what if she hears of it first? Kaycie is something of a local celebrity. The story could easily get out, especially since she's already on her way back."

"I'll call Sandy," Pen said. "She's closest to Mary of all of us. She can go and tell her in person." She picked up her phone.

"Meanwhile," Amber said, once the call was finished, "let's eat." She looked around the room. "What? We have to eat, don't we?"

Gracie glanced at her watch. "It is close to lunch time." A long sigh. "Since there's no reason for us to stay in China much longer, we'd better make the best of it."

The hotel concierge told them of an excellent restaurant nearby and they headed toward it. Pen couldn't help but feel the atmosphere was a little too celebratory, given the day's events, but the others were right. They needed to eat and it might as well be the food they'd all come to enjoy here.

Golden Dragon turned out to be a small storefront place with lots of red trim and paper lanterns hanging inside the front windows. Inside, the dining room was much larger than they would have guessed and they were shown to a small table near the back. The specialty, it turned out, was dumplings. Within minutes, trays of the tiny bundles were being delivered. Amber was put in charge of understanding and explaining what each of the little packets contained. Between rounds of dumplings, bowls of rice and vegetables showed up on the table.

A new batch of dumplings had arrived when the financial aspect of their current job hit Pen. "With Clint gone, there's no chance a judge will review Mary's divorce settlement and make any changes."

Gracie paused with chopsticks midway to her mouth.

"Don't you see? Our entire goal has been to gather evidence to prove Clint cheated Mary in their divorce and he owed her a bigger share. He's dead now. The whole question will become entangled in his estate. Unless he got a sudden burst of good-heartedness that none of us know about, it's fairly certain he didn't include Mary in his will. All the money they earned together, the money he's been squirreling away in various banks—it's going to someone else."

"Most likely Kaycie."

Pen nodded. "If he'd already been prowling around other women on the side, who knows—but it most certainly won't be Mary."

"Oh, god," said Gracie. "Mary's going to know this, the minute she gets the news. She'll be devastated. What can we do?"

Amber piped up. "Well, it's simple enough. We have to steal the money."

THIRTY-FOUR

TWO SNAGS INTERRUPTED their seemingly brilliant plan, the first coming when Amber tried to sign into Clint's accounts she had discovered earlier.

"Someone's tampered with them," she told the others quietly when she tried to log on later that afternoon in their hotel. She signaled Pen to turn the radio up, their customary precaution against possible listening devices in the rooms. "Either that, or the servers here in China aren't allowed to go to these other servers."

"Could it be possible Clint discovered you were spying and changed his passwords? It might have happened even before we left the States," Gracie said.

"Yeah, I thought of that. It's most likely the case. Even if he didn't discover my little visit to his bank, he might have been in the habit of changing his passwords regularly. Just my luck, he did it at a crucial time for our purposes."

"So, don't you just hack again? You figured out a way before."

"I tried. That's what I'm saying. My normal channels aren't coming up for me here. I need to get back home."

"Yes, well, that's proving to be a problem, too," Pen said from across the room. "I've been on the phone with the airline and all flights are full for another day. I could book us as far as Tokyo but then we would sit there eighteen hours until another U.S. flight is available. I might get one seat, for Amber, and the rest of us could come along later?"

"I don't like us splitting up," Gracie said. "We know Sandy is taking care of Mary. I don't know that an extra twenty-four hours will gain us anything."

Amber seemed skeptical but Pen agreed. She went back to the phone. Fifteen minutes later she said, "I have us on the six-fifty-three flight tomorrow evening."

She didn't mention the horrific upcharges for changing their reservation on such short notice. That knowledge would do nothing to put the others at ease. At least they would soon be heading home and could pursue their goal.

"Since we're stuck here another whole day," Gracie said, "how about we get out and do a little more sightseeing? It's a fantastic place and we've hardly seen any of it, being so wrapped up with Kaycie and Clint."

Amber rolled her eyes and kept tapping away at her tablet, but Pen agreed. Eventually, they convinced Amber to come along to a temple with a rare white-jade Buddha on display, grab some dinner and take a nighttime stroll along the Bund, an area made famous for its lighted reflections of the buildings across the Huangpu River.

Their restaurant that night was called Red. Pen found it a little disorienting that every single thing in the room was red—walls, carpet, light fixtures, tables and chairs. A black vase of red flowers on their table and the waiters' dark hair above their red uniforms provided the only things she could focus on. The chef had come from Beijing, bringing that city's specialties, and the food was reputed to be the best in the city, so she put aside her qualms about the overdone décor.

"Okay," said Amber, "I get it that red is the theme here,

but *why*? I thought the Chinese were backing away from flaunting their communist status."

"The manager told me red is the color signifying luck to the Chinese."

"Well, this must be the luckiest place in the city," Gracie said with a wry grin.

Their food arrived and, they were relieved to see, was not red. The Peking Duck and sweet bean sauce were delicious. With groans of pleasure coming from Gracie, Pen felt justified in choosing the place. Amber wasn't quite in the spirit; she toyed with the vegetables and thin pancake, apparently still in a sulk over the fact she couldn't get her computer hack to work.

Gracie tried to lighten the mood. "I really enjoyed seeing that jade Buddha. Seemed a little funny that they kept the smaller one tucked away in a special room with dim lighting and no cameras allowed, but the bigger statue—that reclining Buddha—it was every bit as elegant and its display case seemed more an afterthought of the gift shop."

"The white jade on both was truly remarkable," Pen said. "I've seen special traveling displays of some beautiful jade in my time, but those were fantastic."

"And his jewelry—rubies and emeralds and sapphires mounted into his carved bracelets and necklaces—Amber, are you actually here with us?" Gracie gave an impatient little tap at Amber's wrist.

"Yeah—no, it was great. Sorry, my mind is writing computer code in my head."

"Come on, let's skip dessert and take a walk," Gracie suggested.

A steady drizzle greeted them as they stepped outdoors, making Pen thankful they'd each invested in an umbrella the first day of their visit. Traffic whooshed through the busy street and people trudged along with their heads down, heading home to their concrete block apartments after a long day.

Three streets over, the three women passed through a tunnel, a method the efficient Chinese used to do away with the need for many stoplights and pedestrian crossings. It was dimly lit and damp but within a couple of minutes they were climbing the stairs on the opposite side, emerging onto the wide promenade known as the Bund. Across the river stood Shanghai's tribute to innovative architecture—buildings shaped like spaceships, a sphere, walls that appeared wavelike.

"Look at that one," Gracie said, pointing. "It's so tall it's disappearing into the clouds. And the one with the round globes built into it—it looks like something out of the Jetsons cartoon."

"It's called the Oriental Pearl," Pen said. "Rather striking, for a radio and TV tower, isn't it?"

Amber perked up, pulling out her phone and shooting pictures of the brilliantly lit structures. Pen, as was her habit nearly all the time, watched the people come and go. She often found inspiration for characters in her novels from some little action or exchange she witnessed between strangers.

She'd no sooner had the thought than she noticed a little girl tugging at her father's sleeve. He leaned forward to listen to what she had to say. Then the man bent down and in one quick move, picked up his daughter and pulled her slacks down. He held her over a large trash bin and the girl proceeded to urinate into the open container. When she finished, he pulled her garments back in place and set her feet on the ground again and the two strolled away, hand in hand. Pen blinked—had she actually witnessed what she thought she did? Oh, yes, she thought. This is a vignette for a book.

She told the others about it as they walked back to their hotel. Amber laughed out loud. Gracie commented on the number of times she had scrambled to find public restrooms when her kids were younger. "Sometimes, you do whatever works," she said.

They agreed to sleep late in the morning, have a leisurely breakfast and check out by noon. It allowed an hour to get to the airport, the requisite two-hour lead time for an international flight, and a little breathing space.

"I want to make one final recon of Clint's office at Tong Chen Enterprises," Amber said.

Pen halted in the middle of the crowded sidewalk.

"I've gotten in there once," Amber argued. She took Pen's elbow and resumed walking. "I can do it again. Clint may have left something behind that could be very beneficial to us. Who knows? A notebook with all his passwords in it, a copy of his will?"

"That won't happen," Gracie said, giving her a stern look.

"Okay, I know. But there might be something. It wouldn't take me but a few minutes to check. I need to do this."

The hotel doorman stood aside for them and Pen led the way in. Neither of the women believed Amber would find anything but she was adamant about trying.

THIRTY-FIVE

SANDY SAT AT her desk, twirling a pen between her fingers, unable to concentrate on the stack of loan applications in front of her. Not something a banker should skim over in haste, she reminded herself. Pen, Gracie and Amber would be leaving Shanghai in a few hours—if they hadn't already. She never could keep track of time across the international dateline. Her personal phone rang, startling her.

"Sandy Werner?" said a male voice.

"Speaking."

"This is Billy DeWitt at the gym. You're Mary Holbrook's friend, aren't you?"

"Yes. Is everything okay?" She hadn't spoken with Mary since the day before yesterday, when she went over to deliver the news about Clint's death.

"Well, she hasn't been to work in two days," Billy said, "and hasn't called in either. It's not like her. I tried her cell phone and didn't get an answer."

Sandy looked at the stack of applications and pondered what to do.

"Sorry," Billy said. "I wouldn't be calling you except Mary listed you as her contact person. I just thought you should know."

"Yes, thank you. It's fine. I'll go check on her."

Sandy clicked off the call and glanced at the time. Ten

a.m. was a little early to leave for lunch, but Billy's tone worried her. Mary had been understandably shocked to hear of Clint's dying, but she'd handled it well. They'd been divorced a couple of years, after all. She certainly didn't seem as if she would take to her bed over the news.

Still, Sandy knew she needed to find out. If her workday slipped away she would take the paperwork home and work on it tonight. She went out to her car and steered toward the 101. As she parked in one of the many empty slots, she noticed Mary's apartment building seemed even more drab for some reason. Had she never noticed it was such a crappy place?

She closed her eyes, gripped the wheel and opened them again. Okay, so the landscaping was nothing but gravel with a couple of lanky palm trees, which offered no shade at all, and the building could use a coat of paint. Otherwise, it wasn't in a bad neighborhood and most of the tenants appeared to keep their clutter to a minimum. Most likely her perception was all in her mood. None of the group seemed very perky since events with Clint had gone so wrong. She called Mary's number, thinking to give a little warning before just appearing at the door, but if her friend was screening calls it wasn't only Billy she was avoiding.

Sandy got out of her car, hoping Mary hadn't fallen into another depression. It had been sad and frightening to see how Mary declined after the divorce. Please let her be okay, she thought as she took the sidewalk toward the back of the building.

She listened at the cheap hollow-core door for a moment before knocking. A television talk show's raucous laughter came from inside. Sandy knocked. The TV sound diminished a bit and she swore she saw movement at the window blinds.

"Mary, it's me. Can I come in?"

A full minute passed.

"Mary? Come on. I really need to talk."

She sensed movement behind the door and finally it opened. Mary wore a shapeless caftan that must have come from her heavier days. It hung from her shoulders now.

"Hey."

"Hey. You okay? Billy's worried that you haven't been at work."

"Come on in. I know I should have called him. My phone ran out of minutes and I haven't felt like dressing up enough to go out and refill it."

"But you're doing okay in general? Not sick or anything? If it's because of the news about Clint, I'm here if you want to talk about it."

Mary shrugged. "Nah, not really."

But Sandy noticed three empty soda cans and a near-empty bag of tortilla chips on the end table near the chair Mary had obviously occupied. Junk food and sloppy clothing went completely against Mary's new lifestyle, so all was not right.

"I took the rest of the morning off, thought maybe we could grab some lunch. I've been in the mood for one of Brannigan's turkey club sandwiches. Sound good to you?"

Mary stared down at a soda stain on her caftan. "I don't know…"

Sandy stepped closer and gripped both of Mary's shoulders. "Talk to me. Or don't. But I can tell this thing is really eating at you. You don't, in some way, feel guilty about Clint, do you? Nobody chased him over to the Far East and nobody put him on a boat in a stormy sea—well, except himself. He made those choices."

"It just keeps coming back at me, when I said water torture would be too good for him. And now this—"

Sandy almost laughed. "Mary, Clint didn't drown because you said the words 'water torture.' That's crazy."

Mary looked up at her, finally. Her eyes brimmed but the smile was back. "Well, when you put it that way. I know. You're right. I'm just being..."

"You're being hard on yourself, trying to take the blame for something that was purely an accident."

"What if it wasn't?"

"Wasn't an accident?" Sandy struggled to wrap her thoughts around the idea. "He goes off fishing with some charter boat operator, there's a storm and he's swept overboard...how...what are you thinking?"

"Oh, I don't know. It's silly. From the minute Clint said he would be working in China I thought how weird that was—for him. He has no experience in international business. And the talk about Chinese mobsters and rackets and stuff like that..." She exhaled sharply. "You know what—I've had too much time and too much sugary junk. To start thinking someone over there might have wanted to be rid of Clint? Clint Holbrook from Arizona? Silly."

Sandy was happy to see the smile return to Mary's face. "Yes. Silly."

She glanced around the room. "I'm going to sit here while you shower and dress, and then you and I are going out to lunch. First, use my phone to call Billy and reassure him, okay?"

Mary took the phone and made the call. Sandy heard her tell the boss she would be in later and would teach her afternoon classes. She breathed a sigh of relief. Looked as if she would get to those loan applications today, after all.

Mary was midway through a salad—greens with chicken,

cranberries and a sweet-sour dressing—when her expression turned glum again. They had been discussing the other Heist Ladies' plan to come home tonight and how their mission had taken a turn.

"Mary? You okay?"

Mary poked at her salad with the fork, shuffling bits of food around on the plate. "It just hit me—what you said. I'll never get my share of all that money from Clint now, will I?"

Sandy pondered the question for a moment. "I don't know. I would guess it's pretty certain a divorce court judge won't look at the case. But when I talked to Pen she hinted that they may have some other avenue to pursue. I wouldn't write it off yet."

"Life is just so freaking unfair, you know. I should have known better than to get my hopes up. Every time I do—I mean, like, every time in my whole life I've counted on something—it falls through and things only get worse."

Sandy watched her friend slump against the banquette seat.

"Do you honestly believe that?" She said it quietly but she could tell Mary heard her. "Every single time?"

Mary raised one shoulder in a half-shrug.

"Yeah, Clint dumped on you. It happens. The right and fair and wonderful thing doesn't always happen. But it damn sure gets worse if you believe it will."

She had Mary's attention now. A scowl wrinkled the space between her eyebrows.

"You may never get that money, but will it be the end of things? Look how far you've come in the last few weeks. Even at that low point when you were homeless you still had a lot of gumption. You got healthy and fit. You have a job you love. You made an *amazing* transformation. Now there's a setback and you're ready to go back to square one, to let a dead guy ruin the rest of your *life*? Get with it—pick yourself up and start over again."

Mary actually smiled. "Okay, now you're starting to sound like a cheesy musical number."

"Sorry. I guess I revert to clichés when I'm riled."

In her agitated state she'd knocked a spoon to the floor. She bent down to retrieve it. When she looked up, Mary's face was calm.

"Thanks, Sandy," she said. "Thanks for believing in me."

THIRTY-SIX

"JUST REMEMBER, you must—absolutely *must*—be back before we leave for the airport," Pen said.

Amber nodded impatiently.

"Take your ticket and passport with you. I can manage your bag, but we can't take the chance you won't be able to check yourself in if we become separated. We'll leave the hotel at noon. If you can't be back here by then, go directly to the airport."

Amber gave an irked smile. "Yes, Mom."

Pen ignored the sarcasm. They were all tired and the circumstances were wearing them down. Amber mumbled a small "Sorry" and went back to her own room. She scooped clothing from the closet and dresser drawers and smashed it into her suitcase. She tossed in her bag of toiletries, made certain her documents and iPad were in her tote bag, and wheeled the large suitcase across the hall to Pen's room.

"Just in case," she said before turning away. She called over her shoulder, "I *will* be back in time."

Out on the street she took a deep breath. For all her bluster, this was a huge city and she felt barely confident about smoothly negotiating her way around with public transportation and her limited knowledge of the language. She watched for the correct bus, the one that would get her to Tong Chen Enterprises with only a couple of stops along the way. She could have easily walked the distance but as Pen had reminded her, time was of the essence and it was way too scary to think of missing the flight and having to straighten out the resulting mess.

Settled into a seat, she calmed down. Yeah, maybe she should have gotten an earlier start, but it was only ten-thirty. Plenty of time. The bus roared into the left lane. Uh-oh, this didn't seem right. She looked at the lighted printing above the front window but the writing was all in Chinese characters. Had she accidentally boarded an express bus? Shit.

She twisted in her seat, watching the neighborhood disappear as the bus entered the ring road. Oh god. She forced her pounding heart to slow down then reached for her phone. Her finger scrolled through the contacts before she paused to think about the situation. *What was I thinking?* Telling Pen she was lost—she'd never hear the end of it. She'd best figure this out on her own.

Maybe it wouldn't be all that bad. She would get off the bus the very next time it stopped and figure it out from there. Surely, someone could tell her how to get back. She told herself not to worry about it.

I'm smart and competent and I've done a fair amount of travel. I can do this.

The bus stayed on the ring road nearly twenty minutes, every one of them taking Amber farther from her destination and closer to missing her flight, every mile diminishing her bravado. Finally, it pulled to the curb outside a train station. She got off and looked around for any signage she could read. The few signs in Roman lettering didn't help much. The destinations all contained the same set of letters—Qingsun, Chondau, Guisang. Even if she could remember the name of the neighborhood she needed to reach, the train was probably not the way to get there.

She had paused near a vendor, a man cooking a massive wok full of noodles on a portable cart. An impatient Chinese man who looked close to a hundred pushed her aside to get to the food. She stepped aside and rummaged in her deep tote bag for the address of Tong Chen Enterprises. Where had that scrap of paper gone? She remembered tucking it into the coin pocket of her wallet. Operating by feel she undid the clasp and touched the little slip.

Luckily, the first time she went there she'd asked the hotel concierge to copy the English version of the name into Chinese characters. When the pushy old man stepped away with his cup of noodle soup, Amber held up the address to the vendor.

"Can you tell me how to get to this place?" she asked, remembering belatedly to repeat the question in Mandarin.

The vendor squinted at the paper, made a dismissive gesture and turned away. Amber felt a surge of panic. The blare of a car horn caught her attention. Behind her, across a wide median and divider, idled a line of taxis. It was a risk-your-life move as she dashed between cars to cross over to them. The driver of the first car she came to gave her a tired look.

She held out the slip of paper with the address. He read it and nodded.

Hĕn yuan. Very far away. Shit—how far?

She was running low on cash. *Duōshao qián?*

He named a figure, which she barely understood. What option did she have? She nodded and got into the back seat. He clicked the button on the taxi meter and pulled into the stream of traffic. As the money ticked away, she vowed she would never, ever admit to Pen how harrowing this little adventure had become.

She decided to visualize Clint's office, the layout and

the types of paperwork she'd seen, envisioning herself arriving there and finding something of value to their mission. There were huge rolls of blueprints on a big table, a diagram of the jobsite on one wall. When Clint was there he'd worked on a computer. Had he left it at the office or was it a personal one he carried everywhere? She had no way to know so she kept her thoughts positive. All this effort had to be worth something. Surely, Clint didn't pack up everything in the office every night and take it to his hotel. There must be important documents somewhere in that office.

It was eleven-thirty when the taxi deposited her in front of Tong Chen Enterprises. She approached the front door with all the confidence she could muster.

"Miss?" a voice said in English. A uniformed guard stood at a small podium inside the door. "Your employee badge?"

Badge? She'd never had a badge when she came the first time. Of course, she'd arrived with the morning rush of employees and most likely had scooted on past the checkpoint without realizing she was expected to stop.

"My badge." She patted her chest where a lanyard might hang, if she'd had one. "Oh, no! I must have left it at my desk when I stepped out for lunch. It's the temporary offices of Redwing Holdings… Clint Holbrook is my boss. Do you want to come up with me? It's in my desk drawer."

Amber gave the whole spiel as quickly as possible with a little California-girl spin and a series of hand gestures indicating *upstairs*. The guard's patient smile stayed in place but she could tell he didn't get half of what she said.

"Please go ahead," he said.

Whew. Thank goodness—aside from the fact she'd lost another two minutes. She rode the elevator with three men in business suits, one of whom must have just finished a large serving of garlic.

Clint's office down the hall on the tenth floor was dark. She wondered what would happen with the construction project he'd begun. Most likely, the work would continue under the supervision of the second-lowest bidder. She tried the doorknob but of course it was locked. However, it was a cheap lockset and she was willing to give breaking and entering a try.

With a scan of the corridor in each direction she pulled a plastic card from her wallet. Thinner than a credit card, it would, she hoped, have the flexibility to be maneuvered between the door and the jamb…and, *yes*. It worked.

She slipped inside, locked the door behind her and left the lights off in case someone who knew the situation came along and noticed. The large window in Clint's private office provided almost enough light—enough for her to see the project diagram on the wall and the heavy roll of blueprints on the table. Aside from that, no computer. It looked as if he'd had the good sense to take it back to his hotel each night, although Amber snickered a little, remembering the totally inadequate security on the machine.

She opened the top desk drawer, finding only blank stationery and a handful of ballpoint pens imprinted with the company name. *Who actually uses letterhead anymore*, she wondered as she shuffled through the pages. Email and attachments were ubiquitous these days. The next drawer excited her a bit as she spotted a leather portfolio of the sort a man would use to carry important documents. Sadly, however, there was nothing inside but a fresh yellow legal pad. She tossed it back into the drawer.

She looked at the time. 12:15. She'd already missed her airport ride with Pen and Gracie. This recon of the offices had certainly been a wasted trip. It appeared every trace of Clint Holbrook had been removed.

Amber set her bag on Clint's desk and pawed through it. Clearly, she would accomplish nothing further here, so her mission now was to get herself to the airport so she could leave the country. The cab ride would cost at least three-hundred-fifty yuan but her wallet was empty of cash and the other compartments in the bag yielded no money either. She would have to find an ATM somewhere. The plane would begin boarding in an hour.

THIRTY-SEVEN

GRACIE PACED THE international departure lounge, scanning the corridors which teemed with people, watching for the one head of curly hair among the thousands with smooth dark hair. She glanced toward Pen who sat with their carryon bags. Boarding had already been called for first class and business class passengers, but they had agreed—they would wait until the moment before the doors closed if Amber had not yet arrived.

There had been a series of texts: Leaving Clint's office.

The next one: Got cash. Found a cab.

The next one came what felt like an interminable time later: At airport. Check-in line long!

So, Amber was here somewhere. It didn't necessarily mean she would make the flight. Gracie watched the steady queue of coach passengers thread their way past the gate agent. The crowd was thinning at an alarming rate. She imagined them aboard the aircraft, inching their way toward their seats, stowing their too-many items in too-few bins, flight attendants edging along the crowded aisles to assist. For the first time in her life, Gracie willed the process to take longer.

At last she spotted Amber's familiar bouncy gait. Her curly hair, pulled into a fluffy knot at the top of her head, made a perfect beacon. Gracie sent a thumbs-up toward Pen before dashing out into the crowd.

The last of the passengers had disappeared into the long Jetway.

She ran to Amber, grabbed her hand and gave a tug, wanting to give the same lecture she used on her kids to hurry up. No purpose to that—Amber was already nearly in tears.

"Come on, sweetie. We'll make it."

Pen was speaking to the agent at the boarding pass scanner when the other two dashed into the glassed-in area.

"Ah, yes," they heard her say, "here they are now."

"The aircraft door closes in one minute," said the agent. "Do not dally in the Jetway."

As if they needed to be told. They rushed in, thankful to see the first-class cabin had settled early and they were easily able to take their seats as the safety briefing video began. Pen's seat was next to Amber's, with Gracie across the aisle. The way the semi-private pods were arranged, conversation wasn't easy. When the little video screens shut down and she felt the plane lift off, Pen leaned forward to see around the divider.

"So—what happened?"

Amber paused, deliberating how much to say. Catching the wrong bus, breaking into Clint's office, the mad scramble to the airport and almost missing the flight. Most likely Pen only wanted to know about the mission to find important papers.

"The blueprints and building plans were there, but nothing personal at all. Not even a coffee cup. Nothing that would say 'Clint Holbrook worked here'. Don't you think that's weird?"

Pen admitted it was. "The question is, who cleared it? Clint was only leaving for a few days to go fishing, so why would he take away absolutely everything?"

"I wondered if Rudy Tong or someone in his company

did it. I don't know…that building, that company…the whole place has a very sterile feeling. But to send somebody in and clear a guy's office within a day after he dies—that's cold."

Pen nodded. She remembered the remark about Chinese mobsters and whether Clint had gotten himself—purposely or inadvertently—in with them. And what if the office had actually been cleared before Clint's death? Did someone at Tong Chen Enterprises know their American contractor wouldn't be coming back?

A flight attendant paused beside Pen's seat. "Mrs. Fitzpatrick, may I bring you something to drink?"

Pen requested tea, something which always calmed her nerves. Something she needed after the tense morning.

Beside her, Amber sat upright. "What if Clint had left a bunch of his private stuff there, like maybe even his computer? And what if the Chinese took it all away. They've probably already hacked it."

Pen nodded.

"So, it means they'll know and have access to his money. If we don't find it and steal Mary's share away, we don't even have to worry what the American court would do. The money's going to be gone. My god, I'll bet it was that slimy lawyer of his. I'll bet he's working with those guys at Tong Chen."

That got Pen's attention. "You're saying…this whole thing could have been planned far in advance? Give an American contractor the job, bring him over, gain access to his money, kill him?"

"I know. It does sound pretty far-fetched."

It did, and yet it didn't.

Amber twitched in her seat. "But I won't have secure internet access to find out what's going on for another fifteen hours."

THIRTY-EIGHT

KAYCIE STARED INTO her closet, her mind numb. Black was not her color—it simply wasn't good for anything other than a chic cocktail dress, preferably off the shoulder and over-ridden by a diamond necklace of stunning design. She had nothing to wear to the funeral. She didn't even *want* to own anything appropriate for a funeral. She was twenty-six years old, for heaven's sake, and the idea of widowhood had never once crossed her radar.

She walked out of the closet and picked up her purse from the bed. But the idea of going shopping was too daunt-ing and she tossed the purse back. Unpacking had been overwhelming, too. The suitcases from the China trip sat in the corner of the bedroom where the Vandergrift door-man had left them when she arrived home. She stared at Clint's bag, knowing she would have to choose a suit for him to be buried in. She couldn't face the task.

She threw herself onto the bed and wept. Novels always showed the heroine crying until she had no more tears to shed. Kaycie wondered when that would happen. Her en-tire face had felt like a leaky sieve for three days now, with no sign the waterworks would ever quit.

People had called—she ignored the recorded messages. The buzzer had announced a few—she'd turned them away. Channel Three's news department had come nosing around, the journalists sympathetic, but it was so obvious they really only wanted to cover the tragic story. She'd screamed at Hal Erickson to get out of her face. She would regret it, she knew. One day soon she had to go back to work there. Or not. Maybe she would move to L.A. and start fresh. Or not. She couldn't think straight.

Her mother was the only person she could even think about seeing. Sylvia had brought Kaycie's favorite Chinese takeout food the night she arrived home. The sight of it threw Kaycie into spasms of uncontrolled weeping.

"Chinese food, Mom? Really?"

"It's your favorite. I only thought—"

"I've just come from China, had to leave my dead husband behind…and you *thought*…"

Sylvia had looked crushed. "Honey, you're so right. Let me order us a pizza."

"I can't eat. I'm going to bed. See yourself out."

Sylvia had called more than a dozen times in the following two days, apologetic and worried. Kaycie knew there was business to take care of, arrangements to make—she would eventually have to face it all, and having her mother by her side might help.

She rolled off the wrinkled bed and headed toward the shower, ignoring the suitcases and the gaping closet door where no appropriate clothing awaited. Okay, there was something her mother could do. She detoured back to her purse and dug for her cell phone, hoping it held enough charge to make at least one call.

"Mom, I need a black dress. Can you go to Neiman Marcus and find me one? I don't care what it looks like. I'm only wearing it for one day." *And then it's going into the trash because I can't handle any more reminders.*

"Sure, honey. Anything else? You have shoes and a bag?"

Leave it to Mom to think of the details at a time like this.

"Everything else is fine." Kaycie knew her voice sounded flat and rude but she couldn't muster anything more right now.

"I'll do it right now and be there before noon. Think about lunch, sweetie. It will do you good to get out of the house."

Whatever. Kaycie hung up without committing.

She dropped her robe on the bathroom floor and got into the shower, steeling herself for her mother's visit. She had to start dealing with this, had to see people, get out of this cave-like condo with the drapes closed tightly and the suitcases in the corner. She told herself to start acting like the competent woman she knew herself to be. Then she felt the tears well up again. It didn't matter how many times she washed them off, they always came back.

She turned off the hot water and let the cold blast her until she was shivering. It was horrible but at least she no longer felt numb. When she couldn't stand it another second, she shut off the valve and stepped out. A towel wrapped around her body felt snug and comforting, like one of Clint's big bear hugs. The tears started again. She gave up trying to stop them and meandered to the closet where she dug out an old pair of sweats and a shapeless sweater from her college days.

Without bothering to dry her hair she went to the suitcases. Clint's was easy—she simply wheeled it into the far corner of his closet, parked it and closed the door. She knelt in front of her largest bag and unzipped it.

The door buzzer startled her. Mom surely couldn't have shopped for a dress and gotten here already, which meant she'd come by to convince Kaycie she should join her on the shopping trip. *Come along,* she would say, *you always love browsing in Neiman's.*

Kaycie was tired of the battle. She walked through the living room and pressed the buzzer to admit her mother, then left the front door cracked open a little while she headed back to the bedroom. It was inevitable—she would have to put on something suitable to be seen in public.

A tap sounded from the living room.

"Mrs. Holbrook?" came a male voice.

Oh shit. Who have I let in? She scurried to the door.

It was Clint's attorney, Derek Woo. She hadn't seen him since Shanghai, when he'd come to the clinic to break the news and later at the hotel to escort her to the airport.

"I'm sorry," he said. "I think you must have been expecting someone else?"

Kaycie nodded and waved him in. "My mother. She'll be along any minute."

"I won't take much time then. How are you holding up?"

Didn't her puffy red eyes and her hair, all kinked and damp from the shower, give him a clue? She made a dismissive gesture. She should probably invite him to sit down but, truthfully, didn't really want him to stay.

"What can I do for you?" she asked with a nod toward the file folder under his arm.

"I brought a copy of the death certificate. You'll need it for certain things, such as filing an insurance claim."

She reached for the folder.

"There's more. We should probably sit down." He looked toward the large sofa in the living room.

"What more? What do you mean?" This whole week had turned to pure hell—what could be worse?

He gently took her elbow and steered her toward the nearest chair.

"I'm afraid…well, I've just learned…" He took a breath. "Clint's body has not been recovered. I was unable to bring him back with me."

Kaycie felt the room tilt and her vision narrowed to a small tunnel.

"They told me there's no chance. The boat was twenty miles offshore in an area known to have many sharks. He won't be found."

She heard the words *I'm sorry* coming from a great distance as the tunnel closed in around her.

THIRTY-NINE

MARY PICKED UP her cell phone and pressed the button so it would light up and show the battery level. Yep, it still held enough charge. Why wouldn't it?—she'd checked it ten minutes ago, and ten minutes before that.

"Either make the damn call," she muttered to herself, "or put the whole idea out of your head and get on with the day."

She punched the digits of Kaycie's number, the one given to her by Debbie when she'd made her exploratory call and acted surprised at the news about Clint. Everyone wanted to be the first to tell her, assuming as the ex-wife she wouldn't otherwise know. Well, it was true—no one official had bothered to tell her. She was actually surprised when Kaycie answered.

"Hi, Kaycie, it's Mary Holbrook."

A stammer? A sob? Mary couldn't decipher the sound.

"I've just heard the news and I wanted to offer condolences."

This time it was definitely a long, exhaled breath. "Yeah, you too."

"I wondered if there's going to be a funeral. I mean, there are several old friends I should tell. I won't come myself, not if it's going to be painful for you."

"Painful? This whole thing is so painful, I can't even describe it. Do whatever you want. It'll be a memorial service at Tanich on Tuesday. I don't know if that's the right thing, considering..."

"Considering?"

"The body. Oh god, you haven't heard. Clint's body... well, they haven't found him."

"What? Oh my god, Kaycie, I had no idea."

"I just found out. The attorney came by and he brought the death certificate and it's two pages of printed stuff from the Philippine government. One of the pages looks like a diploma or something—red ribbons and a gold seal and all this fancy writing and signatures and everything. At least they're written in English."

"Kaycie, slow down and take a breath."

Mary felt her concentration shooting all over the place. Clint's body was still over there somewhere but they'd sent paperwork? She forced herself to take a deep breath also.

Kaycie had barely paused. "And I feel so rotten because there I was about to go in for a stupid surgery that was nothing but a vain attempt to look different, and if I'd been with him instead maybe I could have done something to save him. And, god, Mary, the lawyer said the water was full of *sharks*."

She stopped talking only because she was now sobbing.

Somehow, the news that Clint's body had probably been torn apart by sharks was more disturbing than the fact he was dead. Mary backed up against her kitchen cabinets and sank to the floor, her back pressed against an uncomfortable knob, her forehead resting on her bent knees.

Kaycie was babbling on and all Mary could think of was, how could events have suddenly taken this bizarre turn? Over the phone she heard a buzzer in the background and Kaycie paused for a blissful second.

"That's got to be my mother," she told Mary. "Sorry I'm not more coherent right now. I gotta go."

"Sure. Bye." The connection was already gone.

Mary sat there until the cabinet knob at her back reminded her to get up.

"What the hell," she said to the empty room. "What the effing hell?"

She dialed another number from her contacts list. "Sandy, I really need to see you guys."

"Mary, what's the matter?"

"It's complicated. Is there sometime all the ladies can meet?"

"It's Sunday, so most likely anytime will work. I'll call them. Shall we come to your apartment?"

Mary glanced around, taking in the small space. She'd meant to clean this morning and had instead wasted the time. But the alternative was to find something decent to wear and catch the bus and ride across town... "Sure, that's great. As soon as you can get here."

"You okay? Never mind. I already asked that. I'll round everyone up. We'll aim for an hour—say, two o'clock?"

Turning over at least part of the burden to Sandy's efficient ways gave Mary the energy to pick up the dust cloth she'd left on the bedroom dresser. Within an hour the bathroom sparkled and the small apartment looked as good as it ever would. If they'd been at Sandy's there would no doubt have been tea and cookies or some fancy little spread, but she didn't have anything beyond a bag of potato chips so they'd have to make do with it.

She washed her hands and put on a shirt that wasn't sweaty. It was 1:55.

"YOU'RE SAYING THERE'S going to be a funeral but no coffin and no body?" Gracie looked as if that was the most foreign idea in the world to her.

"How do they actually know? Maybe Clint managed to swim ashore somewhere and he isn't actually dead," Pen said.

"His lawyer delivered a death certificate issued by the government over there. He's really dead."

Amber sat cross-legged on the floor within easy reach of the chips. "There's something about this whole thing that seems off. I checked the regional weather reports before we left Shanghai. You know, to see if we were going to be in for airport delays or anything. There was absolutely nothing in the way of a major storm in that part of the world."

"But we left more than a day later," Pen said.

"Yes, so any major system following the jet-stream would have been headed right toward us. There was nothing but a nice sunny high-pressure ridge over the Philippines."

"So, maybe the storm Clint's fishing boat got into was a small, localized thunderstorm or something."

"I thought of that," Amber said, "so just before I left to come here I Googled news reports of weather-related accidents for that day."

She had their attention.

"Nothing. Zip, nada." She crunched down another chip. "In fact, I even found the fishing reports for that day and it talked about perfect conditions and great fishing—it listed some hot spots by name. Local fishing guides would surely know about them. None of the stories mentioned an accident involving an American."

"What are you saying?"

"The storm story is b.s." Amber looked frankly at the rest of them. "Clint's personal stuff was completely cleared from his Shanghai office. Kaycie was packed off home before she could think to ask any questions."

"Someone wanted this thing quietly finalized and filed away," Sandy said.

"Precisely my thought," said Pen. "And who would do that? Perhaps the person or persons who killed him."

FORTY

"YOU KNOW WHAT this means," Sandy said after they'd decided to open the bottle of wine Gracie had brought along. "We need to move as quickly as possible to get that money out of those accounts Amber found."

"It's not going to be easy," Amber said. "As soon as our plane landed yesterday I started trying to get back into them. Even looking for a work-around to the passwords, it's as if all the U.S. bank accounts are frozen."

"It's standard procedure," Sandy said. "Until the probate court reviews his will, not even family members have access to the money. It's to keep them from clearing out all of it before the government gets its share."

Pen spoke up. "But a man like Clint, sophisticated enough to move money around the way he did and to have a lawyer handling his affairs—he would have set up a trust. Those don't go through probate."

"True." Sandy seemed puzzled. "Maybe *frozen* isn't the right word."

"It could be that he set up several additional layers of security," Amber said. "I have to admit I'm not mentally a hundred percent right now, and maybe I just haven't thought of it yet. I'll get un-jetlagged and then work on it some more."

"I'll go to the funeral," Mary said. "I ran the idea past Kaycie and she said, quote, do what you want."

"It's not a bad idea. Maybe you can learn something. In the movies, the cops always go to the victim's funeral so they can catch the killer watching from the sidelines."

They all chuckled at Amber's assessment.

"The media will probably be there," Pen said. "The story has shown up on the morning news, at least on Channel 3 where Kaycie works."

"Oh, great. It means I'll have to buy a dress. I don't even own a dress."

"You're close to my size and I probably have something," Gracie offered. "No point in buying an outfit you won't likely wear again."

Mary nodded acknowledgement but didn't quite say she would accept the offer.

"So, what are our next steps?" Sandy asked when the room had been silent for several minutes.

"I'd say we need to talk to the Philippine authorities," Pen said. "I definitely do not believe it's common to issue a death certificate without a body. Without an autopsy how do they determine what to fill in as the cause of death? The whole thing, as Amber said, seems very much 'off'."

Gracie yawned, perhaps involuntarily. "Oh, god, another long trip?"

"None of us are ready for that," Pen admitted. "It would be completely exhausting. I think we can accomplish a lot over the phone. I may speak with Benton about it—if that's all right with everyone? I need to think of an angle, a way to approach the authorities so it seems I have a right to the information."

Mary's face brightened. "Remember the day I went to the plumbing shop and snapped photos at Debbie's desk? One of those documents was a letter from an insurance company. You could pretend to be calling about that."

"Great idea," Sandy said. "They come around the bank all the time, wanting information on deceased clients so they can decide on paying claims."

"Was Clint's policy for life insurance?" Gracie asked. "I thought it was something to do with his construction project."

"I'll go back and re-read the letter," Amber said.

"Send me a copy of it. Either way, the government in Manila doesn't know what type insurance he had," Pen pointed out. "Nor do they care, most likely. Let me give it some thought. I'll figure something and bluff my way through."

FORTY-ONE

PEN CAME IN from her terrace overlooking the sprawling city. She'd carried her cup of tea outside and enjoyed the view, then watered her potted geraniums and swept up a few fallen leaves—all stalling maneuvers while she worked out what she would say during the phone call she would soon make. It wasn't so different from writing lines of dialog in a novel, she reasoned. All she had to do was put herself in the role of the insurance investigator and speak to what was probably a low-level bureaucrat in a government agency. She'd actually written such scenes—now she would be living the conversation.

Amber, bless her heart, had done the groundwork. The girl would make a fine research assistant, Pen thought. She wasn't clear exactly what their youngest member did for a living—possibly supported by her parents who lived in Santa Fe. The thought brought her full circle, back to the task at hand. If she didn't hurry, she would be too late because of the time difference.

She pulled up Amber's email on her computer, locating the telephone number for the Philippine Statistics Authority in Manila. Before she could overthink the situation and talk herself out of it, she dialed the number.

A female voice answered in Tagalog, a phrase so rapid

Pen had no idea if she'd actually uttered a comprehensible sentence.

"Do you speak English?" Pen asked.

"Yes, of course, ma'am." It was clipped and chirpy but Pen understood.

"I am calling from America. I need a copy of a death certificate for an American citizen who died in your country."

"I will transfer you. Please hold."

To another English speaker, Pen hoped. She waited through a series of clicking noises on the line, hoping none of them were disconnecting her. Eventually, a man answered and she repeated her request.

"What is your purpose?" he asked. "Are you a family member of this Mr. Holbrook?"

"I'm with Assured Life Insurance Company. We have official paperwork to file regarding the death." She hoped the man wouldn't attempt to verify the fictional company she'd created for purposes of this call.

"When did you say he died?"

Pen thought back to the day Kaycie went to the clinic and looked frantically at her own calendar. "I'm not certain, but I believe it was either the fifteenth or sixteenth."

"Of this month?"

"Yes, that's correct."

It sounded as if he chuckled, but the phone connection was a little shaky. She couldn't be certain.

"I will check. Do you know who performed the autopsy?"

"No…wouldn't that be an official coroner or medical examiner?"

"Many doctors here are certified to do autopsies, ma'am. There are more than four hundred here in Manila alone."

Pen nearly dropped the phone. Seriously? It was an astounding number.

"I will check," he repeated. The line went quiet. Only a low fizz of static told her the call hadn't been dropped.

She waited fifteen minutes, wondering if the man had gone home for the day and simply forgot she was on the line. She'd nearly given up when a female came on the line.

"May I help you?"

Oh, no—don't make me go through the whole story *again*. Luckily, Pen had asked for the man's name. She explained she had already been talking to him.

"Yes, yes. He have other customer. I find your information."

"Thank you. The deceased's name is McClintock Holbrook." She had to spell it—twice.

On hold once more, Pen glanced at the clock in the bottom corner of her computer screen. It was four minutes to the hour. She would almost bet money the entire staff of that Philippine records office would clear out any time now. She found herself holding her breath as another minute ticked away.

With one minute remaining, the woman came back on the line.

"No death certificate here for that name," she stated. "How long you say it was?"

"A bit over a week."

"Oh, that explain. Sometime it is two, three weeks certificate to arrive in our office. Sometime a month or two. Call back next week."

With that flat statement and the clock hitting the hour, the line went dead.

Another week to wait—minimum. Perhaps a month or two. Pen wanted to smack her head against the wall. In a week, the lawyers or the courts would surely have hold of Clint's estate. By the time the Philippine government acted, all the cash might be dispersed. It would be quicker to turn up in Kaycie's life again and simply ask to see the document. If they actually needed it. The main purpose was to find out who performed the autopsy and what they listed as the cause of death. That was certainly something she could come right out and ask Kaycie.

She dialed the number Mary had given.

FORTY-TWO

"She sounded very surprised to hear from me," Pen told Sandy later that evening. "You know how, if you've traveled with a group, it's easy to become chums with your fellow tourists but once everyone returns home they are never in contact again. Despite the fact I was with her on the day she was due to have surgery, she acted hesitant, cool. She certainly wasn't in a mood to share information from the death certificate."

"Not surprising. And I'm not sure what we would gain by knowing, anyway. Did you learn anything at all?" In the background Pen heard an electric can opener and pictured Sandy opening food for the two cats.

"One thing, and it required spur-of-the-moment thinking on my part, of which I'm rather proud. I said a dear friend was traveling to the Philippines next week and wanted to take a fishing trip. Would she tell me the name of the charter company Clint used, as I would most definitely not want my friend going out with someone so irresponsible."

"She believed that?"

"I think she was simply too stunned at the audacity and rudeness of the question to think of a way to refuse. She told me it was a man named Tiko Garcia with a company called Best Fishing."

"I'm surprised she remembered it."

"She told me she was unpacking. There was a brochure among their things and she even gave me the phone number. I tried it and was told Tiko is out with some customers. I'll give it another go later."

"You might do some online research, or ask Amber to do it. See if there are other businesses nearby. If Tiko isn't willing to talk, maybe someone else remembers the day he claims to have lost a customer overboard."

"An excellent idea. It can't be a common occurrence and there had to be talk around the docks. That is, *if* they stuck with the same story locally as the one they gave Kaycie. If the story differs, I'd love to hear their version."

"Also, what about the crew? I imagine at least one crew member goes along on each trip. These rich guys like someone to bait their hooks, hand them a beer...things like that. Maybe you can get a name and speak with that person separately from Tiko."

"Sandy, you're brilliant. I shall make the call while Tiko's away."

Within five minutes she had the crewman's name—Angelo Reyes. Using a young and flirtatious tone gained her the man's phone number, after being told he was not working today.

Angelo answered on the first ring, as if he was expecting a call. From the tone of his response it clearly wasn't an American woman with questions about an accident. She'd taken the approach that she was a dear friend of the victim's wife, who was stricken with grief because of all the unanswered questions, a woman who hadn't slept in a week.

"I didn't see nothing," he stated flatly.

"You do remember Mr. Holbrook—a man in his mid-forties, chubby, balding, something of a braggart?"

"Braggart?"

"You know—he talked about himself a lot." It was Pen's impression of the man.

"Si—this one, he did that."

"We heard there was a bad storm? He fell overboard?"

He hesitated. "Storm? Si—if that is what they say."

Pen wished she could see Angelo's face. She would bet he couldn't make eye contact.

"Angelo, please just tell me. Was there a storm? Was the sea very rough?"

"The man fall over, but only Tiko see him. He send me below to get more bait."

"And Mr. Holbrook—he simply *fell* over?"

Another pause. "The deck, it is slippery. He not have life jacket."

"Why wouldn't Tiko have reported it that way? Why did he say there was a storm?"

"Ma'am, I do not know. The rules, they say life jackets."

Well, an operator who broke the rules and then lost a passenger might certainly fudge the truth to save his own neck, she supposed. She asked what happened next but Angelo remained unforthcoming; she had to pry for every detail.

"Did Tiko shout for your help?"

"He yell, yes. Another boat nearby, it come. We all start to look."

"It must have been very frightening. Did you look for a long time?"

"In ten minutes you know if you will find someone. He not come to the top anyplace."

A commotion started in the background, as if Angelo had walked into a bar or crowded room. He didn't seem to hear much of what she said after that. She thanked him and hung up. Most likely she had learned all she would get from him anyway.

She went to her kitchen and flicked the switch on the electric teakettle, debating her next moves. Calculating the time difference, she realized it would soon be getting dark along the Pacific Rim. Perhaps Tiko's charter boat would be pulling into port about now. When the kettle shut off, she brewed a cup of tea and carried it to her desk.

As the overseas call rang, she decided to go back to the insurance-investigator tactic with the charter boat's owner. He would surely give as gentle a spin as possible to a grieving widow's friend, but with an authority figure he might feel compelled to relate details.

"Best Fishing—we have the best fishing experience in the islands," came the voice of the woman who'd earlier told her Tiko was out on the boat. "Ah, yes, the English lady. He docked the boat a minute ago. I get."

Pen waited, almost hearing the overseas phone rates tick by as she sat there on hold. In nine minutes a man's voice came on.

"Tiko Garcia."

She went through the spiel about being with Assured Life Insurance and asked the same sorts of questions she had posed to Angelo. Tiko was more experienced at covering his rear end, obviously. His responses were rote, his facts never wavering. Mr. Holbrook refused to wear his life jacket, he slipped on the wet deck and fell over the side. As Angelo had, Tiko dodged her direct question about the storm, repeating only the parts about the life jacket and the wet deck.

"Who else assisted in the rescue effort?"

"My deck hand, Angelo."

"Did other boats come along and help you look for the victim?"

"There might have been one or two. There's always boats nearby—it's a hot fishing spot."

"But no one ever caught sight of Mr. Holbrook in the water?"

"That's right. Look, lady, my customer is outside with his catch. I gotta go take their picture." He hung up without waiting for her response.

Pen chafed at the abrupt end to the conversation, yet she couldn't think what else she would have asked. She felt sure Tiko was hiding something but darned if she could figure out what.

Amber had provided three more leads and Pen decided to stick with it and follow them now. Time really was becoming of the essence. These numbers were for businesses near the dock where Best Fishing operated. Pen pictured a row of wooden shacks and a couple of docks with small-ish, rusted boats that creaked as the water bobbed them against the pilings.

The first number she dialed was for Willie's Crab Shack, most likely a walk-up little eatery with a couple of plastic tables and chairs out front. The man who answered said yes, he was the owner. Didn't remember the day in question but since he wasn't especially friendly with Tiko it wouldn't be unusual that he'd only heard about the missing man secondhand, a couple days later. He stayed busy serving up crab tacos and rarely looked at the boats as they came and went. According to him.

An American man answered the number she called for Island Bait and Tackle, which Amber had noted was immediately next door to Tiko's office. He said his name was Stink. Pen suppressed a vision of the bait shop and got on with her questions.

"Yeah, I heard about that." He had a laid-back voice,

which made her think of someone who'd lived the island life for a very long time, or he smoked a lot of pot. "Kind of a fat guy wearing a polo shirt with a couple buttons down the front?"

Pen gave the best description she could envision, since she'd only seen Clint in a business suit.

"Yeah… I suppose that coulda been him. You know, I woulda swore he went out with Alphonse, not Tiko. But, you know, my memory's not what it used to be. You're prob'ly right. That's what I told the other guy, too. Stay down here long enough and the days all blend together, ya know?"

"Other guy?"

"Yeah, the one who came out here a couple days ago, all white shirt and tan slacks, from the insurance company? You know him? Maybe not—it's gotta be a big office. That corporate shit, that's why I moved down here."

"I'll look him up. Do you remember his name?"

He laughed. "Ha—I barely remember my own name some days. Hang on, let's see…"

He set the phone down with a *clunk* and she heard the crisp sounds of paper rustling in the background.

"Yeah, okay. Here's a card he left behind. It's…geez, I gotta get me some glasses…it's Bradley Muggins. Weird name, huh."

Pen couldn't very well ask the name of the insurance company or the phone number on the card, but she figured Amber could come up with those. She thanked Stink for his help, her mind flying ahead. So, a real insurance investigator was asking questions, too.

FORTY-THREE

"ME? OH, NO-NO-NO-NO-NO." Mary groaned as she said it. "I'm no actor. I can't make up these stories and playact the way you guys do. You're so good at it. I'd suck."

"You won't suck," Sandy said. "In fact, you won't even be acting. This is the real you, going in to ask legitimate questions. You're going inside and you'll ask Derek Woo about Clint's insurance policy, whether you were listed as a beneficiary."

"That's the thing—I'm not supposed to know the policy exists."

"He doesn't know that. For all he knows, you and Clint talked all the time."

Mary gave the others a sideways look. "All the time. Right."

They sat in the parking lot of a three-story office building near downtown Phoenix. Sandy was behind the wheel of her Mazda, with Pen in the passenger seat, Amber and Mary in back. Gracie had left to deliver one of her kids somewhere. Over lunch, Pen had filled everyone in on her calls to the Philippines. Pen's overriding feeling, after making those phone calls, was that Tiko Garcia and Angelo Reyes both knew a whole lot more than they had admitted to her. Garcia, in particular, was out-and-out lying. She had made that point several times during today's lunch.

The more they discussed the situation, the more they felt Derek Woo was involved. The attorney seemed to be everywhere Clint went in his last weeks. The insurance letter confirming Clint's new life insurance policy indicated a copy designated for Mr. Woo.

Part of their mission this afternoon was to learn whether Clint might have had a generous moment—okay, that possibility was slim—in leaving at least part of the proceeds from his policy to his ex-wife. Maybe he'd heard about Mary's hopeless financial situation and decided to do the right thing. Maybe pigs could fly.

The other purpose for the visit was to see what other information they could glean about Woo. Too many things pointed to his playing some part in Clint's death: his Chinese connections, his knowing so much about Clint's finances, the way he showed up in Shanghai within hours of the boating accident to tell Kaycie. How had he known to be there?

"Mary, I can go with you," Amber said. "I'd hold your hand and you could pretend I'm your daughter. I could do a good fatherless-child imitation."

They all looked at her and laughed. Strawberry-blond Mary and lily-white Clint had produced this half-black, very Mediterranean-looking girl?

"Um…your adopted daughter?" Amber's dark eyes sparkled.

"Yeah, no. I'm fairly certain Clint's lawyer would know Clint had no children." Mary squeezed Amber's hand. "But thanks for offering."

"Perhaps Sandy should go along. She could pretend to be *your* attorney," Pen suggested. "Mr. Woo might not be so quick to dismiss you if you have counsel alongside."

Sandy spoke up: "Only problem with that is he's met me. He knows I'm a banker, not a lawyer."

"Okay, well, somebody's got to go in there or we'll sit here all afternoon debating it to death." Mary opened her door. "Amber, I vote for you going along. Only you're not going to be my daughter. I won't explain to him who you are, you're just a friend. What you're there for is to be extra eyes and ears. I'll get Woo tied up in conversation and you spy around."

"Ooh—I love it." Amber grinned and opened her car door too. She slung her spacious bag over her shoulder. "Who knows what I'll come out with."

They walked across the parking lot together.

"If I have to, I'm going to admit to Mr. Woo that I'm dead broke," Mary said. "He told Kaycie Clint's insurance coverage was very generous. Well, then, I'll come right out and ask for some of it."

"Throw in some tears and get him to turn his back on me," Amber said with a wiggle to her eyebrows. "I'll snatch up any piece of evidence I can find."

Mary pulled open the tall glass doors to the lobby. "Just be careful. The man might be dangerous."

They rode the elevator to the third floor without a word. The car was filled with suited lawyer-types. Double doors to Suite 301 faced them when the elevator door opened for the final time. A plaque to the side said Danby & Associates, with a long list to follow. It was impossible to tell how high up the ladder Woo had made it. The women exchanged a glance, a subtle thumbs-up.

Mary didn't hold hope for much time with Woo. When Pen had called from their lunch place to request an appointment, she'd been told there was a two-week wait unless she could take a fifteen-minute space today which opened up because a conference call had been cancelled. She'd grabbed it, and here they were.

A receptionist pressed one button on an intercom and Derek Woo appeared at the door which connected the spacious reception area to the heart of the operation.

"Ms. Holbrook? And?" He glanced at Amber.

"My friend, Ms. Zeckis."

Mary hitched her shoulders straighter, wishing she'd had warning of this meeting, wishing she'd worn something nicer than stretch capris and a warm-up jacket to lunch. She took a deep breath and set aside her insecurity. The unfashionable outfit might work in her favor, since she was here to beg for money.

Woo led them to a small suite where a huge wooden desk dominated one room, a narrow table and six upright chairs filled the other, separated by a wall of glass with mini-blinds, which were open at the moment. Mary caught sight of a small beverage setup with coffee maker, mugs, and a dorm-sized fridge in the conference room.

He seated himself behind the desk, indicated the two visitor chairs for the women, and got right down to business. "What can I do for you, Ms. Holbrook?"

She took a deep breath. "I don't know if you know about me. I'm Clint Holbrook's ex-wife."

"I'm aware." A yellow writing pad sat beside his hand, a closed laptop computer in front of him. He made no move to touch either one.

"I understand Clint had life insurance. I wonder if I was named as a beneficiary?"

He shuffled for the right way to politely dump her and get on with his day. "I'm afraid not. At least as far as I know."

No point in delaying this. Mary played the weeper card,

thinking of the saddest times in her life to bring on the tears. "Mr. Woo, this is so hard for me to admit." She reached toward Amber, who gave her hand an encouraging pat. "Clint left me penniless. Our home…the one we lived in together for eighteen years…gone…" She used the sleeve of her warm-up to wipe her eyes.

He stared at his yellow tablet.

What was it going to take to budge this guy? Mary sobbed out the story of losing the house and living in a homeless shelter, building the tears into full-fledged sobs.

He began to look uncomfortable. "I don't know what to tell you. Have you spoken with someone at the insurance company?"

Her words came out in an incomprehensible torrent. Amber picked up her cue, jumping out of her seat and standing at Mary's side.

"Do you have some water?"

Woo, anxious for anything that would get the women on their feet and, hopefully, out of his office, was quick to comply. He went to the fridge in the other room.

"Quick," Amber whispered. "Follow him. Get him standing with his back to me and keep talking. I just had a brilliant idea."

Mary staggered into the small conference room and edged around Woo. When he handed her a tiny bottle of water she had him in the perfect position. Amber pulled a small plastic thumb drive from the pocket of her jeans and jammed it into a USB port on the side of his computer. A flashing green light came on.

She signaled Mary to keep talking. Woo reached for a tissue box on the conference table and held it out to her. Mary grabbed his arm, keeping him facing toward the far wall.

The moment the green light quit flashing, Amber pulled

the thumb drive out and seamlessly slipped it into her pocket at the same instant Woo turned around.

"I'm very sorry for your situation, Ms. Holbrook, but there's nothing I can do to change your ex-husband's policy."

Mary grabbed for his sleeve again and missed. She sent Amber a frantic look, but Amber had picked up her bag and slung the strap over her shoulder.

"Come on, Mary," she said. "I guess he's done all he will."

Mary shot Woo a withering stare and blew her nose loudly into his tissues.

"I can't believe you went along with Clint on this."

"Clint was my client. Carrying out his wishes is my only duty in the matter."

Amber took Mary's elbow and steered her toward the door. She kept up the sobs until they'd passed through the reception area, grabbing the attention of a suited man who was most likely Woo's next appointment. In the elevator, both women nearly got the giggles.

"Overplayed the weeping widow thing a little bit there, don't you think?" Amber said as they exited the building. "Blowing your nose like a foghorn—seriously?"

"You said I had to keep his attention. Did you find anything at all? There was really *no* time."

They joined Sandy and Pen in the car.

"I'm hoping I hit the motherlode," Amber said, patting her pocket.

FORTY-FOUR

KAYCIE WOKE UP on a white sand beach with gentle waves lapping at her feet, the distinct smell of ocean water surrounding her. She was wearing the cotton shorts and tank top she'd gone to bed in and she could tell by the way the sun felt on her skin that she'd not taken time to apply sunscreen or moisturizer.

She looked around. There was not a single sign of human life. As the waves began to reach her knees, she stood and moved inland, walking through deep sand. It reminded her of her honeymoon on Barbados, except there'd never been a place without the imprint of man—a grass palapa or shack, a boogie board, a footprint. When she realized this, her anxiety level rose. *Where am I?*

The views in both directions revealed only sand, sea, palm trees and dense bushes. Inland, the ground rose and she could see a jutting hill in the distance. Gulls swooped low over the water, squawking constantly. But behind their chatter some other sound came through—a whistle. She focused more intently, looking for the bird who made such an unusual call. Then she realized it couldn't be a bird. It was a tune, a recognizable song.

Just as she was about to shout out, movement at the edge of the foliage caught her attention. A man. Fragments of the tune came to her on the wind—something from a Disney movie—"Whistle While You Work." As soon as she identified it, the man turned to her.

It was Clint.

Tears clogged her throat when she tried to call out to him. "Honey Bear! You're *here*." But it came out all muffled and he didn't hear her. He turned back into the tangled bushes.

She ran, impeded by the soft sand but determined he wouldn't get away again. Away from the swooshing of the waves and the bird cries, she began shouting his name. He walked into a thicket and she kept her eyes on the spot as she followed.

A small clearing appeared and there he was, kneeling in front of a fire. She realized Clint's hair had grown long and tangled and he had a full beard. His clothes were tattered. A ring of stones surrounded the fire pit and a pile of boxes sat nearby, all with the FedEx logo.

Kaycie startled awake, panting. She was on their king-sized bed in the Scottsdale condo. Her heart raced and she closed her eyes quickly, hoping to recapture the dream. But the vision, she realized, had been Clint's face on Tom Hanks' body and the scene was from the movie. Clint hadn't really survived, wasn't living on a deserted island somewhere. She would never be able to watch that movie again.

She rolled over. A bright strip of light rimmed the dark bedroom drapes. She'd probably slept until noon again. Noon. Was this the day she'd agreed to have lunch with her mother?

She sat up and rubbed her face. Sleep granules caked the corners of her eyes and her hair felt greasy. She didn't have the energy for a shower; she would have to cancel the lunch plans, although she dreaded making the call. Mom was increasingly becoming a pain, insisting Kaycie get out and do something. She had even suggested going back to work might be good for her.

Kaycie couldn't imagine dressing, having her hair and makeup done, and appearing on camera. She started to fall back against the mattress and give in to more sleep, except she felt the need to pee. She stumbled to the bathroom. Whose idea was it to put a skylight in here? The room was too damn bright. She grumbled and sat on the toilet, burying her face in her hands.

She'd no sooner finished than she heard the insistent, nagging sound of the door buzzer coming from the living room. Her cell phone sat on the bathroom vanity and when she pressed the button to wake it, the device faintly glowed with the numerals 11:58 before they faded and it went dead.

It had to be her mother at the door. Sylvia had learned from the past week's experience that Kaycie wouldn't necessarily show up for meals or shopping simply because they had an appointment together. Last night she'd pestered Kaycie to agree to lunch. Now she was here to enforce.

Kaycie pulled up her shorts, noticing they were loose. The waistband elastic must have stretched out. Not bothering with a robe, she walked through the living room and pressed the buzzer beside the door. Now, if she could find some coffee and clear her head before she had to face her mother's judgment.

The kitchen was a disaster. That cleaning woman certainly wasn't doing a very good job. Then Kaycie remembered. She'd sent the woman away twice because she wanted to be alone in the condo. She rummaged through food cartons on the countertop—things her mother had dropped off—and found several mugs. All were caked with the sludgy residue of half-finished coffee. The dishwasher reeked—a skillet Mom used to prepare garlic shrimp sat there because Kaycie had forgotten to add the coffee cups and run the cycle. She closed the machine tightly.

An upper cabinet held one clean cup and she'd barely reached for it when a knock came at the front door.

"C'mon, Mom. Just let yourself in," she muttered.

The coffee maker's basket held a nasty clot of grounds. Geez, it might have been simpler to shower and dress and go out for coffee.

The knock came again. She dropped the coffee basket into a sink filled with used forks and spoons, and stomped to the door. When she flung it open, ready to snap at her mother, she was startled to see a strange man standing there.

"Kaycie Holbrook?" he said. "I'm with Cooper Life and Casualty. It's about the insurance policy your late husband purchased."

FORTY-FIVE

"I NEED ICE CREAM," Amber announced when she and Mary climbed back in Sandy's car.

"So, what did you guys learn in there?" Sandy asked.

"First, Cold Stone. There's one just around the block." Amber buckled up and refused to say another word until Sandy started the car.

Once they had parked in front of Cold Stone Creamery, time had to be devoted to making choices. Amber went straight for the double chocolate and had the clerk stir in brownie chunks and walnuts. Even Pen couldn't resist that particular combination. There were plenty of empty tables outside so that's where they gathered.

"You have one of those cat-who-caught-the-mouse looks," Sandy said, dipping into her maple with caramel and pecans. "What did you learn in there?"

Amber grinned and pulled the tiny thumb drive from her pocket. "If this baby worked, we have all kinds of good stuff."

"What is it?" Pen asked.

"A cloning device. I had planned to use it on Clint's computer, if I'd found it, in Shanghai. With luck, now I've captured everything on Derek Woo's computer."

Spoons paused in mid-air. "How is that possible?"

"A buddy of mine from school invented it. It's not on the

market yet, but he's hoping to get a patent and make a fortune from it. He and I each have one and we've practiced with each other's computers."

"So this isn't something legal?" Sandy asked, eyeing Amber sideways.

Amber waggled her fingers. "Let's just say the less you know the better."

"Okay, then, I'm not asking." She went back to her maple ice cream.

"When do we learn the results of this little magical thief?" Mary asked, dropping her empty cup into a nearby trash basket.

"As soon as I get to my computer."

"Okay, ladies, let's finish up that ice cream and get on the move," Mary said.

Forty-five minutes later they were crowded into Amber's tiny efficiency apartment, watching over her shoulders as a series of boxes appeared on her computer screen. Amber hit a key now and then but for the most part the process seemed to happen on its own.

"Okay...*okay*..." Amber said. "I'm getting some logins to bank accounts. Can't tell yet if this is Derek getting into his own stuff—" She sat up straighter. "No, wait. This is one of Clint's account numbers. I've typed it often enough I know it well."

Sandy fidgeted, fighting her impulse to turn away and ignore the process.

Amber flicked over to a different box on the screen. "And here's the email he received—the bank confirming the change of password on the account. I *knew* it. I knew something changed on that one, and it happened after Clint died. Derek Woo has been all over the place in these accounts."

Mary was practically bouncing on her toes. "Do you

think you can get in there now, retrieve half the money for me?"

Amber moved one of the boxes aside and looked at others. "Well, if it's going to work, this should do it. I've tracked Derek's keystrokes so I know what he enters as a password."

She made a few more moves, rapid changes hard for everyone else to follow, but no one protested. They saw a sign-on screen, watched Amber carefully copy and paste information. Saw her click the Log In button.

Up came a message in red. The user name/password combination you entered is not a valid one.

"Rats," said Mary. "What went wrong?"

"My guess is he's changed them again. I'll have to do some more digging. You all don't have to wait around. It could take awhile."

The reminder about the time of day made Mary look at her watch. "Oh, god, I've got a class to teach in a half-hour."

"I'll drive you to the gym," Sandy said. "It's quicker than trying to catch the buses."

"Thanks—I'd never make it otherwise."

"Coming along, Pen?" There wasn't much option. They'd all arrived in Sandy's car.

"Keep working on this information, Amber," Pen said, "and let us know what you come up with."

Amber nodded and the others saw themselves out. She decided to concentrate on the lawyer's emails next. If he'd changed the banking passwords more than once, there could be something more recent in the data files. But rows and rows of code rolled by without a hit on anything usable. Either that, or she was growing bleary-eyed from staring at the screen too long.

She locked her screen and logged out, sticking the precious thumb drive in her pocket before she picked up the basket of dirty laundry she'd gathered earlier and walked out the door. Maybe a walk to the laundry room and back would help clear her head.

She'd thrown dark colors and lights into two machines, tossed in soap pods and started them when the idea occurred to her, a place she hadn't yet looked in the computer files. She race-walked back to her apartment.

Narrowing her search to the data added during the time Clint Holbrook was in China, Amber found what she was looking for in the folder called Trash. More than two dozen emails had gone between Derek Woo and Rudy Tong, Clint's customer. She copied the coded lines and opened them in a word processor for easier reading.

As her eyes scanned the messages she realized she had hit the jackpot.

FORTY-SIX

THE EMAILS WENT back almost a year, to the time right before Clint's company was awarded the bid for Tong Chen Enterprises' construction job. The correspondence was conducted in English for the most part, since it appeared Derek didn't speak much Mandarin. The occasional Chinese words were easy enough for her to look up. She took the messages in order, to make sense of the sequence of events. Right away, she found an interesting fact. It seemed Derek Woo and Rudy Tong were cousins.

Amber called Sandy and asked whether the rest of the Ladies should be in on this discovery.

"Why don't you read everything first," Sandy suggested, "make copies of the important ones and come up with some conclusions for us."

It was the most responsibility the team had ever given their youngest member and Amber was determined to do the job well. She started again, reading with a more critical eye.

Knowing about the relationship between the lawyer and his client's customer put a new perspective on the whole story. Perhaps it was not so coincidental, then, that Clint had been awarded the bid, something the Ladies had wondered about from the beginning—why an American from Arizona with seemingly no contacts in China happened to win such a lucrative contract. With Derek in the picture it all began to make sense. A few kickbacks, shaving costs on materials…there were lots of ways a cousin could better his own situation in such a deal.

She found one set of communiques where the deal was fairly well spelled out: Rudy Tong would award the contract to his cousin's client; in return, Derek Woo would steer Clint toward allowing him more financial control, give Derek access to his bank accounts and allow him to handle payments and transfers. She wondered if Clint actually knew Derek had changed his account passwords, *and* which of the several banks Clint used were accessible by Derek. All of them?

Amber thought of the accounts she'd located early in her dabbling into Clint's background. The fact she'd been unable to get into them later made her think things changed around the time Clint left for Shanghai and Derek Woo began taking charge. It could hardly be a coincidence.

But how would this lead the Chinese to want Clint Holbrook, unimportant plumbing contractor from America, to die? He was, after all, constructing a building for Tong Chen Enterprises.

She took a deep breath and stretched her shoulders, realizing she had been at the keyboard more than an hour without a break. While she ran to the laundry room to transfer her clothes from washers to dryers she thought about it. What she'd read so far didn't lead to any conclusions. One thing she did know—Clint's lawyer and his client sure had talked a lot about him behind his back.

She hurried back to the apartment and continued her task. Moving along in time, she saw how the two Chinese had planned exactly when Clint would travel to Shanghai and where he would stay. Rudy Tong knew what room Holbrook would be given, and there was a hint he could have set up surveillance of the premises. Another little flurry of messages when Clint's lawyer learned he planned to take Kaycie along. The men weren't too happy about that.

Amber made notes. When she came to an exchange of messages where Rudy Tong expressed displeasure with Clint's using space in the Tong Chen offices, he commented to the effect that he wished to be rid of him. It hardly came across as a death threat, but Amber didn't know the subtle nuances of the way these men communicated. Their different cultural habits, the familial bond—being rid of someone *could* mean wishing him dead.

She printed copies of the most inflammatory messages, not completely convinced she had anything that truly posed a danger to Clint Holbrook's life—at least not yet. She realized the data she'd taken from Woo's computer was up to date as of the moment she took it, but most likely he and Rudy Tong were still in touch and she was missing a treasure trove of information if she couldn't continue to follow along. The past would become irrelevant and Woo would come up with explanations for everything she'd gleaned so far.

She paced her tiny apartment. There had to be a way to follow his moves in real time. She and her buddy, Bernie, had toyed around with this kind of stuff in their spare hours in school. Now if only she could apply that knowledge…

A final trip to the laundry room gave Amber the mental space she needed. By the time she got back to her room and dumped the laundry basket on the futon, she'd devised a series of steps in her mind. At her computer again, she wrote programming code until the room had gone dark and the night outside was black. Working in the glow from her screen, she began to see Derek Woo's text messages coming in fast and furious.

FORTY-SEVEN

AMBER YAWNED HUGELY at the Village Inn breakfast table where the Heist Ladies had gathered. An early meeting was all Sandy could manage—the bank's auditor would be in her office by ten and she knew the grueling experience would go on all day. Gracie had shuffled her kids off to school. Mary and Pen were the only two who appeared as if they'd enjoyed a restful night and were alert this morning.

They should have met at one of their homes, Sandy thought. This place was full of seniors with their early-bird habits and nothing better to do than eavesdrop on others' conversations. The only upside, other than the restaurant being centrally located, was most of those old folks probably had no better hearing than a stone.

Even so, she kept her voice low as she asked Amber to expand on what she'd found out about Derek Woo.

"I don't know how valuable it's going to be, all the work I put in on this," Amber said, mirroring Sandy's near-whisper and helping herself to a second cup of coffee from the carafe the waitress had left on their table. "He's still in contact with his cousin—I did learn that—but they are being super cautious. They'll say things with references like 'the usual place' and they talk about people using initials, most of which I don't recognize. I'm watching out for TG or AR, figuring if Derek has knowledge of Tiko or Angelo in the Philippines, those names might come up."

Mary seemed sobered by Amber's revelations this morning. "This whole thing started with you guys wanting to help me with my situation. It seemed so harmless, gathering financial data on Clint so we could get a judge to take a look. Now we're possibly tracking killers?"

"I feel like a spy," Gracie said, cutting a wedge from her blueberry pancakes. "All this hacking and watching is kind of exciting."

"Perhaps we should turn everything we've learned over to the police and let them scrutinize Clint's death," Pen suggested. "We're ill-equipped to take this investigation of ours all the way to a conclusion."

She dipped a toast triangle into her soft-boiled egg. "Although I have to agree, it's somewhat thrilling to see what can be done with surveillance these days."

"It's also highly illegal," Sandy reminded. She turned toward Amber. "Not that we won't stand behind you. We're in this together."

"It won't come out," Amber said, as if reading her thoughts. "Other than the emails I'm printing for you to look at, there's no hard evidence. My programs have a self-destruct feature that erases everything the moment the thumb drive is plugged into any other computer but mine."

"Amber, you keep one copy of the emails," Gracie suggested. "I'll take the others. My house has a fireplace."

The comment brought a chuckle. It also gave an even more clandestine feel to the meeting.

"What we need is some definitive proof that these men conspired to...you know. Just one scrap of real evidence, and we can turn it over to the police to investigate. Agreed?"

"The problem is, we don't even have evidence that Derek

actually went to the Philippines himself. He was in China, but I haven't found any phone calls or emails originating from the islands," Amber said.

"He didn't have to be there," Gracie added. "If he was the one directing that boat guy, telling him what to do."

"Yeah, guys like Derek Woo and Rudy Tong aren't going to be the actual…killers." Amber only mouthed the final part. A tiny woman with a fluff of white hair was watching from the neighboring table.

Pen gave the woman a hard stare, forcing her back to her bacon and eggs. "We need to tread very lightly," she said. "I've learned one other thing. There's an insurance investigator looking into this case. Apparently, Clint's large new policy is not what you might call a shoo-in."

Sandy glanced at her watch. "I've gotta go. Today's going to be a busy one." She put money on the table for her share and slid out of the booth.

Privately, she thought the Ladies would be hard-pressed to come up with anything on their own. The death happened in another country, after all, and *if* it was true Rudy Tong was connected somehow with Chinese mobsters and this really was a murder…well, the Heist Ladies were in far over their heads. It wouldn't have taken a lot of cash to bribe a man like Tiko Garcia to sail his boat into shark-infested waters and give his passenger a shove over the side. She would speak to Pen later about consulting her friend Benton for advice.

Sandy thought about all the new information on her way to work. Pen's discovery of an insurance company's involvement might be more important than they realized. She parked at the bank and pulled out her phone, jotting a quick text to Pen: Can you find that ins investig? Maybe we shd talk with?

FORTY-EIGHT

KAYCIE HAD PUT off the insurance man as long as she could.
His look of disbelief when she'd claimed to be meeting her
mother for lunch was almost funny, but only in retrospect.
She knew the picture she'd presented yesterday morning—
wearing sloppy shorts and top, no makeup and her hair in
knots, the condo a complete mess. No way had she been
on her way out the door, but the man was pleasant and gra-
cious. No doubt he'd come face to face with the recently
widowed, many times.

The surprise visit had one positive effect—Kaycie realized what she looked like through someone else's eyes and it
snapped her back to reality. Today, she was freshly showered
and wore one of the dresses she often wore on air for Channel 3. Her swollen sinuses still felt like hell and the sleeping
pills she was taking every night left her groggy until noon
the following day, but he didn't need to know that. She was
walking and talking and wore makeup. Little else mattered.

The one thing she did not do was to invite him back to
her home. Fixing yourself up to face the world was one
thing. Having the house ready—that was something else.
She'd called Inez, the cleaning lady, and apologized pro-
fusely for being rude the other day. She offered double the
woman's regular rate if she would put off someone else and
come clean the Holbrook condo today.

The sun was bright when she went outside to the covered parking space where her little Mercedes sat next to Clint's big Cadillac SUV. Another reminder. What was she going to do with all these possessions? Clint had been big on toys and gadgets. He had an antique car collection she had only seen once, garaged in a big warehouse-like storage facility out in Glendale. He'd bragged to people that he had more than a million dollars tied up in those cars. She could ignore the things she didn't see everyday, but the things she encountered all the time—like the Cadillac and his clothes and such—each item was a painful reminder.

She almost blew off her appointment with the insurance guy and turned back, but the man would only come around again if she didn't go see him instead. She took her keys from her purse and pulled out his business card, too. Bradley Muggins. A smile curved her lips. What a name.

The city looked different as she drove toward the address on Central. When she tried to pinpoint what had changed, she realized it was simply the otherworldly feeling of having been away—first to China, then locked away in her condo for more than a week. A return to real life was more a plunge back into the ordinary.

Mr. Muggins—she smiled when she said his name to the receptionist because it sounded like a character in a children's book—met her in his office cubicle. His desk was clear, although there were piles of folders on the adjoining credenza and file cabinet.

"How are you today, Mrs. Holbrook?" he asked, followed by an offer of coffee, tea or water. "You seem a little more—" He stopped. There really wasn't a good ending to that sentence. More dressed? More alive? More ready to face the world?

She waved away his blunder and accepted the coffee,

which he signaled someone outside the cubicle to bring. Her sinuses still ached and she hoped the burst of caffeine would help.

"I brought the certificate you requested," she said. "Unfortunately, they only gave me one copy."

He reached for the papers she held out. No comment. He studied the two stapled sheets while Kaycie accepted her coffee in a foam cup, holding it to warm her hands which were suddenly ice-cold in the air-conditioned room.

"It lists the cause of death here as drowning," he said, "although apparently there was no autopsy."

"He uh…they uh…his body was never found. They said they searched the water for a long time but there were a lot of shark—"

She set the untouched cup on his desk and reached into her purse for tissues. It hadn't become easier to tell this story. Would it ever?

"I'm sorry. I know this is upsetting." He looked over the papers and gave her a minute to compose herself. "There are some standard questions I have to ask, just things the company needs ticked off a list before they can pay a benefit."

She sniffed and nodded. "I understand."

"Your husband's health, in general, was good?"

"Yes." Clint had a routine physical every year.

"Did your husband—I'm sorry this is a difficult question," Muggins said. "Did your husband ever mention having suicidal thoughts?"

"Clint? He loved life. There he was, having a ball on a fishing trip. He—" She saw what he was getting at. Asking whether Clint might have bought insurance and then chartered that boat so he could die quickly. "No. Absolutely not."

"Sorry—it's just one of the things I'm required to ask."

She swallowed the choking feeling in her throat, blinked her eyes quickly and nodded.

"I'll need to keep this document a few days to have it verified," he said.

"You can't just make a copy?"

"Normally, a funeral home will obtain several copies for the next of kin because each insurance company and agency needs an original. I understand—you only have this one. It will have to be reviewed upstairs, but I'm sure you'll get it back in due time."

Due time. What on earth did that mean? She fidgeted with the clasp on her purse.

"There will be a delay in payout. I need to let you know. Normally, if all is in order, a beneficiary will receive payment in a couple of weeks. But this is a very large policy— a million dollars—and the circumstances are unusual. The foreign death certificate and the fact your husband only held the policy since last spring." He tucked her papers into the file folder and pushed it to the far side of the desk, well out of her reach.

"How long is this delay?" she asked.

"Hard to say, exactly. Do you have enough money available to live on until we're able to finalize our determination?"

"Oh, yes. I'm…well… Yes, I'm sure I do." She stood. He stood and gave an awkward handshake.

"We will be in touch," he said, turning so she had little option but to leave the cubicle.

A young assistant, the girl who'd brought the coffee, stood ready to escort Kaycie out. As she rode the elevator down, she pondered the meeting. Muggins had been businesslike with his questions, so why did she have the feeling he wasn't telling her everything?

His parting question about her finances caused her to

pause in the parking lot as she opened her car door. What did she truly know about their financial situation? She'd brought in her own salary, which she kept in a small personal account in her name. But Clint's money—it was a mystery. He'd always handled everything, paid the mortgage, bought the vehicles, applied for his own insurance. She wouldn't have even known about this policy without Bradley Muggins' visit.

Her salary had been absent now for several weeks and she had no clue whether it was enough to cover expenses or not. She loved the Scottsdale condo but had no idea what the mortgage was costing. She slipped into her seat and sat a moment with the door open. She needed to find out the answers to these questions. How much money did she truly have at her disposal? How would she find out?

All of Clint's checkbooks, bank statements and financial information was kept at his office downtown. She would go there and ask to see everything. There was also an accountant somewhere who prepared their tax returns and generated all kinds of printed reports that Clint brought home and pored over each month. The thought of going through Clint's business space and all those papers intimidated her. It would be so much simpler to call his lawyer. Derek Woo surely had access to the accountant and could get the information for her.

She breathed a sigh and started the car. It was a plan, anyway. Call Derek, make sure she had enough money. If all else failed, she could contact the station manager and say she was ready to return to work.

She didn't feel ready. Not at all.

FORTY-NINE

PENELOPE READ SANDY'S text message again. Yes, it really would be a good idea to talk to the insurance investigator the bait-shop guy in the Philippines had told her about. In fact, she'd intended to do it days ago but a call from her editor had sidetracked her. Of anyone, this Bradley Muggins could answer the question about whether Mary was named as a beneficiary on Clint's life insurance policy. She texted back an affirmative and went to her desk where she'd written notes from her overseas calls.

Somewhere on her computer was the message Mary had sent—what seemed like ages ago now—with the photograph of the insurance letter she'd seen in the office at Holbrook Plumbing. Pen paged through various email folders until she located it, thinking with a bit of envy of the way Amber so quickly found any and every tidbit of information on her own computer. Well, Pen decided, I'm not apologizing for not being twenty-one anymore.

Once she'd found the message, she opened the attached photo and enlarged it enough so the letterhead was readable. Cooper Life & Casualty, it said. The rest of the print was too small to make out, even with her reading glasses, but it was most likely from a home office far away. She looked in her old-fashioned telephone directory and found the Phoenix office, dialed the number and asked for Mr. Muggins.

"Ah, yes, the Holbrook case," he said. "I'm working on it right now as a matter of fact. And what is your interest in the policy?"

Ah…how to answer *that* question. She could claim to be Mary, an almost-related person, but then he would likely ask for some bit of personal information to identify herself and she would stumble and be locked out forever. Plus, she knew her accent gave her away as not being born and raised in Arizona. She decided to begin with the truth and then move on to the next-most-believable lie.

"Penelope Fitzpatrick? The writer?"

She confirmed it.

"My wife is probably your biggest fan. There's one of your books on her nightstand right now. So, how is it you're mixed up in this insurance claim for Holbrook?"

"I'm a close friend of Clint Holbrook's ex-wife, Mary Holbrook. She's been quite distraught over his death and I offered to phone on her behalf. Mary is in possession of a letter from Cooper Life and Casualty about a policy on Mr. Holbrook but it doesn't state names of the beneficiaries. Quite frankly, Mary is in a bit of a financial pinch and I wonder if there is a chance she was named on this policy? If so, it would be a big help to her."

Pen realized with a sinking feeling, now she'd raised the question, this might lead the insurance man to question Mary's role in Clint's death.

"Was the ex-missus in close touch with him in recent months?" he asked.

"Well, no. Which is why she is uncertain about this policy. It's somewhat awkward, I suppose."

"Not for me. It's not unusual at all for the relatives— past and present—to come crawling out of the woodwork when there's a big insurance policy at stake."

"Mr. Muggins, I assure you Mary Holbrook is not 'crawling out of the woodwork.' A number of her friends are very concerned for her. She's a hardworking woman who helped her husband build his business for many years, and she's become very concerned."

Pen took a deep breath and backtracked. This call was not going well. "I'm sorry. You are the investigator, but haven't you discovered a lot of inconsistencies in this case?"

She heard the sound of his hand rubbing across a growth of whiskers.

"What are you ladies up to?" he asked.

There wasn't much choice but to spill the whole story, how because of Mary's destitute financial situation her friends had chosen to help get her ex to release some of the money they'd earned together to ease the pain for her and, essentially, right the wrong he'd done to her two years prior.

"We know he got involved with the Chinese, supposedly working in Shanghai on a large building project. But they seem to have organized this fateful fishing trip for him, then cleared out his office quite quickly. We haven't found contact with anyone else in Clint's company, and it's as if the Chinese wanted to be rid of him so their own people could take over. We know there was no storm in the area the day they claim his boat was overtaken by weather, so the claim he was washed overboard seems false. His lawyer has also become suddenly active at moving money between Clint's various bank accounts."

She refrained from saying only this morning Amber had located another account and attempted to access it, only to find, an hour later, the balance had vanished.

"You suspect this lawyer is making illegal transactions with Mr. Holbrook's money?"

How to point the finger at Derek Woo without doing

the same to Amber...? Pen felt the sticky wicket closing around her.

"Well, I suppose I would say we're suspicious about it. We discovered the lawyer is a cousin of the client in Shanghai. If the lawyer has access to Clint's money, it's most likely enough to make it worth paying someone in the Philippines to kill him for it."

There. It was out.

"Murdered? Is that what you think?"

"Well...don't you think it's a possibility? The evidence in favor of an accident is fairly slim."

"Ms. Fitzpatrick." He sighed loudly. "I don't even think he's dead."

FIFTY

THE INSURANCE MAN'S statement hung between them, as if a bomb had gone off in the room, leaving a stunned silence. Finally, Pen spoke.

"Can we meet and discuss this?"

"I'll discuss the case with anyone who has relevant evidence," he said. "The faster I close this one, the sooner I get on to the rest of the pile on my desk."

"I can be at your office in thirty minutes."

When she arrived, Pen found a tall slim man in a white shirt and tan business suit. Sandy hair skimmed the top of a balding pate and his pale brown eyes could be golden in the right light, she guessed. She shook his hand, taking in his crowded cubicle with stacks of folders on top of the file cabinets and two empty coffee mugs pushed to the side of his desk. One folder lay in the middle of the desk and she saw it was labeled Holbrook.

"Needless to say, I was shocked when you said you didn't believe Clint Holbrook is dead," she said, after declining an offer of a beverage.

Muggins was watching her intently. "People try to fake their own deaths all the time. We see it more often than you would guess. Most are males, and they fall into two categories financially—those who are in debt up to their eyeballs and see dying as the only way out, except they don't really want to die. Mr. Holbrook certainly fits the model, with multiple mortgages on the Vandergrift Towers condo and a hefty lease on the downtown office suite."

Pen mentally filed the information. "And the other category?"

"Often they're successful enough at what they do for a living but they're disenchanted. Their present life isn't good enough. Sometimes there's a woman on the side and the guy has a picture of the two of them running off to live on some beach in paradise, especially if there's a dowdy wife at home and he knows a divorce will cost a fortune."

Pen thought of the hints the Ladies had found about Clint already starting to nose around other women. Although Kaycie was hardly dowdy, maybe the lust was gone. The Ladies did know for a fact he'd been moving money around—perhaps to avoid the cost of divorce, exactly as he did last time.

"Those are the ones who give up the deception and come back home the soonest," Muggins said. "The shine wears off the new girl about as quickly as it did the old one, and he'll decide he misses his hometown and his kids."

Pen was fascinated. "So, let's say a guy does sneak away and no one's the wiser. He can't collect the large insurance policy, can he?"

"Absolutely not. In fact, usually the wife he left back home can't collect it either. That's why we're keeping an eye on Kaycie Marlow Holbrook. You'd be surprised how often the wife is in on it with him. In his mind, the ideal situation is that he vanishes and escapes all his responsibilities. The little wife waits at home, goes through the grieving widow routine and collects his life insurance. Then she tells friends and family she's feeling like getting out more, she wants to take a big long trip. She joins up with her husband and the two have a grand old time with all that money."

"I sense a *but*…"

"But she'll tire of it soon, for all the same reasons the men do. Missing the family, the kids. Women can very seldom disappear forever. They have to stay in touch."

"But, *she's* not dead. I mean, on the record, she's still very much alive. Can't she come and go as she wants?"

"She can. But eventually, the plan falls apart. What kind of life is it—for either of them—seeing your spouse a few times a year, at most. Never being able to tell anyone where you've gone, who you're seeing. They crack. Sooner or later they all crack."

"The ones you know about."

He finally smiled. "Yes, true. If they truly did get away with it, we wouldn't know, would we?"

"What do you do about that—how long do you keep pursuing them?"

"It's not my job to fix somebody's messed-up life. Once I have enough evidence that the insured is pulling a scam, we simply deny the claim for benefits under the policy and move on to the next." He waved a hand toward the stacks of folders. "Whether Clint Holbrook is dead or not, whether his wife collects the benefit or not—I'll still have a job."

"Do you actually believe the wife is an accomplice this time?"

"Kaycie Marlow?" He let out a long breath. "I'm not willing to say for sure, yet. I've talked with her and she's certainly playing the grieving widow to the hilt. She and her home were a mess when I showed up there. She seemed distraught."

"So…"

"I don't take anything at face value. We'll continue to

watch her awhile. Most likely if she doesn't press for the insurance benefit money, we'll let it go. If we're not out that million dollars, it's really not our concern what the two of them do."

Pen nodded. Besides being pertinent to someone she knew and was trying to help, this was all so intriguing.

"All right," she said. "For the sake of argument, what are the clues you look for?"

He opened the Holbrook folder and pulled out a document with a red ribbon and gold seal on the front, extending it to Pen.

"Death certificate for an American citizen, issued in the Philippines. Or Thailand, Mexico, Nigeria, South America or the Caribbean islands." The light brown eyes met hers. "Not that travelers don't legitimately die in those places... but they rarely die and their body vanishes all at once."

Pen read the details on the certificate in her hand. It certainly looked complete and genuine.

He read her mind. "There are guys in Manila who can make a document that looks more real than the real one. You know what I mean? Sometimes they're a little *too* perfect."

"But still—"

"The guy was eaten by sharks—yeah, that's a popular one. C'mon. The sharks ate every last stitch of his clothing, his shoes, his wallet? If it really happened that way, something would have surfaced, washed ashore, showed up somewhere. I can't tell you how rare it is for a body to disappear at sea and *never* leave a trace. You remember that case some years ago, where the guy kills his wife and weighs her body down with cement blocks—she still floated to the surface. Drowning's not a smart way to do this. We always look twice at those."

"Good to know. Although I will tell you up front that

I'm not a fan of water. You won't catch me in the ocean on a good day, much less as my final resting place."

He took the certificate back and laid it on the folder.

"What is the other thing that alerts you, or the thing that trips up the person trying to stage a fake death?"

"They don't understand the procedures for how a death is handled, and there are a lot of places along the way where they slip up."

From the research for her books, Pen could think of one or two examples. Her quizzical expression made Muggins go on.

"Think about it. In a normal death, say, a guy has a heart attack in his own bed—there's the body. EMTs are called—there's the recovery of the body, where it's taken into official custody for autopsy. Then a funeral home takes charge—the disposition of the body, when it's decided whether it will be buried or cremated. We've got none of that with Clint Holbrook. The very fact that a death certificate shows up but there's been not one official sighting or handling of a body—the whole thing doesn't wash."

Pen had never actually considered those things but it was true. Taken one thing at a time, death involved certain steps which always happened.

"So, what about that death certificate?" she asked, nodding toward the document. "It sure looks like it was issued by the government."

He shrugged. "Could have been. Most likely not. Forgers can even get hold of the official paper stock the government uses, if a little cash changes hands. These guys are good. Only thing is, Clint and his attorney should have paid a little more and included an autopsy report signed by a doctor, and they didn't add the crowning touch—photos of him in a coffin and a crowd of mourners at a funeral. Lots of these fake-death scenarios include those things."

"Seriously?"

"Oh yes, ma'am. We've seen it all. Well, I've heard the tales. When the policy is a large one and even with excellent documentation and so-called proof of the death, the home office sends an investigator, or a team, to the location. They've been known to order exhumation of remains, only to find a coffin filled with rocks. In one case, they enlisted the help of a cremation service who burned cow bones rather than human remains. Those folks are doing prison time."

"What about Clint Holbrook? Is he facing prison time for this?"

"Depends. Cooper Life won't press charges. We'll just deny the claim and we're not out any money. It's not a crime to disappear and pretend to be dead, as long as you don't defraud someone in the process. What gets a lot of these guys though is that they do commit some kind of financial fraud—tax evasion, unreported income, offshore accounts. That kind of thing. In Holbrook's case, it's going to depend on what he really did and where he went."

Pen stared at the beribboned death certificate. Where Clint went—that, indeed, was the question.

FIFTY-ONE

PEN LEFT THE offices of Cooper Life and Casualty, her head spinning with new information. She couldn't keep this to herself. Call all the Ladies together, or decide who needed to hear it first?

There was no point in keeping information for later—she would only have to repeat everything multiple times. She composed a text she sent to all. Big news. Need to meet. Can you make happy hour at my house, 5:00?

By the time she'd reached her car and started the engine she had all four affirmative replies. She stopped at the wine store on the way home and stocked up on some good cheeses to go along with a bottle of Merlot.

Amber came first and it was hard to hold the news for the others, but Pen knew telling her would open a flood of questions, and it would be far simpler to handle them once.

Sandy and Mary were the last to arrive, together, in Sandy's car. Pen shuttled them all into her living room with the views overlooking the city. As concisely as possible, she delivered the gist of her earlier meeting with Bradley Muggins.

"He's not dead?" Mary's face went pale.

"The insurance company doesn't believe so," Pen said. "The investigator seems a very sincere man. I don't believe he's lying about this or that the company is simply trying to avoid paying a claim. I posed the hypothetical question to my friend Benton and he says he has seen this sort of thing before. He says not to believe the man is dead until you have seen and identified the body. Apparently, there are cases where a substitute body, unclaimed from a morgue, has been used to autopsy and bury in someone else's name."

"Can we open that wine now?" Amber asked. She couldn't sit still, and the moment Pen nodded assent she went to the long granite bar to get the bottle.

Gracie was staring into some blank spot in the distance. "You know...it does make sense in a way. What the man said about how some type of evidence would have shown up. You'd think a bit of clothing or papers from a wallet, or something..."

"He essentially said the same thing," Pen said. "It's extremely rare for a body to be lost in water and never show up without a trace. It's the type of case they always examine closely, especially when the insurance policy is fairly new and a claim is filed right away."

"Did Kaycie file the claim?" Sandy asked.

Pen thought about it for a moment. "He didn't say. He has the death certificate the lawyer delivered to her."

"If this insurance company is taking a closer look at Kaycie, they must believe she was in on it. Didn't you say the vanishee—is that a real word?—the one who vanished often has a cohort to collect the money so they can live happily ever after." Sandy accepted the wineglass Amber handed her.

"Instead of thinking we're tracking a murderer maybe we need to direct our efforts toward what little Miss Kaycie is up to," Amber said. "I mean, wasn't her scheduled surgery very convenient? She would have been at the clinic, happily getting her new boobs and planning to meet up with Clint the minute she looked good in a bikini again."

"Except for this—surely she knew they would come to inform her of his 'death' at some point," Pen said.

Amber set the empty bottle down. "So, she thought the news would come later. Events at Clint's end of the line began happening faster than Kaycie anticipated."

Pen thought of something. "Yes. When I called the various business operators near the boat docks, one man made a comment about thinking he'd seen Clint get on a different boat, not Tiko Garcia's."

"So, Clint went off with someone who delivered him to some other place…"

"And Tiko continued with his part in the play, saying the words he was supposed to…"

"Kaycie, by being in surgery the day of his disappearance, would be above all suspicion," Gracie said. "Unfortunately, she hadn't thought it through well enough to realize she would immediately need to go into the role of grieving widow, which would not include continuing with her surgery and enjoying a week or two in the spa."

Mary was fidgety, drumming her fingers on her spandex-clad knees. Pen had got up to fetch the platter of cheese and crackers.

"I don't know… I'm not sure she's that good an actress," Pen said. "The insurance man said he dropped by their condo to see her a few days after she got back from China. She had no idea he was coming, and he said that girl was a wreck. I have to wonder why she would be crying and moping around the house in sloppy clothes if she thought she was on the way to collecting the insurance money and joining Clint somewhere?"

"Maybe she was *expecting* the insurance man? Getting into the role for when the doorbell rang?" Amber suggested.

"I was with her at the clinic when the lawyer showed

up," Gracie said. "Kaycie was so shocked at his words she nearly fainted."

"Because the news came a lot earlier than she expected? Disappointment she would have to leave before her surgery was done?" Sandy asked. "Sorry, I know that's cynical and not kind."

"Not that I'm any fan of Kaycie Marlow, but I think he skipped out on her, too," Mary said.

No one spoke for a full two minutes.

"You do know," Pen said, "if the insurance company, or the law for that matter, is looking closely at Clint's finances—watching for him to make a move toward his money—they'll catch us if we take it."

"Ooh—not good," said Amber.

"No, not good at all," Pen said.

They all looked toward Mary.

"I hate to abandon our mission to get your money back for you," Sandy said, "but I agree with Pen. It wouldn't be smart for any of us to have a hand in taking money from Clint's accounts. In fact, I'm worried they may already have seen traces of Amber's searches. Can they do that, Amber? See evidence of a specific computer looking at a bank account? Could they possibly trace back to you?"

Amber dabbed salt from her lips with a napkin. "The technology's there, yeah. Whether they can identify me and come after me…hm, I just don't know."

"So it's back to Plan A," Gracie said. "We know he's hidden the money out there somewhere. We find out where he's gone, try to get the case to court—"

Mary spoke up. "I say we find the jerk and turn him in."

She said it with a smile but there was a definite edge to her words.

FIFTY-TWO

PERFORMING COMPUTER SEARCHES for Clint's money was one thing. Tracking a man who was determined to hide required a whole switch in methods and attitude, the Ladies discovered. Happy hour at Pen's house had now morphed into a full-fledged dinner with an array of food delivered from a nearby Thai place. Cartons sat on the coffee table and the women had filled their plates and scattered around the living room on couches and cushions.

For a good ten minutes, hardly a word was spoken as they concentrated on their churning thoughts and the scrumptious Pad Thai and Green Chicken Curry.

Mary had excused herself to go to the bathroom when Pen brought up a point.

"You know...there's another tactic we could take. Do nothing. Wait it out and see if Clint surfaces again, as the insurance man suggested he probably would."

"Meanwhile, Mary is living in a dumpy apartment making barely minimum wage," Sandy said. "Even if Clint is caught, odds are he won't move right back to Phoenix and take up his business where he left off. His life has changed forever now. There are guys who disappear—not necessarily playing dead—but they go away and turn up in another part of the country where they've been living under a different name for decades."

"Plus, it just isn't right. He stole money, cheated on his taxes, left Mary penniless and now he's most likely doing the same to Kaycie. How many other women are going to fall under his charms and end up the same way?" Gracie stabbed a hunk of tofu from her Pad Thai as she said it. "He *could* come back, but he might have run through all the money before he does."

"You're right, of course," said Pen. "I only thought… these next actions will test our resolve. We need to be sure we're ready for whatever comes up."

"I'm ready," Amber said. "I am *so* ready."

Mary came back at the moment they were all laughing over their youngest colleague's kick-ass expression.

"Okay, then. What's the plan?" Gracie asked.

Silence for a time, as thoughts raced.

"I think we need to ask ourselves, who is likely to know where Clint has gone," Pen suggested. "Unless he did this entirely on his own, someone knows. If nothing else, the man with the boat in the Philippines—not Tiko Garcia, but the one the bait shop guy mentioned—he took Clint somewhere and dropped him off."

"And then…"

"Clint would have needed an identity, some cash, maybe credit cards in a different name." Pen thought of the checklist the insurance man had described to her. "He has to be ready to hit the ground running, to feed himself and have a place to stay. Someone created those false documents for him."

"And which of us wants to go over there, travel to the seedy underbelly of a society we know nothing about, to root out this fake-ID supplier?" Sandy asked.

Amber looked as if she might jump at the chance but Pen put a quick halt to that idea.

"None of us," said Pen. "For one thing, the supplier of the documents is only one link in the chain. He, or she, likely just made up a packet of papers and cards and handed them over to someone. He may have never even met Clint, much less know what he planned to do with the materials."

Mary set her plate aside. "So, it's pretty hopeless, isn't it?"

"Well, darlings, I never said *that*." Pen gave a cat-like smile. "We have resources."

She had everyone's attention now.

"The insurance company, for one. Mr. Muggins told me they have investigators who travel the world tracking down people, especially when there's a lot of money involved."

"But didn't he also say they would just deny the claim and be done with it?"

"Most likely, yes. But he's intrigued with this case, especially after what I told him about Clint's moving so much money around right before his trip."

The ladies looked skeptical.

"I also placed some calls before you arrived. I spoke with Benton. Although he retired from the prosecutor's office some time ago, he stays in close touch with his old contacts—golf games are apparently where men do their best talking. He agreed to make a call to an old colleague, Dave Fresnell at the U.S. Attorney's office, and find out whether Clint is on their radar for any of his activities. If he's not already being watched, they or the IRS might be willing to open a case, based on his offshore accounts and the convenience of his disappearance."

"That's good," Sandy said. "It's a start, and it begins locally. They'll most likely interview his employees. Mary, it's possible you could get a call from them. It wouldn't be unusual for a U.S. Attorney to want to know specific office procedures if they feel a business owner has been break-ing the law."

Mary took a shaky breath. "I'm afraid I wouldn't be able to tell them much. From the little bit we've learned in the past few weeks, obviously Clint changed his business practices drastically since I was there."

Pen gave her a reassuring smile. "That's all right. Sim-ply tell them so."

Gracie carried the empty plates to the kitchen. "Among the others who could know something about this would definitely be Derek Woo. I'm betting he's in this up to his earlobes."

"I can track him," Amber reminded. "With those cloned passwords, I'll be able to see his moves and watch his emails."

"Don't forget Kaycie. Even though Muggins didn't seem terribly concerned about her involvement, it's possible—even just a little bit—that she's such a great actress she has faked all this grief and knows exactly where to meet up with Clint at a prearranged time and place."

A wave of unease went through the room. How on earth would they be able to find Clint with all his connections and resources?

FIFTY-THREE

AMBER CARRIED HER laptop to a shady spot by the pool at her apartment complex. She set a cereal bar and a yogurt smoothie on the small table beside her lounger. A Tuesday morning in early October was the perfect time to have the place to herself since everyone else in the building was a student. The wireless connection wasn't as strong out here, but who could pass up a balmy eighty-degree day?

She signed onto Derek Woo's email account, pleased to see in the background that he was not currently logged on. A scan through today's messages didn't bring up any names she knew, nor any subject lines containing something from her list of sensitive words—Clint, Holbrook, Philippine, fishing, drown, or China—terms the lawyer had used regularly before and immediately after Clint's disappearance. She considered adding a search for simple terms, such as *go* or *travel*, but those might return so many results she'd bog down forever.

Still, doggedness was one of her best traits. She smiled at her reflection in the screen, then looked around to see if anyone was nearby who might have noticed her preening. The pool area was still empty.

She decided to go back through Woo's old emails. With the new belief that Clint was not actually dead, clues could abound, little comments that previously had not seemed relevant. She performed a search on Tiko Garcia's name. Not a single email appeared on the list. In Woo's Trash folder, same result.

"Okay…this is weird," she said to her computer screen. "You were here a few days ago. Where did you go?"

She clicked over to another folder, one she'd discovered Woo created for correspondence specific to Clint's trip to China. When she'd first cloned his computer and decoded the password, the folder contained emails back and forth with Tiko Garcia, arrangements for Clint's fishing trip, as well as notes between Woo and Holbrook about the arrangements. All those had vanished. Checking a similar folder pertaining to Clint's business with Tong Chen Enterprises, she found the same results.

"So you're a tidy man, Mr. Woo. You like to empty your trash regularly."

She tried to remember other names from his earlier correspondence. Rudy Tong—no match. Tong Chen—no match. Seriously? A lawyer who deletes all files on a client's business dealings? Well, bigger people than you have tried to delete emails only to learn someone, somewhere can find them again, Amber thought.

She grinned, although having to hack into the server and dig around for Woo's mail was a pain, a chore she would have to go back into her apartment to perform since all her code guides were in there. She closed the lid on the laptop and sighed before downing the last of her smoothie. Her mother nagged constantly to get Amber outdoors. While her parents hiked the mountains around Santa Fe and Pecos, Amber had been a perfectly content kid when algorithms and formulas danced in her head. She gathered her things and went back to her little apartment.

PEN AND SANDY stood outside the downtown high-rise Clint Holbrook had once claimed he built. Even though his statement had turned out to be a gross exaggeration—or an outright lie—the man's construction business had occupied an entire floor, and Pen wondered how things up there were going now. Was the company in complete disarray (as Mary secretly hoped it would be), or was the business ticking along just fine as employees handled the details to finalize the project in Shanghai and whatever other jobs were under contract?

Pen reminded herself that Clint never had come back asking about the bid for the so-called concert hall project. But that was then and this is now. She remembered the procedure from her first visit and the two women signed in at the security desk in the ground-floor lobby.

"Holbrook Construction?" the guard said. "Not sure you'll find anyone there now."

He issued visitor badges anyway and Pen led the way to the elevators. When the doors slid open on their floor, a dim and hollow feeling greeted them. Beside the door to Holbrook Construction the narrow side window showed only blackness within.

Sandy cupped her hands around her face and stared inside. "There's an empty desk," she said. "That's about it."

A sound at the end of the hall caught their attention. Two burly men in coveralls stepped out of a freight elevator, pushing a large, wheeled cart ahead of them. The women slid close to the wall to let the men pass, but they halted directly in front of the Holbrook door.

"These offices appear to be closed," Sandy offered.

"Yeah, no kidding," said the man in the lead. He had pulled a key from his pocket. "We're just here for the furniture."

Pen noticed their coveralls had patches with an embroidered name: Stockwell Business Interiors. The man with the key was Pete; the other was Julio.

"Holbrook Construction is moving?" she asked, although she was fairly certain she already knew the answer.

"No idea where the company went, ma'am. We just pick up leased furniture when it's a case of non-payment. Three months in arrears, so unless you got the money to get this account up to date, we're takin' everything."

The ladies exchanged a look.

"I'm a little upset about this," Sandy said. "My boss is going to flip out. We had this guy preparing a bid for a job. He's got all our plans and specs. If I don't go back with our paperwork I'm in big trouble."

"I don't care about no paperwork," Pete said as the door swung open. "Far as I know these desks and files are empty, but if you find what you need you're welcome to it."

The men headed toward the reception desk, where Pen remembered a secretary sitting the morning she had called on Clint Holbrook with her proposal that he bid on a concert hall. They picked up a lamp and a silk potted plant and set them near the door.

"May I?" She stepped behind the desk and pulled open each drawer. All empty.

The trash basket under the desk held a few wads of paper. She picked it up and dodged out of the men's way.

"We're startin' in here and workin' our way toward the back," Pete said. "You want papers from the other offices, knock yourself out."

He wheeled the secretary's chair toward his partner and tipped the desk on its side, then began removing the legs.

Sandy and Pen dashed through the double doors to the inner rooms.

"What are we looking for?" Sandy whispered as Pen opened the first door on the right.

"Anything that might be a clue. I don't even know where to begin."

The room she entered held a drafting table with lamp and a high stool. Two rolled sets of plans lay on top of a two-drawer file cabinet. A quick glance showed standard blueprints, nothing pertaining to Shanghai. They left them behind.

Four other doors along the corridor opened to empty rooms. Pen remembered her first visit, the feeling the place was largely for show. Now, it appeared no one had ever worked in most of this vast shell of a space.

The conference room where Clint had taken her the first time looked exactly the same. No doubt the table and chairs were rented pieces too. She wondered if that extended to the small fridge and coffee machine. For all the money he made, Clint Holbrook apparently had spent more on renting than owning much of anything.

Clint's private office beyond the conference room was lavishly furnished but the impressive pieces didn't affect the women, knowing now the whole scene was a façade.

"He must have squirreled away nearly all the cash that passed through his hands," Sandy said. "Three months past due—that goes back way before he left for China. Do you think Clint had been planning his disappearance for quite some time?"

"I don't know. He talked about other projects and certainly seemed to take my concert hall bid seriously. It's possible he simply spotted a quick way out."

Sandy took the desk and Pen opened a door in the paneled walls, revealing a bank of file cabinets and a safe. The door to the latter was not locked.

"Go through everything," Sandy said. "I think we have a little time before the repo men reach this room."

"Or not. When you add it up, there isn't a lot of furniture in this whole suite."

Sure enough, they heard sounds of the men hauling the drafting table onto their wheeled cart. The women yanked open drawers and stepped up their pace.

For the most part the search was an easy one—nearly every file drawer was empty. The safe held two empty checkbooks, an expired passport in Clint's name and a roll of old silver dollars. Only the coins might be of value, if a person took the time to take them to a dealer and have them appraised. It hardly seemed worth the effort, but Pen put the items in her purse to give to Mary. Better she have them than the moving men.

Similarly, Sandy discovered the desk held only a few personal tidbits. A tacky keyring from Las Vegas, four pads of Post-it notes, a scattering of paperclips and a couple business cards.

"It's as if the whole office has been cleared of paperwork," Sandy said, picking up the business cards on the chance they might provide leads.

"My thought exactly. It doesn't seem possible a man was actually conducting business here and there's no trace of it now."

"So, did Clint take everything away before he left for China, knowing he wasn't coming back? Or do you suppose someone else came in here after his so-called death and wiped the place clean?"

Pen thought of the description Amber had given of Clint's borrowed office in Shanghai, the space empty only days after he vanished. "I've no idea."

FIFTY-FOUR

THE TWO REPO men were knocking at the door, literally. Time for Sandy and Pen to clear out. They grabbed the few items which might provide clues, the business cards and old passport.

"Find what you were looking for?" the man called Pete asked.

"Unfortunately not. The offices are empty."

He only shrugged. "We get that a lot."

"Well, we shall be out of your way then."

The elevator stopped on the next floor down and a young woman got on. She eyed the two older ladies. "If you went upstairs to Holbrook Construction, it was a waste of time," she said, pressing the button for the second floor where a tag said the cafeteria was located.

"We discovered. Did you know Mr. Holbrook or the employees?"

"Only one. Tamara. We ate lunch together sometimes."

Pen smiled. "Yes, I remember Tamara. So, did the business move away?"

"She didn't say anything about that to me. One day she was at lunch, the next day she wasn't. After about a week I went up there to be sure she was okay. Whole place, locked up and dark."

The car slowed.

"Well, this is my stop. Morning coffee break. They have a really good mochaccino here."

Pen stepped out of the elevator, nudging Sandy along. "That sounds good to me."

They followed the girl, chatting their way to a long queue waiting for service.

"I really need to get in touch with Mr. Holbrook," Sandy told her. "Do you suppose Tamara would have a number or a new address for him?"

"Dunno. I think I have her number in my phone." She pulled a cell phone from her pocket and began thumbing across the screen as people ahead of them inched forward. "Yeah, here's one time she called me and we met somewhere else for lunch."

Sandy took the number. Pen made a show of looking at her watch several times.

"I'm afraid I don't have time for a coffee after all," she said. "I'm running late."

Sandy gave her a pseudo-impatient look and the two walked away.

"Well, at least *one* thing this morning went smoothly," Pen said as the two got into Sandy's Mazda in the parking garage.

"I'm not sure what a secretary can tell us but I'm willing to find out." Sandy pulled out her phone and tapped the number she'd just received.

"You might be surprised. The office staff are often the eyes and ears of a business."

"True. With otherwise-boring work, gossip often runs the place." She perked up when the call was answered. "Hello, Tamara? This is Sandy Werner with Desert Trust Bank. I'm trying to reach Mr. Holbrook of Holbrook Construction and can't seem to locate him."

"Sorry, I don't work there anymore."

"Oh, I'm sorry to hear that."

If Tamara wondered how a banker had her personal phone number, she didn't ask.

"I've got some questions about the company and it's the type of thing better discussed in person. May I come by, or possibly meet you somewhere?"

A long pause.

"You could come by the bank and meet in my office if you're not feeling certain that I am who I say I am."

"Look, it's not that. I really don't care, unless you want to offer me a job. Right now, if I don't get a paycheck real soon I'll have to give up my apartment."

"Tell you what, then. Let's call this a job interview. We're short a teller at one of our branches."

Sandy had no idea if this was true but it was likely. At suburban branch banks, tellers came and went like butterflies. If she could do a good turn by providing Clint's cast-off employee a job, it could be a win-win for everyone.

"Come by in an hour." She gave Tamara the address and hung up. With raised eyebrows she turned to Pen. "Well, at least she'll talk to me."

She dropped Pen off at her Scottsdale home, hit the 101 Loop and arrived at her desk only five minutes before Tamara came walking through the door. Introductions and a little chit-chat paved the way into the conversation Sandy wanted to have.

"Tell me about the last few weeks at Holbrook Construction," she said.

"Is this part of the job interview?"

"Holbrook is a client of the bank and the questions are pertinent, so let's say yes, it's part of the interview. Everything said in here is in strictest confidence."

"Well, the office had been really quiet. Other than one

lady coming in on a weekend who talked to Clint about some charity thing, no new jobs had come in for awhile. Not that he was worried or anything. We were in the midst of a huge project in China, and Clint was going to be away for several weeks."

"And he did go? All as planned?"

"I sure thought so. I mean, yes, he went. I don't know how the job was going over there. He touched base every few days for messages and updates in the office, but truthfully it was deadly slow."

"What happened next?"

"Well, more than a week went by when I didn't hear from him. Once I'd cleaned up the whole office and organized all my files and such, I was reading a paperback romance novel a day, sitting there at my desk twiddling my thumbs. The design engineers had finished their work a long time before, and even the draftsman didn't need to be around. I was half tempted to forward the phones to my cell and just go out and have fun all day. Just my luck, I worried Clint would call and request something I had to be at the office to get for him." She shrugged. "So I didn't."

"Was it unusual that you didn't hear from him for a whole week?"

"Well, yeah. I was starting to get a little worried. Then one day the attorney calls. Derek Woo is his name. I'd thought he was in China with Clint—something the boss said one time—so I have no idea if Mr. Woo was calling from there or if he was back in the U.S."

She shifted a little in her chair across from Sandy.

"Anyways, he tells me over the phone that Mr. Holbrook says my job is done. I'm finished as of that day. There would be a severance bonus which he would electronically deposit in my account." Her mouth pinched in anger. "Some bonus.

It was barely a week's pay. I've got my rent, some credit card bills. It's been two weeks since he told me this, and I've had one week's pay to live on."

She seemed to remember her purpose in being here was a job interview with the bank.

"I'm a good money manager, really. This just hit at a bad time. I never missed a day of work and I'm not the type who whines about emptying wastebaskets or washing the coffee pot. I like to stay busy at my job."

"I'm sure you do."

"It just kind of hurt, too, that Mr. Holbrook himself didn't call. He still hasn't called, if not to thank me for my efforts, then at least to say goodbye. Getting laid off by that lawyer just didn't feel right."

Sandy realized with a shock Tamara had not heard about Clint's *accident*. It presented something of a quandary—tell her Clint had been reported dead, or let her believe he might still be alive? Neither was a good answer, and she couldn't take the chance Tamara would let slip to the wrong person that the death was now suspect. She gave it a moment's thought then broke the news, in its official version, that Clint was believed to have perished during a fishing trip.

Tamara's face blanched. "Oh my god, I had no idea. Why didn't anyone tell me? I just assumed he wasn't coming back because he'd decided to move the whole business to China."

Sandy shook her head, giving the stunned young woman a few moments to absorb the news.

"I'll tell you what. I'm going to give a recommendation on your behalf to our HR department. There will be a background check, of course, and a formal interview with someone there. Call this number to set it up." She handed over a business card. "Good luck. I'm sure you'll ace it."

She watched Clint's former employee get up and walk away looking as if she'd been slapped.

FIFTY-FIVE

AMBER PORED THROUGH the huge volume of emails that showed up once she cracked the code into Woo's deleted files. Certain names showed up in abundance—Tiko Garcia and Rudy Tong. When she searched China or Philippine she got an Alphonse Ruiz, several others with surname Tong, the Beautiful Life Haven clinic where Kaycie had gone for her surgery and a scattering of others with the dot-ph suffix that normally went with Philippine websites and servers. It seemed a lot of crossover for a lawyer to have with his client's personal business.

As someone in the group had pointed out, why was Derek Woo connected in *any* way with a fishing trip for his businessman client? Somehow, he had to be involved in Clint's disappearance, but so far she'd not found a direct link.

However, when it came to opening and reading each individual message, she had a long way to go. The task felt daunting and she experienced a rare wave of discouragement. It could be she would never find the answers.

Beside her on the desk, her phone let out a quick chirp and she glanced at the screen. A single word reminder message: EAT

It was noon. She closed her eyes and stretched her arms over her head. Yes, it's really that bad, she thought. I have to program a device to tell me not to get so wrapped up with my computer that I'll starve. She stood and worked the kinks out of her back and hips with a few yoga stretches. She knew what Sandy or Pen would say—just wait until you're older. You won't be able to move if you don't get some exercise.

"Yeah, yeah," she said as she went to the fridge for a glass of orange juice.

The tangy cold revived her and she found a packet of string cheese and an apple to add a little protein and fiber to her lunch. She paced the length of the room, munching on the cheese, thinking about the task ahead. With each pass by the computer she clicked an email message from the list and quickly read it.

Derek Woo to Tiko Garcia: Client arrives tomorrow

Tiko: All is ready

Woo to a company called Manila Charters: Destination set?

Manila Charters reply: Yes. The sender's name was Alphonse

These all seemed to be about Clint's arrangements for fishing—maybe even his disappearance—but the messages were so brief she had no idea if they meant anything special. She sat down and took a huge bite of her apple. Going through the messages, she began saving them to a separate folder where the Ladies could view them without the clutter of Woo's other mail traffic.

"I swear, this man must spend as much time online as a teenage girl," she said as she went through the list.

She paused when she came to a message that mentioned papers. It felt different. The term ID was in there. She flagged the sender, a C. Sanchez, and looked for other correspondence between the two. Nothing.

A few days later something from the same server in the Philippines, but the identifier was Bureau of Documentation. Was there such a thing? The language in the message seemed almost juvenile, not really what a bureaucrat would use. Same server as the one that mentioned identification papers? It seemed like more than a coincidence, but when she performed a search on the domain name ownership, it wasn't the Philippine government.

WHOIS listed the domain owner as David Tong. Now, *that* could not be a coincidence.

AMBER READ OFF the names she'd collected from Derek Woo's emails. The Heist Ladies had gathered at her apartment after Sandy called to say she and Pen had discovered something interesting about Clint Holbrook's downtown offices.

"Stop me if you've heard of any of these," Amber said. "Tiko Garcia." All raised their hands. Tiko had already been much discussed.

"Alphonse—no last name." Only Pen knew of him, and only the briefest mention from the bait shop guy at the beach.

"David Tong." Blank looks all around.

"Perry Tong." None.

"C. Sanchez. I don't know what the C stands for." Nothing.

She got the same response with the rest of the people and companies she'd unearthed from Woo's collection.

"I'll consolidate the messages and send each of you copies. Maybe reading everything in context will bring something to mind. I've looked at them so often, my mind is numb."

Sandy took the lead next, filling Gracie, Mary and Amber in on what she and Pen discovered. Clint's office furniture had all been leased and, this morning, was hauled away.

"The whole top floor of the building is sitting there empty," Pen said, sounding amazed.

"Even before the repo men showed up, the place had basically been stripped," Sandy told them. "There was not a file folder or computer in the whole suite. A couple of rolled up blueprints and some paperclips. The trash cans didn't even hold anything of value. I think someone came in and cleared the offices, knowing the furniture would be repossessed. It had to have happened recently because I spoke with Clint's secretary, Tamara, and she talked about filing and keeping the place neat up until she was summarily dismissed."

"You think it was Derek Woo?"

"Or someone he sent there… I have no idea," Sandy said.

"He must have missed that little drawer inside the safe. Otherwise, he would have taken the empty checkbooks and the old passport. Well, I would guess. Who knows what the man's up to." She reached into her purse and got the roll of silver dollars, holding it out to Mary. "This is pitiful, I know. I just picked them up so they wouldn't be taken by someone else."

A sad smile came over Mary's face. "I remember these. At one point way, way back Clint collected coins. Just the spare change that came through our little retail store. Whenever he spotted an old coin he would stick it aside and take it home to look it up in a book. Guess he got too important to do that later on."

Amber sat at her keyboard for a couple of minutes, creating an email containing the messages she'd mentioned, to forward to the whole group. Something that had nagged at the edges of her mind suddenly clicked into place.

"I wonder what happened to the computer Clint carried with him?" she asked the group. "When I went to his office in Shanghai it was gone. Obviously, it never made it back to the downtown offices here…"

"He must have taken it back to the hotel room each night he stayed in Shanghai," Gracie said. "Then, I suppose the question becomes whether he took it with him to Manila. Surely the man operating the fishing boat would have turned it over if Clint had it with him that day."

"On a fishing boat?"

"Well, you know… Some people can never leave their computers behind." She was looking at Amber when she said it.

"Hey. This is like an extra arm to me."

"Just teasing."

Pen spoke up. "Still, this is a very important question. If Clint did take the computer to Manila with him, most likely Derek Woo took possession of it. But if he left it behind in the Shanghai hotel, Kaycie probably brought it home with all their other things."

The room went quiet for a long minute.

"Am I the only one thinking we should tell Kaycie our suspicions? If she does have Clint's computer there could be tons of valuable stuff there," Amber said.

"And if the investigator was right, she could be in cahoots with him. Then what can of worms are we opening?" Gracie's eyes were wide.

Pen looked around at the group. "Perhaps the best idea is to approach gradually and see how it goes. We can say we're suspicious of Derek Woo and have been since before the trip to China—some plausible reason will surely come to mind. Something about him masterminding the movement of a whole lot of money. We'll ask if we can see Clint's computer. Depending upon her answer, we'll know what direction to take."

"So, like, if she's nervous and refuses to let anyone see it, we'll be pretty sure she's in on the fake death scam with him," Amber said.

"But she might hand it over, thinking all the juicy stuff has been erased," Gracie added. "Little does she know we have an expert hacker in our midst."

Mary leaned forward in her seat. "I wonder if she would listen to my story. I'd bet money Clint never told her a darn thing about how he left me, financially. If she has a clue he's up to the same old tricks… Well, it might make the difference."

Sandy sighed. "I think Pen's right. We take it slowly and see what her reactions are. This will take some finesse."

FIFTY-SIX

KAYCIE WADDED THE letter and tossed it into the kitchen trash. What the hell was going on? A demand notice on their mortgage? No way was the condo payment four months in arrears. She missed Clint with a stab of pain so physical it made her heart ache. He would have handled this. He always managed things so well.

"I'm Kaycie Marlow. I smile on camera and give out science fair awards and show up at celebrity gala events. Clint handles the money." A sob welled up in her throat.

Someone at the bank would straighten this out, but it was going to be up to Kaycie to make the call and point out the error. She picked up the crumpled letter and smoothed it against the granite countertop. *Why me*, she thought with a sigh. *I really need to go back to work, get my mind back to my career.*

The phone rang and she picked it up without looking at the caller ID.

"Kaycie, hello. It's Penelope Fitzpatrick."

Fitzpatrick? Oh. The woman she'd met in Shanghai and confided in. A thousand years ago.

"I'm in your neighborhood and wondered if I might stop by?"

"Um…"

"A quick visit. I've been so concerned about you since

China. I'm just five minutes away, if this is a convenient time."

Kaycie remembered the older woman's reassuring manner. Not to mention her connections here in Phoenix. Maybe she would offer a simple answer—an inside contact at the mortgage company, some easy way to make the problem outlined in this letter go away.

"Sure, just buzz at the front door when you get here."

Kaycie flipped through the rest of the mail. The sympathy cards had dwindled to nothing. Nowadays she received only bills and letters in long white envelopes. She didn't want to deal with any of them. She tossed the stack into a corner by the microwave and walked into the master bathroom to check her hair in the mirror. The door buzzer sounded sooner than she would have believed possible. Geez, had the woman literally been sitting in the parking lot when she phoned?

When she opened the door she was surprised to see two women standing there—Penelope Fitzpatrick, looking elegant as ever, and someone she didn't recognize. Red-blonde hair in a cute pixie, cut a little spiky on top, a sprinkling of freckles across her nose and very little makeup. About five-three, athletic and muscular in gray stretch capris and a hot-pink tank top, she appeared to be in her thirties, but Kaycie thought she was probably one of those lucky ones who just looked young for her age. There were a few telltale wrinkles at the corners of her eyes.

Kaycie realized her long appraisal of the woman was being returned.

"Hi, Kaycie. I'm Mary."

Kaycie almost said *no way*, but stopped herself just in time. This was not the woman Clint had described as dumpy and fat, had told his new wife how badly the old one had let herself go. Even in photos she'd seen of the younger Mary, she'd dressed conservatively in muted colors and had a timid look about her.

Kaycie glanced toward Pen. "You two know each other?"

Pen nodded. "May we come in?"

Kaycie stepped back and held the door wider. "Um, sure. I'm not clear what this is about."

Pen reached for Kaycie's hand. "It's as I said a moment ago. I wanted to stop by and see how you are doing. But there is something more. I felt I needed some help in telling you."

"Telling me what? I don't—"

"Perhaps we could sit down. Mary has a story to tell you."

The two visitors walked past her and Kaycie had no choice but to pretend she'd invited them into her living room. She took her favorite corner of the couch before one of them could reach it, the little nest she'd made for herself since being here alone so much.

"Maybe we should start with Pen's story," Mary said from a straight chair near the fireplace. "There's a lot to this."

"Yes," Pen said. "No doubt you are wondering whether our coming in contact in Shanghai was coincidence or not."

Actually, so many questions zipped around in Kaycie's head right now she couldn't seem to put them in order.

"The answer is, somewhat. Two friends and I were there, but it wasn't a pleasure trip. We've been investigating your husband, on behalf of Mary."

Mary took it up from there. "I don't know what Clint told you about me, but I can guess. While I was away, caring for my elderly parents, it seems he gave people the impression I had left him. Abandoned him to run the business on his own, and that he alone made a success of it. Because of my so-called abandonment, he filed for divorce and hid our mutual financial assets. I received a heavily mortgaged house and no means to pay for it. I ended up broke and homeless."

Kaycie had an idea where this was going. "Money? This is all about *money*, and you think I owe you something *now*?"

A flicker passed over Mary's face which told Kaycie she had hit the mark.

"Well, good luck with *that*. I'm not giving you anything. Clint dumped you and he loved me, and there's nothing you can do about it." She tossed aside the pillow she'd hugged to her chest without thinking. "You can just—" She rose from the sofa, her beautiful face strained in anger.

"Kaycie, calm down a moment, please." Pen remained in her seat and smoothed her skirt across her lap. "Mary isn't here to ask anything of you. She—we both—want to tell you something very important."

Mary was sitting back in her chair, arms crossed over her chest.

"Initially, we began watching Clint's activities in hopes we could get some financial help for Mary—that's true. But—" Pen held up one index finger to stop Kaycie from approaching Mary. "We discovered some interesting things about his financial picture and, more importantly, about his recent activities."

"My husband died on a boat trip. Have you not heard about that?"

"We have. One of the friends who is working on our team was with you when you received the news."

Kaycie felt the world shift slightly. *Team?* The moment when Derek Woo arrived to inform her of Clint's accident— she'd been at the clinic in Shanghai with clinic personnel.

Penelope nodded toward Mary and the ex-wife got up and went to the front door. She opened it to admit three other women. One—a fifty-ish blond in a beige business suit—seemed vaguely familiar, but the shocker was the taller woman with long brunette hair. It was Gracie, the American representative from the Beautiful Life Haven clinic. The third looked like a college kid with wild dark curls that could do with a good conditioning treatment. She held a laptop computer under one arm.

"Who the hell *are* you people?" Kaycie demanded. "How did all of you get in here?"

She backed toward the sliding doors to the terrace, feeling cornered.

Again, Penelope took charge. "We're friends, and we have no ill feelings toward you, Kaycie."

She introduced Sandy Werner, who admitted she'd met Kaycie a couple of years ago at the bank. Next was Gracie Nelson, and the young one was an Amber Zeckis. Kaycie barely acknowledged them.

"I'll ask again—what are you doing here and what business do you have spying on me and my late husband."

The three newcomers exchanged looks.

"You haven't told her?"

"Told me *what*? I'm getting frustrated with all of you. Tell me what you want."

Mary stepped forward, getting right in Kaycie's face. "Stop with the wounded little widow act, Kaycie. Clint isn't dead."

The words echoed in her head, bouncing off the marble flooring and stone fireplace. Kaycie felt her vision become a bright pinpoint in a dark tunnel as the white floor came up to meet her.

FIFTY-SEVEN

"So, I THINK we can safely say she didn't know about Clint's fake death?" Amber said it with a grin as she leaned over the back of the sofa and stared at Kaycie on the floor.

The others nodded.

"Shh, I think she's coming around," Sandy said. "Can someone bring a glass of water?"

Kaycie had fallen, almost in slow motion, and Mary had reached out and lowered her to the fluffy white rug in front of the sofa where she lay now.

The blue eyes fluttered, rolled briefly upward, came back to focus on the faces around her.

Pen, at her side, spoke first. "Oh dear, I'm so sorry I didn't give you a bit more warning about the news."

Kaycie blinked and rolled to her side, pulled herself to a seated position by grabbing the arm of the couch.

"Want some water?" Gracie offered, holding out a glass.

Kaycie shook her head and flinched. "Whoa. Dizzy."

"You blacked out so quickly after Mary told you...did you actually understand what she said?"

"Clint? Something about Clint."

"Yeah," Mary said. "He's not so dead after all."

"That's not possible. There's a death certificate. And an insurance man came by..."

"To question you and see whether you were in on the scam," Mary said.

Pen gave her a small nudge. "One step at a time, ladies. Let's help Kaycie up to the sofa, please."

With a couple of helping hands, they parked her in her favorite corner. Gracie draped an angora throw around her shoulders, as their hostess was now shivering.

"From the beginning," Pen said. "Mary, please."

Mary went over the parts Kaycie had disbelieved earlier, describing how Clint had promised to make the mortgage payments on their home but instead let it go into foreclosure, forcing her into a homeless shelter. About the day she'd walked into Sandy's branch of the bank, trying to figure out how long she could live on her last two hundred dollars. How the women, beginning with Sandy, had banded around her to help, hoping to find evidence of where the couple's assets had gone and a way to get Mary a fairer settlement, at least enough to live on until she could establish a career and support herself.

"At least you're lucky," Mary said to Kaycie. "You already had a career independent of Clint, and you can go back to it."

"What do you mean? If he's been found alive, he'll come back home soon. Well, unless he has to stay in China awhile to finish his project over there."

"You're not getting it," Amber said. "There is no more China project. Derek Woo and his cousin pulled some kind of run-around to get the job started with Clint's help, but they don't need him anymore."

She sat beside Kaycie and placed her laptop on the coffee table, opening the lid and pressing a key to start it.

"Clint skimmed money from everywhere he could," Amber said, typing a name in her browser. "He moved money from the jobs he actually completed, mortgaged everything he pretended to own, even leased the furniture in his downtown office."

"Most likely, you don't own this condo any more than I owned the home I'd lived in with him for eighteen years," Mary said. "Three mortgages."

"He has a maxed-out line of credit, and at least six credit cards near their limits. He was, as the old saying goes, robbing Peter to pay Paul and neatly juggling every bit of cash he touched into hidden accounts."

Kaycie listened intently, her blue eyes sharpening.

"So, you're saying he was getting ready to skip out on me too?" Gone was the flighty little television persona. "Is Derek Woo in on this? Did he talk Clint into it?"

"We don't think so. Derek may have supplied some contacts in the Far East, but the disappearance seems to have been Clint's idea."

"I talked to Bradley Muggins, the insurance investigator, quite at length," Pen said. "It's a strange phenomenon known in the insurance trade as pseudocide, where a person fakes his or her own death, to the extent of obtaining official papers to prove it. Sometimes a real body is identified by a cohort—oftentimes, it's an unclaimed corpse in a morgue—and they'll go so far as to have an autopsy and a funeral. In some countries, paid mourners will show up and wail away for a camera which is there to document the event. The spouse, or sometimes a new lover, is often in on it, waiting in the wings to collect a huge insurance benefit. The plan then is to stay apart for awhile, then meet up somewhere and enjoy the money."

"The fact Clint had recently purchased a new policy for a million dollars sent up a dozen red flags to the insurance company. He should have been more patient and waited at least three years," Amber said.

Kaycie's mouth hardened. "I'd been wondering if there was someone new. I didn't want to see the signs so I ignored them. And to think I was about to have surgery, just so I could impress him and keep him."

Gracie patted her on the shoulder. "He's not worth it."

"Why do you suppose Clint was so obsessed with amassing all this money?" Pen asked. "He had plenty, if his idea was to go off and live on some remote island or something. Why take the risk with a new insurance policy, especially knowing it most likely wouldn't pay out."

Mary and Kaycie exchanged a glance.

"If I had to guess," Mary said. "It's because Clint is the kind of guy who can never have enough. No amount of business will satisfy him, no amount of money will be enough. I didn't see that about him in the beginning. He was just a solid, hardworking guy—the kind I'd always wanted to find."

"I saw a bit of it," Kaycie said. "When I met him he was all Mr. Charm. Loved to buy me expensive gifts, take me places, spend money on me. It was a lot of flash."

She looked over at Mary. "Sorry. I really don't mean to rub salt in the wound."

Mary waved it off. "Success really did go to his head. I noticed it even before the big deals came along. I thought our success in the plumbing business just meant we'd worked extra hard and were seeing the rewards of it. For him, obviously, those triumphs were seen as stepping stones to something even bigger."

Gracie, always the practical and organized one of the group, paced into Kaycie's view. "Okay, so here's the way I see it. Mary's barely living on the edge, with nothing to show for the years of hard work she put into making Clint a rich man. Kaycie, you're sitting here in your beautiful condo on your beautiful furniture, and chances are you owe a ton of money—more than it's worth. You can go back to your job in television, but there's no way you earn enough to bail yourself out of the debt he created."

All expressions turned sober.

"Our original mission remains the same—we get that money back for you."

"Yes!" Amber said.

Sandy and Pen nodded agreement.

"So, all we need to know now—well, two things—where is Clint, and where did he stash the money?"

"And that brings us back to the real reason we decided to come here today," Amber reminded. She turned to Kaycie. "Do you have the laptop computer Clint took with him to China?"

Kaycie slowly shook her head. "I have no idea where it is."

"One possibility remains," Pen reminded them. "His lawyer, who has been involved so deeply in Clint's business. Could he have taken it?"

"I can find out," Kaycie said. She picked up the phone. Within two minutes she'd been connected to Derek Woo.

"Derek, it's Kaycie." A short pause. "Better, I think. It's difficult. Yes. Yes, I know. Look, I'm calling today because I realized I didn't make it home with Clint's computer. All our pictures from China are on it." She let her voice break a little at the end. "Those are my final memories of Clint and I'm so upset I don't have—"

The Ladies waited, hardly breathing.

Kaycie remained silent while the lawyer talked. Eventually, she shook her head and ended the call. "No luck. He says he doesn't have it."

FIFTY-EIGHT

KAYCIE'S ANNOUNCEMENT SOLIDIFIED their belief. Clint had planned his disappearance carefully but there was one piece of his old life he couldn't leave behind.

"Technology may end up being the downfall of more than one guy," Amber said.

"Can you find it?" Gracie asked.

"No idea. It could be he took it so he could dump it over the side of the boat, which would definitely cut all ties to his past. Let me think about this."

Pen spoke up. "One thing Mr. Muggins said to me during the rather candid part of our chat was oftentimes men who disappear like this will leave the broadest of clues. Mary, or Kaycie—did Clint ever make a statement to you about his dream life? Something along the lines of, 'if I could ever drop out of society, I'd love to…' Fill in the blank. Did he have a dream spot he would go?"

"Golf," Mary said. "He always wished there was more time to play, to improve his game."

"That could encompass thousands of places. Anything more specific?"

Mary shook her head.

"He loved the place we went on Barbados," Kaycie said. "Several times, when we talked about future vacations, he said he would go back there in a flash."

"A tropical escape features high on many men's lists, apparently," Pen said. "The guy I talked to who ran the bait shop in the Philippines told me he'd left the crazy life of the city to be there."

"So, we start with tropical locations that have golf courses," Sandy suggested. "Yeah, I realize that's not exactly a short list."

"I'll call the resort on Barbados," Kaycie offered. "Maybe it's simple enough to think he just went there."

"And who do you ask for? He'd be a fool to be there under his real name."

She made a face. "True."

"Clint may have a selfish, narcissistic approach to life," Mary said, "but he isn't a fool."

"Still, there must be a way. We tracked someone else to a resort place before," Pen said. "With a photo of him and a good story, I can start working on it."

Kaycie stepped over to the shelves beside the fireplace, to a dozen framed vacation shots of the couple. She gathered the frames in a messy stack and handed them over to Pen. "Take whatever you want. I don't think I can look at these anymore."

Amber turned to Kaycie. "Do you have a file of paperwork that comes with new things you buy?"

Everyone turned and stared. Where had *that* question come from?

"Clint's computer—there would have been some papers that came with it. I have an idea."

Kaycie gave a huge shrug but went into the kitchen where a small desk sat tucked into one corner. While she poked through a drawer, Pen suddenly remembered something.

"Clint's expired passport—we took it from the safe at his

office. At the time, I was thinking of it more as a memento for Kaycie. But it's a little book that could be full of clues."

Pen pulled the booklet from her purse.

Gracie's eyes sparkled. "This could be huge—we'll know everywhere he traveled. If we see repeated trips, it's a pretty good idea where he liked the best."

Mary looked skeptical. "He got that passport ages ago when we were invited to a wedding in England. After that, we never traveled."

Pen could tell Mary was trying not to turn the comment into a dig toward Kaycie, but the fact was Clint had treated wife two to a lot more perks than Mary ever received. She tucked the passport away.

"I can do this later. It will be more efficient to compile a list and report back."

Mary gave a weak smile. "It's okay, Pen. Really. I'm working on putting old hurts aside. Some days are easier than others."

"You're sure?" Pen took the passport out again, along with a small notepad she always had with her. One never knew when an idea for a story would pop into one's head.

While she paged through the passport and wrote dates and countries, Sandy looked at the stack of photos Kaycie had left on the coffee table. She set two aside.

Meanwhile, Kaycie and Amber returned from the kitchen. Amber seemed satisfied with the few sheets of paper she clutched in her hand. Kaycie approved Sandy's choice of photos and removed them from the frames for her.

"It seems the islands are hands-down favorites here," Pen said, closing the passport and looking at her hand-written list. "Although, as Mary pointed out, Clint was hardly a frequent world traveler. In the ten years he held this passport, we have the one trip to England, Barbados twice, Grand Cayman twice."

"He renewed last summer because this one was about to expire and he felt sure he had the China deal wrapped up," Kaycie said.

"Based on what you've said about Barbados, I'll start there," Pen told them. "Amber, you found a Cayman connection before, didn't you, so perhaps you could pursue it a bit further?"

Amber held up the papers she'd borrowed from Kaycie but didn't elaborate on her plans.

"We'll get out of your way," Pen told Kaycie, her way of letting the rest of the ladies know they should continue the investigation on their own.

It didn't matter that Kaycie's reaction to their startling news today seemed as if she'd turned on Clint. Pen had reservations—when faced with choosing a side, she could easily go right back to him. The Heist Ladies walked out of the Holbrook condo, not saying much until they reached their cars in the parking lot.

"All right, then," Pen said. "I am on a mission to find out if Clint is staying at a nice resort on Barbados or Grand Cayman."

"I'll go back and check out the banks on Cayman where we discovered he'd moved money before," said Amber. "And, with the identification number of his computer, I'll see what I can do about locating it."

Sandy offered any assistance she could do from the bank, if Amber would give her a task. Gracie had to pick up a kid at school but said the group could meet at her house next time. She would bake cookies.

Mary stood beside Sandy's car. "Me? I'm going back to the gym, where I intend to whale away at a punching bag for a good, long time."

FIFTY-NINE

PENELOPE WALKED THE length of her terrace, breathing in the sweet scent of the winter petunias she'd planted yesterday, waiting for her international call to connect.

"Hotel Barbadian. Front desk," the pleasantly accented voice said.

"Yes, hello. I hope you can assist me," she said, stepping back inside and taking a seat at her desk. "I'm with the Cayman Islander Bed and Breakfast, and we've run up against a problem pertaining to a guest's payment. As he told us his next stop is Barbados, I wonder if you can check and tell me if he's currently registered?" It was the same line she'd now used with six places, and although she'd received no positive responses, she did notice she was getting quite good at delivering the story.

"I can check that for you, ma'am. What is the guest's name?"

"Unfortunately, that is the problem. He checked in and paid with a credit card that was not his own. By the time we ran the charges and discovered the discrepancy he had already left, so I do not know his real name."

She knew it sounded flimsy. Any of the larger hotels would have required a passport at check-in and most would have processed at least one or two nights' stay before the guest ever entered his room. By posing as an owner of a small B&B she hoped the desk clerk would think she was stupid, not that she was lying.

"I don't know how I can—"

"I have a photo. We host an evening happy hour here and my husband snapped a picture in which this question-able guest appears. If I may email it to you, perhaps you will recognize the man and can tell me what name he used if he stayed with you."

She heard the sound of impatience and pictured the thought process. *Why should I take the time to go through this when you're the one who messed up?*

"We want to offer a reward, provided the information we receive leads us to collect. The man ran up a sizeable bill with us."

"Send me the photo," said the clerk. Implicit in her tone was the unsaid, *I doubt it will come to anything but since there's a reward...*

Pen jotted the email address she was given and entered it into the address line of a pre-copied email she'd already set up. Once it was sent, she dialed another hotel on her list. At some point she should probably get on with other things and wait to see if one of these seven golf resorts responded. She'd always hated repetitive phone calls, ever since she worked for a telemarketer in her early twenties. It had taken her only two days to know this was not the career for her.

Repeating the spiel, receiving the same answers, she sent email number eight. She drummed her fingers on the desk, stalling before making another call. The phone rang before she talked herself into continuing.

"Pen, I got your message. Sorry I was out most of the day." It was Benton Case.

"Not to worry. Did you remember to give your friend a heads-up that I might be calling?"

"Dave Fresnell? Sure did. He assured me he would brief a few others in the office, in case he's not the one you actually get in touch with. It turns out the U.S. Attorney's office has had Clint Holbrook on their radar, as well."

"Really?"

"Dave got a call from Cooper Life and Casualty. Although the insurance company has decided to deny the claim on Mr. Holbrook's life policy, they turned over the fake death certificate and suggested there was probably some financial malfeasance involved. Odds are good the IRS will jump into the act pretty soon, too."

"Oh, my. This is beginning to get fairly complicated, isn't it?"

"Welcome to the world of the law, Pen."

They exchanged bits of personal news and made plans to have dinner together later in the week. When Pen turned back toward her computer screen she noticed an email reply from one of the hotels on Barbados.

Expecting another negative response, she opened it and scanned the words, prepared to delete it. When the words, *Yes, this man stayed here*, jumped out at her, she reread carefully. This was it—she felt she was closing in on their quarry.

The photo you sent matches a guest who stayed with us for a week. Unfortunately, he has checked out two days ago. The name on his passport and credit card was Mack Hudson. We hope this information helps in your search.

Mack Hudson. Hm. Pen remembered the insurance investigator saying it was smart for someone wanting to change identity to use a first name the same or similar to their own. McClintock had simply become Mack. Hudson was a two-syllable name beginning with H. Clint retained the same initials this way. She wondered how long he had practiced responding to the new name, so it would come as second nature. It may have been no effort at all—Mary had mentioned Clint's friends of his youth calling him Mack.

She typed a reply to Joan at the Coral Reef Hotel, informing her the reward would be coming her way if the information resulted in capturing the man.

It was dark outside now, too late to call Dave Fresnell at his office, but it would be fun to share her success with the Heist Ladies. She typed a quick email and copied it to all of them.

Keep it quiet, she said in the message. Best we don't mention it to Kaycie or anyone outside our group. I only wish I could give Mr. Fresnell a current location for Clint. It would be the icing on the cake.

Within five minutes she had a response from Amber. Hang tight. We may have icing for that cake very soon.

SIXTY

THE TECHNICAL HELP guy came on the line right after Amber sent her note about icing the cake.

"Thank you for holding, how may I help you?" The accent was foreign but Amber had no trouble understanding the guy who had the voice of a fourteen-year-old and said his name was Michael.

"My name is Kaycie Holbrook and we need help locating my husband's computer. He misplaced it sometime during a trip he took and now we can't find it anywhere. Men—I swear, always losing things. Is there some way you can send out a signal and see where it is?"

She knew perfectly well there was a way, but it would take the specialized software of the manufacturer and the ability to log into their system. She gave the model and serial number from the registration form Kaycie had given her this afternoon.

He asked a couple of questions, supposedly for security purposes, nothing Amber couldn't handle from the basics she knew about the Holbrooks.

"Okay, let's see here…"

In the background she could hear computer keys being tapped fast and furiously, with an occasional murmured comment. While he typed Clint's information, Amber ran a reverse connection and linked to the tech rep's computer.

"He went to China, hm?" Michael said.

"Yes, that's right. Wow, you're really good at your job." She put enough gaga in her voice to puff his ego a little. "Is that where the computer is now, cause he was pretty sure he had it with him after that."

"I'm checking the data calendar right now. It can only register the location if the machine is turned on and using an internet connection."

More typing, a few *mmm*s.

"Okay, two days after China I see a connection in Manila, Philippines. He logged on there. Wouldn't he remember that? Are you sure he knows you're asking about this? You're not a jealous wife spying on a cheating husband, are you?"

Amber laughed. "You got me."

Michael laughed along with her. "What the heck—it's not my job to worry about that."

By now, Amber had a link and was downloading the program she would need.

"So, after the Philippines does it show him going somewhere else?"

"There's a couple logins in Bangkok, Thailand." More typing. "Let's see…a few days after that there's an airport public server in Dubai, and after that several days in Bridgetown, Barbados. Your man really gets around."

The stopovers in Thailand and Dubai were interesting. Amber already knew about the other.

"Yes, he does. He told me about Barbados. The rat, going to a beautiful island without me. Where did he go after that?"

"I've got a login at JFK airport in New York. Looks like he's making his way back home."

They shared a brief chuckle over that, but Amber's mind was racing. Clint had managed to use his new fake passport—assuming he got it in Manila—in at least three other countries. So far. It must be a convincing forgery. She wondered what country supposedly issued it. Clint was far too Caucasian to convince anyone he came from the Philippines. She would have to run the question past the Ladies.

Michael spoke again. "Yesterday, the computer was used in Albuquerque, New Mexico."

"Anything today?" The program had finished downloading to Amber's computer and she only needed one more thing.

"Not yet," he said. "Maybe he's on another airplane."

If so, Clint's next stop could be Phoenix. She stopped herself. It *could* be anywhere. His making a stop in a neighboring state might have nothing to do with his ultimate goal. She kept Michael on the line long enough to be certain her own computer was now mirroring his, tracking Clint's computer's moves.

She thanked the technician for his help. *Heh-heh*, she thought. I'll get you now, Clint Holbrook.

SIXTY-ONE

"GRACIE—I'VE GOT exciting news." In the background Amber could hear heavy-beat dance music. "Where are you?"

"The gym—with Mary—self-defense—" Gracie paused a moment to catch her breath. "Sorry. Mary and I are doing a little self-defense practice." A couple of panting breaths. "Oh, the music? There's a Zumba class in the next room."

The background sound became slightly muted. Someone must have closed a door.

"I've got good news," Amber said. "Did you catch that part?"

"Yeah. News."

"I have a pretty good idea where Clint is."

"Clint? That's great. Can we catch him?"

Mary came on the call. "Can we get the money?"

"I put my phone on speaker," Gracie said. "So, what's up?"

"Well, it's been kind of like watching a TV series, one where a few hours go by between episodes."

"We were almost finished here at the gym anyway," Mary said. "Should we come to your place?"

"Yeah, fine with me."

When they arrived an hour later, Amber led them to her computer. "It's not exactly like the movies, where there's a blinking red dot on a map and there just happen to be cameras along the way so the followers know exactly where their quarry is the whole way. But I've got the next best thing."

She picked up a notebook where she'd written each time she got a ping on Clint's movement. "I figured out that he has a smartphone with email and messaging. Once I was able to get into his computer, with the help of a sweet guy at Dell, I linked the email coming to the computer with the email app on his phone. The dummy has his location finder turned on, on the phone, so every time he uses it I'm able to tell pretty closely where he is."

She filled them in on Clint's travels from Manila to Albuquerque. "My guess is, he's now in a car. Maybe he got worried about being on planes so much, having to present ID all along the way."

"You have to present ID to rent a car," Gracie said.

"True. So maybe he had a buddy in Albuquerque who loaned him one?"

They both looked toward Mary, who shook her head. "I can't think of anyone offhand, but obviously Clint's life has taken a lot of turns since I was around."

"Anyway…" Amber read from the list. "He sent a text message this morning from Gallup."

"Can you tell who it went to?"

"Not without a whole lot more digging. All I know from this program is the basic functions of the phone. So, that time it was a text. And he received a reply awhile later. He must have been near the New Mexico-Arizona state line, somewhere along Interstate 40."

"He's heading our way." Gracie's eyes lit up.

"Possibly. I-40 stays to the north of us, so he could go on through and end up in California." She set down the notes. "That was about three hours ago. He could be near Flagstaff by now."

"How will we know?"

Amber met Mary's eyes. "Patience. The next time he uses the phone, I'll get another ping."

"He'll stop somewhere for lunch," Mary said. "The man never missed a meal in his life."

Amber heard the signal from her computer and dropped into her chair. A white box rimmed in red had appeared on her screen. A series of numbers strung across the box, and she highlighted them with her cursor and copied them.

"Latitude and longitude," she said.

In another window she already had a program running. She copied the coordinates into a space and hit a key. A map came up on screen.

"He's west of Flag already. I think there's a truck stop out there. Maybe he's stopped for gas and some food. Anyway..." back to the original white box "...he's in touch with someone."

"Can you tell where he's heading?" Gracie asked.

"Not for sure. He could go north at Williams, but the only thing out there is Indian land and the Grand Canyon."

"A person could hide in a zillion places out there," Gracie said.

"Except a white guy without a Park Service job will stand out like a beacon. Wouldn't he be better off to lose himself in a big city?" Mary said.

"I wish we could find out what he's saying in those texts," Amber said. "At the moment he's close to Williams, but it's an easy turn here or there to head back to Phoenix or go west to Las Vegas or even California."

"Las Vegas..." Mary said. "He's had friends there over the years."

"But," Gracie reminded, "he can't go where he has friends. Clint Holbrook is no longer alive. He needs a place where he won't be recognized."

"So, who is he contacting? Someone out there knows what he's done and has either given him some contact names for his fresh start, or he's still in touch with an old friend."

All three looked at each other. "Derek Woo." Mary was the one who said it. "He's hiding behind the cloak of attorney-client privilege."

"We need to get back on his trail, see if—"

A loud knock at the door interrupted Gracie. The Ladies exchanged a puzzled look. Sandy was at work and Pen wouldn't knock so forcefully. Amber nodded, distracted by another ding from her computer. While she stared at her screen, Gracie looked out the peephole.

"A guy in a suit," she whispered. "He's holding up some kind of badge."

Amber got up and opened the door.

"Amber Zeckis?"

When she nodded, he stepped forward. "FBI. You'll need to come downtown with us."

Amber's eyes grew wide as the man took her arm. Two more agents pushed their way into the room, forcing Gracie and Mary to step to the side near Amber's futon bed. The agents swarmed Amber's desk, picking up her computer and all her notes. The items went into evidence bags.

"What the *hell* is going on here?" Mary demanded.

"Sorry ma'am, I can't say. Your friend will be at our office, answering a few questions." He already had handcuffs on Amber and had turned toward the door.

"Wait!" Gracie shouted, but the man kept walking.

The other two agents had simply scooped up everything in sight, short of the paperclips, from Amber's desk, bagged it all, and were also on their way out the door.

Amber turned toward her friends, her dark eyes wide

with fear. "Get my *dad*—he's heading for Sedona. He's the *only* one who can solve this."

Of course she meant Clint. Mary and Gracie both understood. The tough question was, how would they get him?

SIXTY-TWO

PEN LIKED DAVE FRESNELL almost immediately when she met him. In addition to being young and handsome in his well-made suit and trim haircut, as they spoke she saw many of the same qualities that appealed to her in Benton Case. Honesty and a forthright manner, along with a winning smile, told her he would perform his job with integrity, do the legal thing—and he would do the *right* thing.

Along with outlining the reasons they believed Clint had hidden his income and stashed money in offshore accounts, she was open with him about the original reason for their mission: that Clint had cheated Mary all the way to homelessness and they wanted justice done.

"Right now we think Clint Holbrook is making his final maneuvers to gather all this money he has accumulated and disappear forever. Once he gets away, he'll leave two wives and numerous employees abandoned."

"My heart goes out to your friend, Ms. Fitzpatrick, but I'm afraid spouse-abandonment doesn't fall under our office's mission," Fresnell said. "What you've said about his attempting to cheat the insurance company out of a million dollars, setting up unreported offshore accounts, and using false documents to avoid his legal obligation to pay taxes—those are things we can go after. We'll work together with the FBI and Internal Revenue."

Pen felt a surge of irritation. Stand up for the IRS or a mega insurance firm, but think nothing about the struggling woman who is barely surviving every day? But she tamped down the emotion. At this moment, she was after results and Fresnell at least had a kindly manner. If he managed to get his agency moving and they caught Clint, the bottom-line result would be the same.

Her phone rang before she could think what to say next to Fresnell. The name on the screen showed it was Gracie.

"I'm in a meeting, Gracie. Can you make this quick?"

"The FBI just showed up at Amber's apartment and took her away. She was tracking Clint."

"Hold on a moment," Pen said. Looking across the desk at Fresnell she aimed her words at him. "Very fast work. The FBI came for one of my friends, apparently because she was making progress toward finding Clint Holbrook."

He flinched slightly at her accusatory tone.

"I'm afraid I had nothing to do with that," he said. "You've been sitting right here. I haven't made any calls."

It was true.

She turned back to Gracie, who said, "Clint is traveling along the I-40 corridor, and we think he's in touch with Derek Woo. But we're not sure about that part. He's contacting someone, though, at each stop along the way."

Names flew through Pen's head. Maybe Woo, maybe Kaycie? It could even be someone at the offices of Holbrook Plumbing. Just because the women had debunked the image of his huge office suite downtown, the other shop was still up and running. Of course, Clint could only trust someone who knew the story of his death wasn't true.

Gracie was talking to her left ear while Dave Fresnell was saying something else.

"Gracie, let me call you back in a moment. Dave, can

you find out who at the local FBI office has Amber Zeckis in custody? For that matter, I'd love to know who ordered her taken in and on what grounds."

He nodded and picked up his phone. After a good ten minutes of noncommittal um-hmms and silent nods as Fresnell jotted notes on a pad, he hung up and faced her.

"Three agents were sent to Ms. Zeckis's apartment with a warrant issued by Homeland Security when they discovered she had recently traveled to China and hacked the computer of an American citizen working there. The whole thing came on their radar because the Chinese were also keeping tabs on this man and our government was watching both of them. Sort of the spy watching the spy, watching the other spy."

Pen felt her face go pale. "Is Amber in serious trouble?"

"Depends on what she learned. If there are matters of national security at stake, you bet. She's in deep."

"But it wasn't that at all. She's been watching Clint Holbrook to keep track of his movement of money." She fidgeted slightly in her chair. "We had hoped to make a case on behalf of his ex-wife, to get some of his money given to her."

"In China? Seriously?"

"Well, it's where he went." She sat up straighter and squared her shoulders. "We managed to ferret out valuable information, if you'll just give us a chance."

"At this point, I think you ladies have done enough. With all due respect to you, Mrs. Fitzpatrick, and to Benton Case as a longtime friend, this is where you need to step back and let the authorities handle the matter." He stood and extended his hand over the desk.

Pen shook it, steaming at the brush-off.

All right, she thought as she left the building and walked to her car. *You go through your little bureaucratic proce-dures and get your paperwork all lined up and assemble teams. You'll discover Clint Holbrook supposedly died, and then you can go through all the steps to confront and arrest him. Meanwhile, we Heist Ladies aren't waiting around.*

She climbed into her Mercedes and called Gracie's num-ber.

"Now, Gracie, tell me everything you know."

Gracie went into a story about how Amber had figured out Clint's moves from the Philippines back to the U.S.

"He's here in Arizona right now," Gracie said with ur-gency in her voice. "But according to Amber, he could easily head for California or Nevada, maybe the Grand Canyon."

Mary said something in the background.

"Oh—that's *right*," Gracie said. "Amber shouted out just before they took her away, something about Sedona. It must be where he's headed now. Amber thought he was most likely in contact with Derek Woo. We don't know what Clint is driving, though, and all of Amber's fancy little trackers are gone with her computer and phone. How can we find him?"

Pen thought for a moment. "If the two are planning to meet up, maybe I can follow Mr. Woo. His office isn't far from here. Do we know what type of vehicle he drives?"

Mary spoke up. "The day Amber and I went into his of-fice, I saw car keys on the credenza behind his desk. The emblem on the fancy keyring was…let me think… I'm pretty sure it was the Lexus emblem."

"I'm on my way," Pen said, starting her car.

SIXTY-THREE

PEN'S PULSE PICKED up as she pulled into the parking lot outside the building that housed the law firm. The obvious, easy way to locate Woo's car would be if he had a reserved space with his name on it, but she had no such luck. Perhaps attorneys these days had such seedy reputations they didn't want their vehicles too easy to find. She cruised through the lot as if she was looking for a prime parking space for herself, scanning cars for a Lexus. There were no fewer than six in the lot. Four of them were parked on the same row, perhaps a sort of attorney privilege area.

She parked her Mercedes where she could keep an eye on them. Now what? Should she go upstairs and confront Derek Woo in his office? Or wait here until he came out? She was tempted toward the former, considering he might not come out of the office all day, but something told her to wait.

The U.S. Attorney's office was beginning to move on this situation. The FBI had Amber in custody. Clint Holbrook was on the move and was in contact with someone. As far as she could tell, the only person in Clint's circle who could possibly know he faked his death would be the attorney. Something told her she was on the right track. She phoned Gracie.

"Mary and I are driving toward Sedona, but we're still

more than an hour away," Gracie said. "We couldn't stand to sit around doing nothing, and that's the location Amber believes he's heading toward."

"I was at the U.S. Attorney's office when you called, so he's stepping in as well. If you see anything resembling a law enforcement operation, step back and let them handle it. We don't know Clint's state of mind these days. Things could become ugly."

"I wish we knew what type of vehicle he's driving. At least we could bring the police in on this and have them watching for him."

Pen saw movement at a side door to the building. "I see Derek Woo. Must go. Be careful."

"You too," Gracie said as they ended the call.

Woo glanced in both directions as he stepped off the sidewalk. He wore outdoor clothing—khaki cargo pants, a checked shirt and hiking boots—and had his cell phone to his ear. He walked straight to the row of vehicles Pen had been watching. The lights blinked on a black one as he unlocked it, then he slid inside.

Pen wished she could listen in on that phone call. He didn't look like a lawyer heading out to meet a client. This could be his afternoon off and the Ladies could be entirely on the wrong track. But at this point she had no other leads. There was no choice but to follow and see where this led her.

He took a roundabout path through the downtown area, stopping at a convenience store once, which put Pen in the awkward position of having to make a U-turn and park in a neighboring pet shop parking lot. If he glanced in her direction, the move would catch his attention. She pulled between two other cars and sat, her engine idling, until he came out with a covered white coffee cup and a small bag.

Again, he was talking on his phone. She hoped the call and his snack would distract him from paying attention to the cars around him.

When he joined the traffic on Adams Street, she pulled out of her spot and settled in two cars behind him. She'd written these scenes often enough in her books, had watched a million of them in the movies, but had no clue whether her surveillance technique was any good. He might have spotted her ages ago.

Woo cruised west and got in the lane for the I-17 on-ramp. If he stayed on the freeway for ninety minutes or so and got off at the exit for Oak Creek Canyon, it would appear Amber's assessment was right. The man was heading toward Sedona.

After thirty minutes on the road, Woo seemed settled on his way and there was no reason he would be suspicious of another car a mile behind. After all, it was the well-traveled route to Flagstaff and points beyond. Pen pressed the hands-free button on her dash and called Gracie again.

"We're getting close to Sedona," Gracie said. "Another fifteen minutes or so. We must have gotten on the road quite a bit ahead of you."

Or you're driving as if that minivan were a Formula-one racer. She smiled at the image.

Pen described Woo's car. "Once you get there, find a spot where you can park and watch the road leading into town. If Derek stays on course, he'll be a bit ahead of me. Watch for the black Lexus sedan and get into traffic near him. It's going to be harder for me to remain out of sight in a small town."

"And if he does something radical?"

"I shall be on the phone instantly."

"Got it."

An eighteen-wheeler had gotten between Pen and her quarry so she switched lanes to pass it. When she passed the truck, Woo's car was nowhere in sight. She almost panicked. Had she become so distracted by the call with Gracie that she'd passed an exit and not noticed?

Her phone rang while she was scanning the road ahead and she almost ignored it, but it was Gracie again.

"What's happening?" Pen asked.

"We think we just saw Clint. We pulled off at Camp Verde to get sodas. Mary spotted him at the gas station."

"Stick with him. I've lost Derek Woo."

SIXTY-FOUR

PEN HIT THE gas pedal, roaring past three large trucks and a U-Haul trailer pulled by a small pickup, heavily loaded and driven by a small white-haired man. The steep grade as the road climbed toward three-thousand feet had slowed most of the traffic. Apparently, Derek Woo had spotted the slowdown and made his move quickly to avoid being tied up with them.

Pen saw a black dot in the right-hand lane more than two miles ahead, then lost him again as the road curved. Her Mercedes swung into the curve and hugged the road beautifully as she passed more vehicles. The Lexus stayed well ahead of her, but the good news was there were no exits along this stretch. She would have ample time to catch up once they bypassed the slower traffic.

She tried to imagine a map in her head. If Gracie and Mary had, indeed, spotted Clint in Camp Verde, it could mean he had another destination in mind. It made sense. If he felt law enforcement was after him, he would want to stay away from crowds. But, she reasoned, he obviously felt secure enough to have come back to his home country, his home state. What was the man thinking?

Ahead, the black car was in a clear stretch and Pen tucked in ahead of the freight truck she had just passed. An aggressive driver in a dark gray pickup truck with huge tires and darkened windows roared by her, obscuring her view of Woo's vehicle once again. It became a game—her sleek little Mercedes would gain a space, the gray truck would block her. She might worry it was a government agency that somehow knew she was on this quest and was determined to stop her, but the truck's bed was filled with off-road bikes and the driver looked about nineteen.

"I don't have time for these games," she said, flooring her accelerator and putting more than a mile between them before she slowed.

The gray truck seemed determined to even the score, but the sight of a state trooper's car in a small pullout in the median changed his mind. Pen held her breath a moment, praying the officer didn't have his eye on her own movements. She certainly didn't have fifteen minutes to waste with a traffic stop. The cruiser didn't move.

Pen was once again within a mile of Woo's car when her phone rang.

"It *is* Clint," Gracie said breathlessly. "Mary spotted him coming out of the Shell station. He's dressed like he's going hiking and he's getting into a white Toyota sedan. I wish we had binoculars—we'd try to get the plate number."

"Where are you?"

"Far side of the parking lot from him. I'll follow. Here, Mary, take the phone."

Pen heard a shuffle as the women switched things around.

"He's pulling out of the parking lot. I can't read the number on his license but it's not Arizona. It's a New Mexico plate—that bright yellow really stands out."

Which made sense with what they knew of Clint's moves. He'd flown to Albuquerque and most likely rented a car with his new identification.

"We're following him through town. Um, wait. Looks like we're stopping for McDonald's." A little muffled movement. "Yeah, I could eat. Pen, we're getting in line behind him."

"It's a great ploy for following him, but you'll lose him when he leaves the line and you wait for food. Don't do it."

Mary relayed the order, sounding slightly chastened. Pen, meanwhile, saw Derek Woo's car edge toward an exit ramp. The sign said Camp Verde.

"Looks like we're getting close to you," Pen told them. "In case we lose phone signal out here, stick with Clint, no matter what."

Pen hung behind Woo, who breezed past the businesses near the interchange and took a road that meandered south and eastward.

Mary's voice came through, breaking up slightly over the sketchy connection. "Blodgett Basin," she said. "Looks like a campground or hiking area. Clint's driving in."

Pen thought back to her meeting with Dave Fresnell. The U.S. Attorney would not be happy that she and her friends had gone against his orders. But they were so close—unless Clint and Woo got away completely, Pen knew Fresnell would discover what she'd done. Best to 'fess up now. Plus, even with three women against the two men, she knew better than to try to apprehend the crooks on their own.

She looked at her phone. Three bars and she was heading into mountainous terrain. She brought up Fresnell's number and dialed.

"Clint Holbrook and his attorney are heading toward a campground called Blodgett Basin," she blurted when he picked up.

"And how do you know this, Mrs. Fitzpatrick?"

"I, um…"

"Are you and your friends following him?"

"Well, yes." There was no way, really, to deny it.

"Dammit, *dammit*."

She could practically hear him pacing the floor in his office.

"Look, I'm issuing an order to dispatch State Troopers out to the location. Can you please, please stay out of the way and let them apprehend the suspects. I repeat, do *not* try to handle this yourselves."

Pen pictured the man, practically irate, pressing charges for their meddling in a federal case. Worse yet, on a personal level, word of this little incident getting back to Benton. He had trusted her to turn it over to authorities and let them handle everything.

"Yes, sir," she said to Fresnell.

The connection was lost when she went around a bend in the road. Ahead, she saw Derek Woo's car crest the next hill. Mr. Fresnell, with his orders and forms and such, could take forever to respond and the situation was happening here and now.

"Screw that, as the youngsters would say." She pushed her car to its limits and closed the gap with the Lexus.

They came out of the hilly country onto a flatter section and Woo's car slowed. Pen eased off the gas, dropped slightly behind, saw a sign for Blodgett Basin. When Woo turned at the visitor center, it came as no surprise. A quick glance told her the parking lot was fairly full so she risked following, hoping to blend in.

Blending in, she quickly realized, would not happen here. Wearing the suit and heels she'd chosen for her visit to Fresnell's office was, at this point, proving to be like wearing a beacon to a star-gazing party. She stood out among the visitors wearing shorts and tank tops, her Gucci bag in sharp contrast with their backpacks and water bottle holders.

There was nothing to be done but play the role her costume dictated. She picked up a folder of manuscript pages she'd meant to leave at home and adopted an officious stride as she headed toward the campground's business office.

SIXTY-FIVE

"*Pen!*" Gracie whispered sharply and her friend spun around. "Well, I see you dressed for the occasion."

"Don't laugh," Pen said when she walked over to the minivan, noting the others wore suitable casual clothing. "I thought I was attending a business meeting this morning. No idea I would end up out here in the cactus."

Mary was sitting in the minivan, staring intently beyond the campground's buildings. "Okay, I've caught sight of the attorney," she said. "He's heading up the same trail Clint took."

"They must be in contact by phone," Gracie said. "Come on, we have to catch up."

"Mr. Fresnell said he would dispatch State Police," Pen told them. "Should we wait, just keep an eye on the suspects for now?"

Mary gave her a look. "This wilderness area is huge. Once they get away from the picnicking families, they could go off the trails and disappear."

"Mary and I will start after them, keep them in sight," said Gracie. "You can wait here for the police and tell them where we are."

Without waiting for an answer, Gracie and Mary left the minivan and headed toward the signpost marking the trailhead.

"I'm pretty sure Clint took the first right-hand fork,"

Mary said, marching ahead effortlessly while Gracie wished she'd started attending those gym classes. "He won't go too far."

"How do you know?"

"You're already breathing a little hard. He'll be huffing and puffing in no time."

Gracie took a deep breath and let it out, pacing herself so she didn't seem quite so winded.

"Plus, if he's meeting with the lawyer, I seriously doubt that guy will want to turn this into a full day hike. He's surely here to collect a fee or something and get back to his office."

"I don't know," Gracie said. "Did you see how he was dressed? He's ready to spend some time outdoors."

They walked steadily uphill, side by side, conversing in low tones.

"So, what do you think?" Mary asked. "He's going to walk Clint way into the desert and do away with him?"

To Gracie, Mary didn't sound completely unhappy at that prospect. "I guess I hadn't thought that far ahead."

They came upon a picnic area, a half-dozen small three-sided structures with concrete tables and benches under sloping roofs. Only two were occupied—the nearest one with a family with four rowdy kids and the farthest one up the path, where Gracie spotted Derek Woo's dark hair and his distinctive checked shirt. She signaled to Mary and they circled to the walled-off side of the shelter. They edged close to the concrete block wall, careful not to dislodge rocks or make a sound.

Gracie wished she'd been able to call to Pen before they got so close, to let her know specifically where they were. The parking lot was only partially in sight now. Hopefully, their friend had watched their progress on the trails.

"Can't believe it. Do you know how much work and how much cash it cost to set you up?" The voice was Derek Woo's.

Clint murmured something. The breeze carried his words away.

"That death certificate alone—I had to lay out five grand. The fake ID and new passport… Geez, man, you're gonna throw it all away by coming back here."

"I changed my mind," Clint said. "It was harder than I thought, knowing I didn't have a home anymore."

Feet crunched on gravel, Woo pacing. "You damn fool— you already didn't have a home. We cashed everything out and mortgaged the rest. The loan company is starting fore-closure on the condo this week."

"But my wife…"

"She's coping."

"I want to change the deal," Clint said.

Mary grimaced at the whine in his voice.

"I don't even have access to my own money anymore."

"Yes, because Clint Holbrook is dead. You signed it all over so I could handle it. Don't worry. You get yourself settled somewhere—I thought we'd agreed it would be in the Far East until you went traipsing off to Barbados last week. Anyway, you get settled and I'll transfer the cash over to your new account."

"Leaving Kaycie out in the cold. That's just not right."

Mary's eyes widened and a growl escaped her.

"Shh," the women heard Derek say.

Mary dashed around to the open side of the structure. "Not *right*? You *pig*—let's talk about what's *right*."

Clint looked as if he'd seen a ghost. His jaw dropped and his face went whiter than ever. "Mary? You look—"

Derek Woo was quicker on the uptake. He glanced toward the parking lot where Gracie spotted two State Police cars with lights flashing. "We gotta get out of here," Woo said, grabbing Clint by the sleeve. "Now!"

The two men took off, running up the trail.

"Hell no!" screamed Mary, sprinting after them.

Gracie shouted to the family in the other shelter. "Get those policemen and send them up here. Those guys running are wanted by the law."

The four kids screamed and dove under the concrete table. The father looked as if he wanted to gather information, opening his mouth to ask Gracie a question. The mother took off down the trail, shouting to some hikers to help her get the police.

Clint, his lawyer and Mary were fifty feet up the trail now, and Gracie ran after them. She'd closed the distance and could hear Clint wheezing for breath. He'd fallen behind the lawyer, who turned to grab his client's arm. When Woo saw the scene in the parking lot below he came to a dead stop. He calmly faced the women and pulled a gun.

"Mary—don't!" Gracie's shout was carried away on the wind.

Mary was practically on top of the two men when she saw the gun pointed at her.

Gracie froze in place. Quicker than it could register, she watched Mary adjust her stance and kick out at Derek. Her foot squarely caught his hand and the pistol flew, striking a tall saguaro about ten feet away. It discharged and caught the cactus right in one of its arms.

When Gracie glanced back toward her friend, Mary had the lawyer down in the dirt, her knee in the middle of his back and one arm twisted sharply upward.

Gracie ran toward Clint, determined to be every bit as brave as her self-defense teacher, but her job went far easier. Clint was standing still in the middle of the trail, his hands raised when she approached. For good measure, she grabbed one wrist and turned it behind his back just as the two officers ran up to them.

SIXTY-SIX

"DID YOU KNOW it's a crime to shoot a saguaro in this state?" Gracie asked, drawing hearty laughter from the other four.

The Heist Ladies had gathered for a celebratory happy hour at Sandy's house, a decision made when Pen called to say she'd convinced Dave Fresnell to release Amber. Pen had explained that the young woman was poking about in Mr. Holbrook's computer to gather information to solve the case and locate the perpetrator of a huge fraud, not to take the money for herself.

Although the U. S. Attorney seemed a tad skeptical of that argument, based on his longtime friendship with Benton and the fact Amber's findings had, indeed, helped bolster law enforcement's own case, he was willing to let her go. He issued a stern warning, though, and told her unless the two men admitted their crimes, she would most likely be required to testify at their trials. Since one of the defendants was a lawyer, Amber knew the odds of his confessing to anything were about the same as hell freezing over. But she was here now with a smile on her face.

"The saguaro *is* considered a protected species," Sandy said, "although, with tens of thousands of them growing all over the hillsides, I can't exactly think of them as endangered." She had her own thoughts on the silliness of certain laws, but she kept them to herself.

"Anyway, it's one of the many charges against Derek Woo. Along with aiding and abetting Clint on all the stuff he's charged with," Mary said.

Sandy poured wine into five glasses, the best bottle of French cabernet in her pantry, and they toasted.

"To the Heist Ladies, and to another successful mission accomplished."

Amber reached for one of the small plates Sandy had set out and began stacking it with slices of English cheddar, smoked gouda and prosciutto. Both black cats, Heckle and Jeckle, shifted their attention to her.

"Sorry...hungry. They give you one lousy baloney sandwich in that place. I couldn't even look at it, and some other girl in a spangled bra-thing looked more desperate than I was."

Mary and Gracie had gone over the story of what they overheard and how the capture happened up on the hillside. Pen's contribution had been to meet the police in the parking lot and give descriptions, in great writerly detail, of the suspects and their clothing and to send the police charging up the trail after them.

"So, what happens next?" Mary asked.

"As I understand it," Pen said, "formal charges are being drawn up and the men will be indicted. Trials—most likely separate, as it seems the lawyer will be most willing to throw Clint under the bus if that's what it takes to get himself off the hook."

Sandy glanced at Mary, who hadn't eaten anything yet. "What about the money? Our original goal goes unfulfilled if we didn't get some money out of this for Mary."

Amber handed a tiny cracker morsel to each cat and set her plate on the coffee table. "I think it's coming along. When that Dave guy questioned me all afternoon, he had my computer so I showed him some stuff. How Clint and Derek moved money around, and I had lists of the various bank accounts. He wouldn't admit it to me, but he was impressed with how much we had learned—way more than what his guys found out so far."

"By the time they piece together their case," Sandy said, "I think they'll find, in addition to tax evasion and insurance fraud, that Clint did a lot of stupid moves with his money. If they ever untangle the mess with the Chinese, it will be amazing. I have a feeling Derek Woo's cousin Rudy and his gang ripped off more money than we can even guess. The price of Clint's delusions of grandeur."

"Dave Fresnell told me there would likely be a substantial reward," Pen said. "The IRS alone offers rewards when information leads to a prosecution for tax evasion. I suggest any and all of that money should go to Mary."

"But, you all did—"

"There may be more," Amber said. "I told Dave what our original goal was, to get a divorce judge to reconsider the division of property based on Clint and Mary's assets at the time. He said that's not his area of the law, but he admitted he'd had a 'close friend' who was cheated in the same way once. He knows people and will help steer the case toward someone who will go over all the evidence in a fair way."

"It's all I can ask," Mary said. "I never wanted to get rich from this."

"Speaking of getting rich, guess who actually did marry Clint with hopes of getting rich, and guess who isn't getting her wish?" Amber plucked one more slice of apple from the snack plate. "Yeah, poor little Kaycie has to go back to her dreary little glamour job in television. Until all the assets are liquidated and the debt she and Clint acquired as a couple gets sorted out, she has no access to anything but her walk-in closet."

"How did you find that out?"

"They put her in an interrogation room next to me. Boy, that girl's voice can carry when she's screaming." Amber showed the cats her empty hands and they turned back to Sandy. "Last I saw, a uniformed guy was leading her out of the building, I assume to go clear out her closet and find new digs. At least that's what she was screaming at Clint when they passed each other in the hall."

"Ah, Clint. He'll never get it, will he?" Gracie said. "He messes up one great marriage to someone who couldn't be more devoted, then he can't even treat the trophy wife very well. Did he think hoarding all his money to himself would be a satisfying exchange for all he was giving up?"

Mary's eyes were sad. "Who knows what Clint thinks? I thought I knew him so well and he turned out to be *so* different."

SIXTY-SEVEN

DECEMBER TWENTIETH WAS the first cold day of the season for Phoenix. Christmas lights decorated the palm trees at Fashion Square, and Amber teased Gracie about being bundled up in a down jacket, a heavy scarf and fuzzy mittens.

"You don't have a clue that fifty-five isn't actually all that cold. Try growing up in Santa Fe. It's fourteen degrees there right now." She mimicked forming a snowball out of the fluffy white stuff in the display outside Romano's Ristorante. When she tossed it, the flakes drifted back to the ground in a flutter.

Pen arrived, classy as ever in a lavender sweater and winter-white slacks with matching knee-length wool coat, and Sandy came along less than a minute later with hugs for all.

"I'm so glad we decided to get together right before Christmas," Sandy said. "Two months is too long not to see all of you."

"I wonder what Mary's big surprise is," Gracie said. "Her message sounded so mysterious."

"There she is now." Amber nodded toward the front of Macy's where their friend had stepped off the sidewalk to cross over to them.

Mary seemed positively glowing in a hot pink outfit that accentuated her strawberry blond hair and brought out the roses in her cheeks. She had called the meeting, saying dinner tonight would be her treat. She had good news to share.

"I'm so happy everyone could make it," she said. "Let's get inside. I don't care if the thermometer doesn't say it's freezing out here, that wind has a bite to it."

They were shown to a corner booth and everyone went with the server's suggestion of a spiced Christmas hot toddy.

"So? What's the big news?" Gracie asked. "Aside from the fact that you look gorgeous. I'd say you've been teaching more exercise classes, judging by the fit of your clothes."

Mary demurred.

"It's more than that," Pen said with a smile. "You are positively glowing."

"You got your settlement," Amber guessed.

Mary nodded. "Do you want details?"

The drinks arrived and they toasted. "Absolutely—details are a must."

"From the beginning?"

A chorus of *yes!*

"Well. It seems Clint suddenly became cooperative with the law. As the investigation went on, they discovered some interesting things in Derek Woo's backpack, including a map of the area, a feathery brush and a collapsible shovel. He had circled a spot well off the trail where few visitors ever go, and they surmise he planned to get Clint to walk out there with him—maybe on a pretense of getting away from the crowds where they could talk, maybe he said he'd actually buried some of the money out there. No one knows because Woo, predictably, lawyered up the moment they read him his rights."

A plate of appetizers came and they all dug in.

"Clint apparently went on a huge rant against all of us,

yelling and screaming about how we had no business investigating him and how dare we follow him out to the wilderness area. Your friend, Dave Fresnell, is pretty cool. He said he calmly pointed out to Clint that we had most likely saved his life. Once they told Clint his own lawyer had planned to leave him out there as coyote food, he caved. They had so much on him, he knew he was going down for tax evasion and the insurance fraud anyway…"

Mary wiped her fingers on a napkin and took another sip of the warm beverage.

"So, a few days went by and I guess Clint did some soul-searching all alone in his cell. Whatever got into him, he admitted he'd been unfair to me."

"Shall we say it was more like *horrible*?" Gracie said.

"He didn't go that far, but as part of the deal, Fresnell's office agreed to ask for a lesser sentence if Clint would publicly apologize to me and to Kaycie, *and* he had to make restitution based on the years each of us was married to him. Watching how far Mister Mighty has fallen was actually a pretty cool scene, for a courtroom."

"You went to court and didn't tell us? We would have been there as your cheering section," Amber said.

"I know. You've all been so wonderful to me. I just—" She blinked back the moisture forming in her eyes. "It was something I needed to face on my own, confronting Clint like that."

"So you did get your settlement after all," Sandy said with a hint of the romantic in her voice.

"I did. First, the court examined all the documents and ordered everything liquidated—including Clint's business and an antique car collection I never knew about—and all debts paid. They gave decent severances to the employees who lost their jobs. Kaycie, for her short stint in the Mrs.

Holbrook role, didn't get a whole lot. Clint's half of our shared assets will go to cover debt. Anyway, my half isn't a monumental fortune, but it's more than I need. I've found a small house and made an offer. I learned this morning it was accepted."

Smiles and congratulations all around.

"I've bought in as a partner in the gym with Billy. We have some improvements in mind and I'm having so much fun with it."

She settled back in her seat and smiled. "The best part is, after I got everything I needed, there was still money left. I thought of the women's shelter, the one that took me in when I needed it most. They're good people and they do such great work. Once I've repaid Pen, I've donated all the rest to help them."

"Oh, Mary, that's perfect," Pen said, waving off the envelope Mary held out to her. "So kind of you."

"Well, it is the season, right? One thing I learned from this whole experience is that hoarding a big pile of money makes no one happy. I couldn't bring myself to start living as Clint did—I had to help others if I could."

She gave a little shrug and the others teared up slightly. Her gesture reinforced the mission which had originally drawn them together, as simple as that.

* * * * *

AUTHOR NOTE

As ALWAYS, I have a huge amount of gratitude for everyone who helped shape this book into its final version. Dan Shelton, my husband and helpmate for nearly twenty-eight years, is always there for me. And thank you Stephanie, my lovely daughter and business partner, for giving my business and writing career a burst of fresh new energy this year!

Editors Susan Slater and Shirley Shaw spot the plot and character flaws and help smooth the rough bits in the prose. And topping off the effort are my beta readers, who drop everything in their own lives to read and find the typos that inevitably sneak past me. Thank you for your help with this book: Christine Johnson, Debbie Wilson, Marcia Koopman, Judi Shaw and Sandra Anderson. You guys are the best!

CONNIE SHELTON IS the *USA Today* bestselling author of more than 30 novels and three non-fiction books. An avid mystery reader all her life, she says it was inevitable that this would be the genre she would write. She is the creator of the Novel In A Weekend™ writing course and was a contributor to *Chicken Soup for the Writer's Soul*. She and her husband currently reside in northern New Mexico with their two dogs.

Sign up for Connie Shelton's free mystery newsletter at www.connieshelton.com and receive advance information about new books, along with a chance at prizes, discounts and other mystery news!

Contact by email: connie@connieshelton.com

Follow Connie Shelton on Twitter, Pinterest and Facebook